NO SHOW

NO SHOW

SIMON
WOOD

THOMAS & MERCER

Published by Thomas & Mercer
PO Box 400818
Las Vegas, NV 89140

ISBN-13: 9781612184074
ISBN-10: 1612184073
Library of Congress Control Number: 2013936445

For Mum and Dad

Thanks for never stopping me from doing what I wanted to do—not that I gave you much of a choice about it anyway.

CHAPTER ONE

The FASTEN SEATBELTS sign went off with a ping. The passengers on the packed 747 from London rose to their feet, removing carry-on luggage from under their seats and the overhead bins. Everyone moved with the customary jet-lagged weariness, except for Terry Sheffield. The second the jumbo's wheels touched the tarmac, he buzzed with excitement. He was here—San Francisco. His Plymouth Rock. A new life with Sarah awaited him on the other side of those aircraft doors. God, he couldn't wait to see her. After six months of jumping through US Immigration's hoops, he was free to begin his life in America with his wife.

They hadn't seen each other since the honeymoon, six months earlier. They'd kept their relationship alive with regular phone calls. They'd accepted the harsh reality that it would be a struggle from the outset, but that didn't mean they'd found it easy. It was the price of a transatlantic love affair.

None of that mattered now. He was here and Sarah was waiting and nothing could stop them.

The aircraft doors opened, and he filed off the plane with his fellow passengers. He slogged his way through the tedious process of collecting his backpack from baggage claim and submitting himself to the usual unwelcoming grilling by immigration—this time a little extra hostile since he had a green card in hand. It was an agonizing forty minutes, not helped by the arrival of three other international flights only minutes apart. As he finally passed through US Customs, he wished he could have brought a bouquet of flowers through with him, but bureaucracy won every time. Sarah would have to make do with just him. Wasn't that gift enough? He smiled when he thought about using that line on her.

Terry followed the signs for the exit and entered the crowded arrivals lounge. Hundreds of people eager to meet a friend or loved one packed the large area. Their excited voices echoed off the walls as each new face stepped through the doors. He couldn't contain his excitement and had no control over the dopey grin he put on for the world to see. He scanned the sea of faces for Sarah. He expected her face to jump out, but he saw nothing other than wall-to-wall strangers. He slowed his pace and took a longer and more careful look for Sarah, but he still didn't see her. She wasn't there.

Her no show was a punch in the gut. He couldn't believe she wasn't here on time. If the situation were reversed, he would have been camped out in the arrivals lounge for hours.

He was overreacting. It wasn't a big deal. A traffic holdup was no doubt responsible. He knew from his previous visits that Bay Area traffic was a drag at the best of times, especially with the bridge construction delays. She was probably caught up in it somewhere. That was reality, but he wasn't interested in reality. He wanted illusion. Today was meant to be flawless—the ending to a sappy Hollywood movie. Her lateness had killed the moment. Traffic snarls hadn't been part of the plan.

He rode the wave of passengers through to the other end of the arrivals lounge. He still didn't see Sarah, but it was impossible to make out anyone with so many people still pouring in. Even if Sarah arrived now, she'd be looking for him in the wrong place.

He felt pretty dumb standing there with his backpack slung over one shoulder and his carry-on bag over the other. He didn't have much to bring with him. His possessions had been shipped over after he'd sold his house in England and Sarah had moved into their new home.

He dragged himself over to a bank of pay phones. They were the only option available to him until he got himself a cell phone in the US. He pulled out his wallet and dug out a piece of paper with Sarah's phone numbers. No, he had to stop thinking that way. Her phone numbers were his phone numbers too. He smiled, lifted the receiver, and pumped in assorted quarters and dimes collected from his earlier visits to the States. He punched in Sarah's cell number, but the call went straight to voice mail.

"Switch your cell on, Sarah."

"Hi, you've reached Sarah Sheffield."

He smiled at the sound of her voice. It was good to hear it even if it was a recording. He got a kick out of her using his last name. It made their marriage real. After so much red tape, their relationship seemed more like a paperwork exercise than a real marriage.

"I'm not here right now, so leave me a message."

"Hey, I'm here. Where are you? I'll be waiting, but don't make me run off with a different woman, okay? Look, this place is a madhouse. Even if you're here, I can't see you. I'm going to find a Starbucks or something. When you arrive, have me paged. Can't wait to see you. Love you."

He burned the rest of his loose change calling the home number. The phone rang until the answering machine kicked in. At least that meant she was on her way and not at home with her feet up. He left a brief "where are you?" message and hung up.

He bought a coffee and wandered back to the arrivals lounge. He found a spot away from the madding crowd and leaned against a pillar. He sloughed off his backpack, letting it tumble to the floor, and dropped his carry-on next to it. He used his backpack as a seat.

He eyed the doors leading into the arrivals lounge, hoping to see Sarah charging toward him, full of apologies for being late. Instead, he saw his fellow passengers on the London flight pass through arrivals.

Ten minutes passed. Then twenty. With each passing minute, the tedium of watching lovers reunite, friends welcome friends home, and business travelers connect with their counterparts irritated him. He checked his watch again. Another thirty minutes had passed. He struggled to believe the traffic was so backed up that she hadn't arrived yet.

He went to the information desk and had Sarah paged three times over a twenty-minute period. Each page went unanswered.

"She's probably stuck in traffic," the woman at the information kiosk said. "She'll be along soon."

He'd broken a twenty-dollar bill when buying coffee in order to get more change. Cash in big bills was all he had. As yet, he didn't have a credit card or a bank account in the US. He used the change to call Sarah on her cell phone again. He got her voice mail.

"I hope you're close to the airport now. I'm starting to get a little lonely here. Just hurry up and get here."

He nursed his coffee for over half an hour and listened closely to every page, but none were for him. Concern crept in now. What if she'd gotten into a crash on the way over? It was an irrational conclusion, but it wasn't beyond the realm of possibility. He could see it. He'd been a total airhead all day thinking about their reunion, and Sarah wouldn't be any different. She might not have been concentrating on the road. The problem was, if she'd gotten herself mixed up in a crash, there was no way she could get word to him. He hoped he was overreacting.

He finished his coffee, tried Sarah's cell one more time, and got her voice mail yet again.

"Hey, Sarah, I'm worried about you. I know you can't get ahold of me, but I hope you're okay. If you're on your way here, turn around. I'm going to grab a shuttle home. See you in a few."

Home. The word sounded good. This country might be foreign, but with Sarah at his side, it was home.

He had her paged one last time with no result before asking the information person to tell Sarah, if she came looking for him, that he was making his own way home. It wasn't great, but he'd covered all the lines of communication he could.

He followed the signs to the bus courtyard and got on a shuttle van service that went as far as Sacramento. He gave the driver his new home address in Edenville. He didn't know where Edenville was, just that it was somewhere between San Francisco and Sacramento. Sarah had lived in San Francisco until they'd gotten married. Upgrading from her apartment to a house wasn't an option with San Francisco real-estate prices, so she'd settled on Edenville. Besides, she'd wanted a fresh start for the both of them. If they were starting a new life, they should do it in a new home. He'd only seen the house in Edenville in photos Sarah had e-mailed to him.

Terry paid the driver, who loaded his bags into the van. Once Terry had taken his seat, the driver slipped out of the airport. Besides Terry there were only four other people in the van—a couple and two lone travelers.

Progress was slow through San Francisco, but Terry didn't mind. It allowed him to focus on the vehicles coming the other way. He knew it was stupid, but he hoped to see Sarah's car heading toward him. He even looked at stranded cars on the side of the road in case one of them was Sarah's. But he didn't see Sarah speeding toward him or marooned at the side of the road.

A scary thought hit him. Could Sarah have developed a nasty case of cold feet? Six months of separation gave her plenty of time to rethink things. He'd be a liar if he said flickers of doubt hadn't visited him from time to time. He hadn't heard any worry in her voice during their phone calls, but it didn't mean she hadn't been harboring fears. This would be a shitty time to find out—after he'd gotten married, sold his home, dumped his job, and drawn a line under his life in the UK. He had visions of her hiding out in the house, ignoring his calls.

"Please don't be standing me up, Sarah," he murmured.

The woman sitting next to him on the shuttle asked him what he'd said.

"Nothing," he said and squeezed out a smile.

"What's that accent—Australian?"

"No, English," he answered and found himself mired in a conversation about her desire to visit Britain one day. It took him ten miles to break free of the exchange.

Once across the Carquinez Bridge, the Bay Area's influence came to an end, giving way to small towns that punctuated endless fields. Passing from town to town, Spanish town names rubbed shoulders with English ones. It was easy to see who'd been out this way a hundred and fifty years ago. The driver picked up speed, and it wasn't long before he peeled off I-80 for a two-lane highway divided by a grass median. Walnut farms lined either side of the highway. The trees were in perfect rows at forty-five-degree angles to the road. Not a single tree was out of place. The precision amazed Terry.

After twenty minutes, the driver pulled off the highway for what seemed to be no more than a farm track. After a mile or so, the track developed into a road and Terry realized his journey had come to an end. He was in Edenville.

He hadn't been sure what to expect. Sarah hadn't really described Edenville during their phone calls or in her e-mails. He hadn't been expecting the size and sophistication of San Francisco, of course—the town's name summoned up images of small-town America.

The driver came to a halt at the four-way stop. Edenville greeted Terry with a bandstand-style gazebo perched on a square of well-tended grass on his left. At the entrance to the compact park, the town's monument announced that Edenville was the gateway to Lake Solano. The driver crossed the intersection.

They continued traveling down Edenville's main street—and back in time. Buildings dating back to the turn of the twentieth century stood shoulder to shoulder, giving the town a frontier feel. Terry expected Jesse James to come running out of a bank, his guns blazing.

"Do you mind pulling over for one minute?" Terry asked the driver.

The driver eyed his rearview mirror and frowned. "Why?"

"I just want to pick up some flowers for my wife. We've been apart for six months and I want to surprise her."

The driver mumbled something in Spanish before saying, "I have a schedule to keep."

"It won't take a minute. You'd be doing me a big favor."

"Does anyone mind?" he asked Terry's fellow passengers with a roll of his eyes.

Terry saw they just wanted to get home, but no one objected. The driver pulled over and Terry ran into a supermarket, bought a bouquet, and clambered back into the van.

"Thanks a lot, everyone. I really appreciate it."

Disinterested looks greeted him. Terry didn't much care. He had his flowers, and Sarah would love it when he gave them to her.

The driver got on the road again, and it wasn't long before he was pulling up in front of Terry's house. His home on Sutter Drive was located in a quiet neighborhood. All the homes looked to be forty to fifty years old, but well maintained and nothing like their English counterparts. None of the houses were built from brick. They were either stucco or wood-sided, and virtually every home was single story. Bungalows, he would have called them, but he remembered Sarah referring to them as ranch style. He wasn't much reminded of a ranch. He didn't see any two-hundred-acre plots of land and not a hint of cattle.

Terry got his baggage from the driver and overtipped him for stopping.

"Welcome to America," the driver said before pulling away.

Terry walked up to the front door and pressed the doorbell. He hoped to God Sarah was inside. He gave the doorbell an extra push.

Nobody answered the door.

He tried the doorbell again. Sarah wasn't at home.

Stepping back from the doorstep, an irritating thought struck him. He didn't have a key, and he didn't know how long it would be before Sarah got back from wherever she had gone.

"I hope you're on your way back from the airport, Sarah," he said to his absent wife.

He crossed to the other side of the property and tried the side gate to the backyard. It was locked.

"Sod it," he grumbled.

He turned to face the street. A blank street stared back at him. He exhaled, feeling conspicuous.

"Well, I'm not standing 'round here all day," he said.

He tossed his carry-on bag over the six-foot-high obstacle, then unsaddled himself of his backpack and launched it over the fence as well. He gave the street a second glance and hurled himself over the gate. He made it easily, even with the bouquet under one arm, but he wouldn't have scored a perfect ten for his landing.

He left his bags where he'd thrown them with the flowers on top. He walked over to the patio door. The big glass door gave him a view of the interior. Fruit was in a bowl on the dining table, the TV remote was on the couch, and a newspaper was on the coffee table in the living room.

He could have waited on the patio or in the hammock in the shade of a redwood tree, but he didn't want to wait. He wanted to get inside. A message could be waiting for him or the phone could ring at any time, and being stuck in the backyard wasn't going to do him any good. But if he was expecting the patio door to be unlocked, he was out of luck. It wasn't. He didn't get lucky with any of the other windows or doors. All of them were locked.

But the fortress did have one chink in its armor. The patio door had a cat flap built into it. As far as he knew, Sarah didn't own a cat or any other animal, but that flap was going to be his way into the house.

Terry dropped to all fours and slid his arm through the flap. He reached up toward the door latch—and his arm didn't reach.

"Bollocks."

He leapt to his feet and scoured the backyard for an arm extension. He snapped a branch off an orange tree and stripped the leaves off. It looked strong enough.

He stuck the branch through the cat flap and maneuvered it toward the door latch. It took a couple of attempts to position the branch, but when he did, his idea worked like a charm. The branch flexed close to the breaking point, but the latch gave first, unlocking the door.

"Bingo!"

Terry jumped to his feet, grabbed his bags and the flowers, and slid the door open. The first thing to strike him was the smell. The air smelled stale, as if the house had been closed up for some time. His stomach tightened at the idea that Sarah hadn't been around for a while. He shrugged off his bags and dropped the flowers on the dining table.

The answering machine in the living room blinked. Terry pressed PLAY. There were seven messages: his call from the airport, three calls from telemarketers, two hang-ups, and one actual message from a person who left no name or number. From the way the guy spoke, he sounded like a friend. The oldest message dated back several days. Terry erased all the messages, except the personal one. Sarah would probably want to hear it when she came home—if she came home.

He hoped to find a note on the kitchen table, stuck to the fridge, or on the bed, but found nothing. He wandered from room to room. There was no sign that a surprise welcome was waiting for him.

He returned to the kitchen and opened up the fridge. It was low on supplies with little to no food in it. He sniffed an open carton of milk. It had gone sour, and he dumped it down the sink. The only interesting item in the fridge was an unopened bottle of champagne with a red ribbon tied around its neck. Sarah had certainly planned for his arrival in one respect.

The mail slot was in the garage. There wasn't a car in the garage, but there was a whole bunch of uncollected mail in the basket. Most of it was crap—junk mail, coupon books, and supermarket and department store flyers. He examined the postmark dates on the envelopes. Allowing for transit, he guessed that Sarah had been away from home for three to four days. He knew it wasn't longer. They had spoken last weekend, and that was five days ago.

Weekends were the best time to talk. The eight-hour time difference between England and California limited the window of opportunity. A call from the United States at five in the afternoon made for a 1:00 a.m. wakeup call in London. But they had the weekends. On a Friday or Saturday night, they could afford to talk well into the wee hours of the morning.

Messages stacked up on the machine, uncollected mail, and an empty fridge…Had she gone away? She wouldn't have done that without telling him. There was no way she'd leave him high and dry like this. Not a chance.

He checked the closets and dresser. He couldn't tell if Sarah's clothes were missing. If she had gone anywhere, she was traveling light. He did notice one thing missing. When they'd met in Costa Rica, she had been carrying a small San Francisco 49ers sports bag. He'd seen it the last time he'd been over, just before they got married. Though she could have dumped it when she moved, he couldn't find it now. A couple of roller bags and an Eddie Bauer backpack, yes, but no 49ers bag.

There was one way of knowing whether she had packed for a trip—the bathroom. He didn't find a toothbrush, makeup, or any other toiletries.

She'd gone somewhere. She knew he was coming, so why would she disappear on him?

The doorbell rang.

Sarah.

The doorbell rang again, this time sounding more urgent.

He ran through the house, grabbed the flowers, and hurried to the front door. He called out, "Hold on a sec. Coming."

He stopped abruptly at the front door. If Sarah was back, why was she ringing the doorbell? Wouldn't she have a key or be coming through the garage to park the car? Still believing in his heart that it was his wife, he opened the door and found himself staring down the barrel of a gun, with only a screen door for protection. Instinctively, he raised his hands.

A short, muscular black woman dressed in a Christmas tree–green windbreaker was at the other end of the gun. Embroidered on her jacket was a five-pointed gold star with Santa Rita County Sheriff's Department emblazoned on it.

"Don't move a muscle," she said. "You're busted."

Terry nodded.

She removed a supporting hand from the revolver and eased open the screen door. "Now back up and turn around. Put your hands behind your head, interlacing your fingers."

The dining-area patio door squeaked. Terry craned his neck. A second person from the county sheriff's office entered the house, this time a man, much older than the woman.

"You'd better do as the officer tells you, son." His words were calm and smooth, comforting, in fact. The gun he held was not.

Terry dropped the flowers and did as he was told.

"You are under arrest. You have the right to remain silent. Anything you say can and will be used against you in a court of law."

Oh Sarah, Terry thought, *where are you when I need you?*

CHAPTER TWO

"Obviously, you can understand the confusion. To a pass-erby, you did look like a burglar," the sheriff said.

The confusion had taken its time getting resolved. Terry's protests had gone ignored while his arrest had been processed and he'd been reduced to a line of cop statistics—age: thirty; height: five nine; weight: one hundred and sixty-five pounds; hair: brown; eyes: blue. When they got around to taking his statement, the cuffs finally came off.

The sheriff had been the kindly man with the gun who'd entered his home through the back door. Now he held Terry's green card up for inspection yet again, and turned it around to look at the magnetic strip. For a moment, Terry half expected the sheriff to lick his green card, as though its taste would give him a better clue as to its authenticity.

"I suppose," Terry mumbled.

He massaged his wrists. The handcuffs had been off twenty minutes, but he still felt the ghost of their existence. The removal of the cuffs had given him the illusion that he was free. But he was in an interview room, and the sheriff liked to give his gun a touch now and then, as if to remind himself and anybody in the vicinity that he still knew where to find it. The gun was an awesome weapon, rivaling anything Dirty Harry toted. No one needed to be reminded of its existence. The gun possessed plenty of personality.

While the sheriff studied Terry's paperwork, Terry studied him. Sheriff Ray Holman was just like Terry imagined a sheriff to be, but not a modern-day sheriff. He belonged in the Old West. Holman was a hundred and fifty years out of time. He was tall, eclipsing six feet with ease, and lean, with a weather-beaten exterior that only triple-digit summers could inflict on a man's skin. His face was deeply lined with the flesh pulled taut against his skull, accentuating his cheekbones and razor-sharp jawline. His blond hair bordered on red and his moustache wouldn't have been out of place on a seventies porn star, but on him, it was nothing but masculine. Holman dripped testosterone.

"I'm still not sure I understand what's going on here." Sheriff Holman put down Terry's documents. "So why don't you tell me?"

Terry frowned.

"Just so I fully understand." Holman flashed a smile that would have been at home on a shark. The smile tightened his features.

Terry sucked in a deep breath and let it slide out. "I left England to come to the US. As you can see, I have all the correct immigration paperwork."

Holman nodded.

"My wife was supposed to meet me at the airport, but she wasn't there."

"Your wife's American, right?"

"Yes."

"She lived here in California and you in England, correct?"

"Yes."

"That's a funny setup, isn't it?"

Terry sighed. "I know how it sounds, but with immigration laws these days, normal isn't possible. To get through the system, you have to do some things to keep everything moving."

"Hmm. I see. Do you want a coffee or something?"

"No, thanks. I just want to go home."

"So how long have you been married?"

"About six months."

"And where did you marry?"

"Las Vegas."

Holman's eyebrows climbed halfway up his forehead. "Vegas?"

Terry sighed again. It was another of those elements that smacked of tackiness. Getting married in Vegas had been Sarah's idea. They'd joked about having an Elvis wedding. It had been funny at the time, but now, in a sheriff's windowless interview room, it wasn't so amusing.

"The reason we got married in Las Vegas was for simplicity. We were going to get married in the Caribbean, but immigration sometimes doesn't recognize marriage certificates outside of the US. So Las Vegas it was."

Holman frowned at Terry, unimpressed with his fast-food approach to holy matrimony. Terry swallowed at something sour in his throat.

"Why didn't you stay in the US after you were married?"

"Sheriff, what has this got to do with my arrest?"

Holman thought for a second. "Not a lot, I suppose. I guess I'm being nosy. My mother, God rest her soul, was always saying I should keep my beak out of things. I apologize, Mr. Sheffield."

"Am I still under arrest?"

"Technically, yes."

"Can we get this over with so I can go?"

"Apologies again. I'm sure you want to get back to your wife."

"I want to find her," Terry corrected.

"Okay, back to the questions." Holman picked up his notebook and flicked back over his pages.

Terry walked the sheriff through events from the airport to his arrest. He went into minute detail, just so that he wouldn't be asked again.

"Okay." Holman turned the page in his notebook. "One last thing."

Someone knocking at the door interrupted Holman's last thing.

The female officer who'd stuck the gun in Terry's face poked her head through the door. "Sheriff, I have that information for you."

"Come in then," Holman replied.

The deputy stood in the corner farthest from Terry, and Holman joined her, his lanky form towering over hers. She held a sheaf of papers for him to examine. The deputy kept her voice low, but Terry could still hear.

"The house belongs to Terry and Sarah Sheffield. They're listed as co-owners."

Holman nodded. "Good. Thanks, Deputy Pittman."

The deputy flashed Terry an examining look on her way out. He saw the doubt in her eyes. *Sometimes evidence just isn't enough*, he thought.

Holman spun on his heels and clapped his hands together. "It looks like I've got all my answers, and you're free to go. I'm sorry it's taken so long, but we can't afford to let these things go unnoticed. I'm sure you understand."

"Yeah, I'm sure," Terry said bitterly.

Holman opened the interview room door. "I'll arrange for a ride home."

"Hey, hold on a second."

"Yes?"

"Who tipped you off that I was in the house?"

"You should count yourself lucky, Mr. Sheffield. You have some conscientious neighbors. They believe very much in neighborhood watch. Come along, Mr. Sheffield. I think our business is concluded."

Terry remained rooted to his seat. "No, it isn't."

Holman's face creased and his blue eyes lost their sparkle. Suspicion consumed his expression. Terry knew where the sheriff's mind was going. He was thinking about a wrongful arrest suit, but that was the furthest thing from Terry's mind.

"What's outstanding, sir?" Holman asked with a sharp tone.

"My wife."

"What about her?"

"I want you to find her."

"You want to report her as missing?"

"Yes."

"But we don't know that she's missing."

"Yes, we do. She wasn't at the airport, and I have about a week's worth of unopened mail. What more do you want?"

"She could be waiting for you at home right now. You said yourself that she packed a bag."

"Yeah, and she could be in trouble."

"Look, Mr. Sheffield, I understand you've had a traumatic day, but I'm guessing by the time you get home, she'll be there to meet you."

Terry stood. "And if not, then what?"

"Then come and see me in the morning. At this point, I think your fears are unfounded."

"Aren't you listening? She's been missing for days."

"You have no proof of that," Holman said. Terry opened his mouth to speak, but the sheriff stopped him with a raised hand. "You have a pile of unopened mail and a missed appointment. It's not enough for us to call out the cavalry."

Terry shook his head.

"Mr. Sheffield, you're tired. Go home and wait for your wife. Like I said, if she hasn't made it home by morning, call me and I'll file a report."

Terry wanted to object, but Holman was ushering him out of the interview room and along the corridor to the front door. At least Terry could be thankful he wasn't being escorted to the cells.

In the reception area, Deputy Pittman glanced up from her PC terminal when her name was called.

"I'm releasing Mr. Sheffield, but he needs a ride home. Can you take him?"

"Sure thing, Sheriff."

At the end of a silent twenty-minute ride, the deputy pulled up in front of Terry's house. He was glad it was over. But even without leaving the car, he could tell he wasn't arriving to a rousing homecoming. The sheriff's department had kept him so long it was dusk. Every house had its lights on except one—his.

"Thanks for the ride," Terry said without much gratitude.

"Take it easy, Mr. Sheffield. And don't get into any more trouble."

A bit late for that, Terry thought. "I'll do my best."

The deputy watched him walk up the path to the front door before driving off.

Slipping his hand in his jeans pocket, he fingered his pocket change before realizing his mistake. He whirled back toward the street in the hope of catching the deputy, but she was already turning onto the next street.

"I don't have any damn keys," he called after her.

• • •

Terry tossed the orange tree branch onto the patio for the second time that day and slipped through the patio door. He hoped he wouldn't have to enter his house this way every time. He switched on the dining area lights.

"Sarah?" he called and got no answer, as expected.

Some homecoming. This was supposed to be his happy home. This place didn't feel like home. He felt like an intruder, a stranger.

"You don't know your arse from your elbow, Sheriff."

Terry spent the next ten minutes rummaging through the house for a set of keys. While digging around he found a garage-door opener with a dead battery before finding the spare bunch of keys in a kitchen drawer. He made damn sure they were in his pocket before the cops could come calling again.

He called Sarah's cell and got voice mail yet again.

He left the house and knocked on the doors of his immediate neighbors. He introduced himself and asked them if they'd seen Sarah. They remembered seeing her, but couldn't recall exactly when.

He couldn't wait for Holman to get his machine rolling. Sarah was in trouble. He knew it even if the sheriff didn't. What to do next was the problem. He could comb the streets calling her name like she was a lost dog, but how far was that going to get him? Sarah had a four- or five-day head start on him. She could be anywhere. Even out of the country. Why hadn't she called him? It had to be serious. There was no excuse otherwise. Maybe she'd run out on him. He didn't want to admit it, but the facts were there in front of him—the unread mail, the unanswered phone messages, her switched-off cell, and the most damning of all, a packed bag. He refused to believe she'd abandoned him. If she'd had second thoughts about their marriage, she could have easily phoned him with a Dear John story. She didn't have to hide from him. And if she planned to run out, why pack only an overnight bag and not clear the house out entirely? As easy as it was to believe in the simplest solution, he couldn't. If he needed proof of that belief, he didn't have to look any further than the fridge. He pulled open the fridge door and removed the bottle of champagne. As well as the ribbon, a greeting card hung around the bottle's neck. He opened the card and read it: *Welcome home, baby. This is going to be great.* Yes, Sarah had skipped out on him for a reason. One so serious she hadn't had the time to call him.

I just wish you'd tell me what's going on.

If she couldn't, maybe somebody else would. He returned the champagne to the fridge and went into the bedroom Sarah had converted into an office. He flicked on the computer and went

18

through her desk while the machine booted up. He found an address book in a drawer.

He flipped through the pages, staring at names and numbers he didn't recognize. He'd heard about some of Sarah's friends as part of some anecdote, but he'd never met them. And naturally, all Sarah's stories involved first names only—John did this and Karen did that. With so few opportunities to see each other over the last couple of years, they'd been selfish with their time together. They came first. Everyone else could wait.

It wasn't like he could even call Sarah's family. She was an only child and her parents had passed away, her father of a heart attack and her mother of breast cancer.

The computer finished its boot-up cycle, and Terry opened up her e-mail program. She might not have left a phone message, but her e-mails might explain what was going on. He felt like a voyeur for going through Sarah's e-mail, but he had no choice. It was better he did it than Holman.

Skimming her outgoing and incoming e-mails, it seemed to be the usual combination of spam, personal and work-related communications, and, of course, their e-mails to each other. Nothing screamed an explanation for her no show.

No matter. He might not have any e-mails that could clue him into Sarah's disappearance, but he did have one thing—Sarah's e-mail address book. He composed a new message to everyone in it. It was the quickest way to get the word out to everyone.

Hello Sarah's friends,
I'm Terry Sheffield, Sarah's husband. Sarah is missing. She wasn't at the airport today to pick me up, and it looks as she might have left town for a couple of days, but I don't know where she's gone. If you know where she is or how to get in contact with her, please let me know.
Thanks,
Terry

He read his message. It was as alarmist as hell considering the e-mail would be going out to friends, business acquaintances, and strangers, but this was the situation he found himself in. It would prove embarrassing if this revealed a totally innocent and understandable explanation, but he was willing to accept having egg on his face.

"Please, let this be a sign of me overreacting," he said to himself and hit SEND.

Hopefully, someone would have some insight.

Sarah's e-mails might not have told him anything, but maybe her browser history would reveal something. It did. She'd cleared both her browser and search engine histories. Was that habit or a sign she was covering her tracks?

He turned his attention back to the names, addresses, and phone numbers in Sarah's address book. None meant anything to him. They would all have to be called. With over fifty names listed, it was a daunting prospect. He checked the time on the computer's clock. It had gotten late. He doubted many would appreciate a call from him at this time of night. Besides, his mind and body were still on London time. Despite being hopped-up on fear, jet lag was getting its teeth into him. He put the address book down. His e-mail plea was enough for tonight.

Despite his exhaustion, his stomach reminded him that it still needed feeding. There was nothing substantial in the fridge and what was in there didn't appeal. He dug out the yellow pages from under the TV and ordered a pizza. His order arrived forty minutes later. The pizza box promised piping-hot pizza and ice-cold sodas, but somewhere along the way the promises had been swapped. Terry ate in front of the TV.

"Welcome to America," he said.

Within an hour, the jet lag got the better of Terry and he fell asleep.

• • •

Two years earlier

"*How's your butt?*" *Sarah asked.*

Terry was facing the Pacific Ocean, watching puffy white clouds drift by and crystal blue water wash against the Costa Rican beach. He turned around to face her. She was sitting on a fallen tree trunk, which was something he wished he could do. He rubbed at his arse through his swimming trunks, feeling the scabbed-over welt.

"*Still sore.*"

She laughed.

"*It's not funny,*" *he said, smiling.*

"*It is. You shouldn't have worn jeans.*"

"*Yeah, well, hindsight is twenty-twenty.*"

Although his backside had been burning for two days, he wouldn't have traded the horseback ride for anything. It hadn't been some pony trek across a beach. It had been eight hours of grueling cross-country terrain. Their destination had been the cloud forest nature reserve of Monteverde. It involved a steady climb through the mountains—usually an easy ride for novices, which Terry and most of the group were. But the rain had changed that. November wasn't rainy season, but no one had told Mother Nature. Ten minutes into the ride, the heavens opened. Previously rock-hard dirt paths turned into clay molasses. The horses sunk in the slop up to their bellies, and novice riders turned into instant experts. It was a miracle no one had fallen and none of the horses had snapped a leg.

Everyone was a casualty of fatigue, but Terry was the only one sporting an injury. He'd worn jeans, his only long trousers. The thick seam and the soaking denim had joined forces on his tailbone to wear through his flesh. He couldn't see the wound, but he'd shown Sarah and apparently, it was an impressive battle scar— quite befitting for an adventure holiday.

He, Sarah, and seven others were part of an adventure-vacation group that was touring Costa Rica. Strangely enough, their guide was Swedish. A Canadian travel company had organized their trip, and the party of nine had come from five different countries. It was the United Nations of travel.

"Are you enjoying yourself?" Sarah asked.

"Time of my life."

She nodded in agreement. "There's so much I've never done."

"Me too. In the last two weeks, I've whitewater rafted, boogie-boarded, deep-sea fished, climbed a volcano, felt an earthquake, and met you."

This last experience had slipped out by accident. He hadn't meant to share that thought, or maybe he had. They hadn't had a holiday romance, but they had formed a connection that Terry hadn't experienced with anyone else. He reddened and looked toward the ocean again.

Sarah stood up and came over to him. She slipped her arm around his. "And it's all coming to an end. In a couple of days, we'll all be going our separate ways."

He wanted to say it wasn't true. It was going to be hard going back to the daily grind. Costa Rica had taken the shine off life back in England. Or was it Sarah that had done that?

"We've got each other's addresses and telephone numbers."

She frowned. "It won't be the same."

She was right. It wouldn't.

"We can visit each other," Terry countered. "I get plenty of holiday allowance, and you work freelance."

Sarah brightened. "You've never been to the US, have you?"

"No."

"Well, it's ski season soon, and you ski. Come and we'll go to Tahoe. We'll have a ball. You'll love America."

CHAPTER THREE

The ringing phone jolted Terry from his sleep. Despite his slumber, his brain felt like a drawer stuffed with dirty socks. It took him two rings to remember where he was and the situation he found himself in. *Sarah,* he thought and lunged for the phone. A half-eaten pizza slice slipped off his stomach onto the floor.

"Crap," he mumbled.

Terry snatched up the pizza but the damage was already done. Tomato sauce and congealed cheese clung to the carpet as he pulled the slice away. He cursed again and chucked it onto the pizza box.

He snatched up the phone before the answering machine kicked in. "Hello. Sarah?" His throat was dry and sleep muffled his vocal chords.

"Terry Sheffield?"

"Yes."

He tugged at the curtains. Sunlight smashed him in the face, and he jerked them shut again. He squinted, looking for a clock. The DVD player displayed 10:10.

"Mr. Sheffield, it's Pamela Dawson."

It was on the tip of his tongue to say, "Who?" but recollection filtered through the haze. Pamela Dawson had hired him at

Genavax, in the nearby city of Vacaville. She was his new boss, and he was their new senior research associate.

"Oh, hi, Ms. Dawson. How are you?"

"A lot better than you by the sound of it."

Terry cleared his throat. "Yeah, I've just woken up. Jet lag, it's a powerful thing."

"Yes, I'm sure." She didn't sound convinced.

He injected some life into his voice. "How can I help you, Ms. Dawson?"

"It's Pamela. We are not formal at Genavax."

You could have fooled me, Terry thought. "Okay then, Pamela."

"I wanted to check to make sure you had arrived as scheduled and that you would be starting Monday morning."

"Ah, we might have a problem there."

"A problem?" A hint of frost breathed out from the receiver. "What kind of problem?"

"My wife is missing. She didn't turn up at the airport to collect me yesterday, and she didn't come home last night."

"And what has this got to do with Genavax?"

Damn fool question to ask, Terry thought. He knew it was a dog-eat-dog world in the US, but American business couldn't be as callous as this, could it?

"I would like to find my wife." He did his best to make his tone civil and not adversarial. He could thank Pamela Dawson for one thing. She'd helped lift the sleep haze that fogged his mind. He was awake and pissed off.

"I understand that, but it shouldn't get in the way of your job."

"I'm afraid it will for the moment. Surely you can understand that?"

"Terry, we went to a lot of time and expense to hire you, not to mention the concessions we made. We hired you on your reputation before your immigration status was finalized. I don't think we've ever done that for anyone else. Genavax has a lot invested in you. I would hate for it to come to nothing."

Wasn't she getting it? Terry collapsed into the easy chair. "I'm not sure I'm making myself clear. My wife is missing. She could be dead, for all I know. I would like to take some time to find her."

"Mr. Sheffield," she said, "I fully understand the predicament you find yourself in, and I sympathize with your plight. But we are not a charity. We have a business to run. Biotechnology is a make-or-break industry. We are not Glaxo or Pfizer. We are a company without an FDA-approved drug yet. That means we have no income. We need every employee to be a team player. You are a team player, aren't you?"

Terry's grip tightened on the phone. He didn't like threats, and he took Pamela Dawson's last statement to be one. He bottled his knee-jerk reaction.

"I need to file a missing person's report with the county sheriff. Can I call you back? By that time, I'll have a better idea of where I stand."

"Of course." She reeled off her telephone number. Terry found a pen on top of the stereo and scribbled the number on the back of his hand. "I'll expect your call."

"Good."

"When you start on Monday, don't forget to bring your green card, passport, and things of that nature."

"I'll call you this afternoon."

Terry went to hang up, but Pamela wanted a final shot. "Oh, Terry?"

"Yes."

"Don't make me regret hiring you," she said and hung up.

"Thanks for nothing," he muttered and tossed the phone at the couch.

A long shower washed away Terry's jet lag and irritation. Afterward, for the first time, he felt in tune with his new time zone.

He didn't bother with breakfast and went straight to Sarah's computer to check her e-mail. He'd received more than a couple dozen replies to his message from the night before. Half of them were bounced e-mail and automatic out-of-town notifications. But the sight of a dozen or so solid replies was encouraging. Each one held potential.

"Someone please know something," he said before opening the first e-mail.

His prayer went unanswered. Everyone expressed their shock at Sarah's disappearance and wanted to be kept informed, but no one knew anything. All of it was supportive, but all of it was useless.

The e-mails had proved helpful in one regard. He now had a sense of some of Sarah's friends. Most had introduced themselves to him in their replies. A couple of people had gone to college with Sarah, while others had worked with her. It hadn't been hard to glean she'd only had a business or professional relationship with the remainder. He found that disturbing. What did that say about his wife? She was either selective about who she made friends with or kept everyone at a distance. That wasn't the woman he knew. Maybe he was different, and he'd broken down her barriers. That thought erred on the side of wishful thinking. If he'd gotten really close, he'd know where she was this minute.

Terry called a cab company then brushed his teeth. Thirty minutes later, a cab tooted its horn in the driveway.

"Where to?" the driver asked.

"The sheriff's office," Terry said as he got in.

After a short ride, the cab dropped Terry off in front of the sheriff's office, and he walked inside. Obviously, Edenville wasn't the crime capital of America. Terry was first and last in line. Holman and Deputy Pittman stopped their work at his arrival.

"Mr. Sheffield," Holman said brightly. "Did your wife come home?"

Terry shook his head. "No."

"I guess you'll be wanting to start the ball rolling on that missing person's report."

"Yeah."

"Would you like me to start a case file, Sheriff?" Deputy Pittman asked without much enthusiasm.

"I don't think so. I'll take this one. Mr. Sheffield deserves my attention. He's had a rough welcome to the US. I want to show him that people here are decent."

"Thank you, Sheriff," Terry said.

"You're welcome." Holman unlatched the counter door. "Follow me into my office, if you wouldn't mind."

Holman led the way into a cluttered room. There was barely room for his desk and chair and a couple of chairs for visitors. Filing cabinets consumed most of the space, and the American and Californian flags dangling from individual poles didn't help matters. The office was painted a utilitarian gray-green, not unlike the color of the sheriff's jacket but with the life drained from it.

"Take a seat, Mr. Sheffield," Holman said. He sat and fired up his PC. "So she didn't come home then?" he said, rephrasing his earlier question.

"No."

"Well, that's not good." Holman's PC beeped. "Give me a second to get this machine working, and I'll pull up the appropriate form; then we'll get this show on the road."

Terry was getting Holman's bedside-manner treatment. His comments were a little too kind, but at least he was making the effort. He seemed to be trying to make up for yesterday's mistake.

The sheriff pecked gingerly at the keyboard as if each key would bite him. After several minutes of manipulation, the PC beeped again.

"Right, we're in business. Can I have your wife's full name?"

"Sarah Lauren Sheffield."

Holman tapped in the information. "Date of birth?"

"October the fifteenth, nineteen eighty-one."

"What was her maiden name?"

"Morton."

Holman proceeded to enter Sarah and Terry's mundane personal details into the computer.

"Okay. How long has she been missing?"

"I would guess it's been five or six days." Terry went on to remind him about the stacked-up mail and the phone messages.

"But you can only be sure about the last twenty-four hours, correct?"

"Yes," he replied reluctantly.

"What's Sarah's driver's license number?"

"Don't know."

"Okay, I'll get it through the DMV. Social Security number?"

"Don't know it, sorry."

Holman sucked on his teeth. "No problem, I can get that too. Let's move on to some things you should know. Describe Sarah for me—height, weight, hair and eye color, et cetera—okay? Those sorts of details."

Terry nodded. "She's five-five with light brown hair with blonde streaks."

The sheriff rattled the keyboard. "Dyed?"

"No, it's her natural hair color."

"Okay. Eye color?"

"Gray."

"Weight?"

"A bit over nine stone."

"Excuse me?"

"Oh. Sorry." Terry did the mental calculation. "About a hundred thirty pounds."

"Have you got a picture?"

"Yes. I brought one. I thought it might help." Terry brought out a snapshot from when he and Sarah had met in Costa Rica. The picture was a little dog-eared. It featured Sarah weighed down by her backpack, smiling with a tropical jungle behind her. She was without makeup and damp looking—not her finest hour, but that was the Sarah he'd fallen in love with. He handed the photo to Holman and the sheriff examined it.

"Does she have any distinguishing marks like tattoos, scars—anything of that sort?"

"Sheriff, she's not a sailor."

Holman cracked a smile. His face creased like it was antique leather. "I didn't mean it as it sounded. So I can take it that the answer is no?"

"Correct, but she does have a heart-shaped birthmark on her right hip."

"Good to know. Who is her employer?"

"She's a freelance journalist. She works features for magazines and newspapers, but I don't know which ones."

"How about friends and family?"

"Her parents are both deceased. I've never met her friends. I just have names in an address book, so I've sent them e-mails asking for their help. None of them seem to know anything."

"Credit cards?"

"Probably."

"But you don't know the numbers?" Holman asked with a sigh.

"Right."

Holman slid his chair back from his terminal and sat back, resting his hands across his trim stomach. "Mr. Sheffield, let's make this a little easier for both of us. Why don't you tell me what you *do* know about your wife?"

"She likes animals and travel, adores horses, and loves me."

Holman exhaled. "That it?"

"Pretty much."

"If your wife is a journalist, it's possible that she's off investigating a story."

"Possible. But she would have left word for me."

"How do you know?"

"I know because she's my wife. She wouldn't have run off and left me stranded."

"How long have you known Sarah, Terry?"

Alarm bells were ringing. Holman was using his first name. Terry knew something was coming. "Eighteen months."

"And how long in each other's company?"

"Why?"

"Indulge me."

Terry didn't like where Holman was going with this line of questioning, but he indulged the sheriff. He totaled up the amount of time they'd spent together. It was embarrassingly short.

"Eight weeks."

"Eight weeks?"

"Maybe nine," Terry added.

"Okay, I'll give you the benefit of the doubt—nine weeks. You've known this woman just over two months."

"We kept in contact by phone and e-mail," Terry interjected.

"Big deal."

"It is a big deal. When you don't have the luxury of living in the same country as another person, you have to make do. You improvise and do whatever you can to maintain that bond. Don't knock it purely because you don't understand it. You don't know me, and you don't know Sarah."

"No, I don't, Terry. I don't know you or your wife, but I'm having a hard time believing in the seriousness of your relationship with this woman. Remind me, where did you get married?"

"Las Vegas," Terry said with a sigh.

Holman shook his head and smiled wryly.

"Who was present?"

"Us, the minister, and two witnesses we dragged off the street."

"Very romantic."

It was romantic. That was how he'd seen it at the time. He'd fallen in love in a tropical location with a woman from another country. And it hadn't been some meaningless holiday romance. Their bond had been strong enough for their relationship to blossom. They'd met up in other foreign countries every few months when they could get the time off from their careers. Their passports were full of immigration stamps proving their commitment to each other. And when their relationship needed to be elevated to a new level, they married. But to Holman—applying cold logic to the situation—Terry's actions were ridiculous. To Holman, Terry was no more a romantic than one of those idiots at a casino who drops a million dollars on red and then watches it come up black. He was a fool.

"Sheriff Holman, what's your point?"

Holman straightened in his chair and leaned across his desk. "My point is, you don't seem to know squat about your wife."

CHAPTER FOUR

Terry walked out of the sheriff's office. He chewed on Holman's remarks and tried to convince himself that the sheriff's doubts were unwarranted, but he failed. True, he didn't know much about Sarah, but their marriage would change that. Whatever Holman thought about the relationship, the sheriff was still obliged to do his job. He had a duty to follow up on Terry's report.

He wandered along Solano Dam Road, Edenville's main street. Sporadic traffic whistled along on the main thoroughfare on its way out of town. Although the look and feel wasn't the same, he was reminded of many villages in England. Edenville felt self-contained. It had its own supermarket, restaurants, a couple of bars, a few stores, a gas station with a mechanic, two banks, and a farmers' market on Saturdays. There was a little bit of everything for everyone. But Edenville, like every English village, would never become a boomtown. Although quaint in a rough-and-ready way, it was never going to be a destination town. Thanks to Solano Dam Road, it was easy to pass through Edenville without a second thought.

Taxis were fine, but Terry needed wheels, so he rented a car from Edenville's only rental center. It took some finagling since he didn't have a California driver's license, but he played the tourist card to swing it his way. He left the center in a Ford Focus. He took to driving on the wrong side of the road pretty well, thanks to Edenville's simple network of roads.

With the car, he had mobility. Wherever Sarah went, he could follow. He bought a map at a supermarket and opened it out across the hood of the car. He put himself in Sarah's shoes. If she'd skipped town, it wasn't like she had a large number of options. The US might be a big country compared to Britain, but for its size, it didn't have a particularly complex or involved road system. Only a couple of roads led in and out of town and a limited number of freeways took you any distance. He could follow, but he stood little chance of catching Sarah. She had almost a week's head start. Besides, Holman had the resources to cast a net far and wide. But who was to say she'd gone that far? She could be in the local area. The surrounding area got pretty rural, pretty quick. Terry could see her crashing in a hundred places within a twenty-mile radius of Edenville. Crashing brought up another possibility. What if she'd had an accident and hadn't been found? He could check out the local area. He had to do this. He couldn't let any possibility go unchecked.

He worked on a twenty-mile radius as a search area, then broke that area into quadrants based on the direction of roads entering and leaving Edenville. He stopped to check every park, campsite, abandoned trailer, unused vacation home, and set of skid marks that left the road—with no success. When the dashboard light came on to tell him to refill the gas tank, he gave up on his search. He was hot, tired, and dehydrated. He was done for the day. He would start over the next day with a wider search. He turned the car around and aimed it back toward Edenville.

His head was pounding and his mouth was so dry his tongue had glued itself to the roof of his mouth. Stuck in the car for hours, he'd boiled, even with the air-conditioning going full blast. He needed to get some liquid into him, but when he wanted a fast-food franchise, there wasn't one to be seen. The only beacon on the horizon was a sign poking high above the walnut groves proclaiming THE GOLD RUSH ARCADE in black text on a gold background. It was punctuated by wagon wheels at either end, and followed by MINIGOLF AND AMUSEMENTS. FUN TIMES FOR ALL AGES. Just to illustrate the point, the rigging for an ancient mine peeked above the fields of walnut trees. The place was bound to have something, even if it was a vending machine.

He parked and went inside. Pinball machines clanged and the latest shoot-'em-up video games wailed at him, which did nothing for his headache. But for all its noise, the Gold Rush wasn't packed with people. It was a school day, and most of the arcade machines were busy playing themselves on demo cycles. He couldn't see the place getting busy until after five. Still, a few teenagers putting the machines through their paces managed to give the Gold Rush an air of respectability.

Terry weaved between the air hockey tables and a bank of NASCAR simulators to get to the combined ticket booth and snack bar. A friendly looking man in his late forties spotted Terry's approach and put down his soda. He wasn't fat, but he carried a hefty paunch, probably from too much soda and too little minigolfing. He looked down at Terry through half-moon glasses.

"Can I get you something?" he asked with a smile.

"The biggest Sprite you can pour and if you've got any headache medicine, that would be fantastic."

The attendant smiled at him in sympathy. "Rough day, huh? Tylenol do?"

"Anything."

The attendant produced a bottle of pills from under the counter. "Working in a place like this, you need them."

By the time Terry had uncapped the bottle and shaken two pills from it, the attendant had placed the giant cup of Sprite on the counter. He tossed the pills back and washed them down with the soft drink. The pills would take their time dulling the pain, but the first taste of Sprite doused the throbbing in his skull.

"Wanna add a round of minigolf?"

"No, I don't think so."

"C'mon, it'll do you good."

Despite the guy pushing the upsell, Terry decided he could do with some light relief. From the moment he'd stepped off the plane, circumstances had thrown him into a conflict. He'd done all he could for the moment, and he needed to take a step back and clear his head. A mindless round of minigolf would give him the opportunity to put his thoughts in order and plan his next move.

"Why not? Sign me up."

"Good decision." The attendant put a golf ball and a putter on the counter. "Ten bucks for the soda and game. The first hole is down the stairs next to the restrooms."

Terry paid.

The Gold Rush had a neat gimmick. The first three holes were subterranean. Rough stucco, pickaxes, and shovels fixed to the walls, and lanterns hanging from the ceiling, helped create the look of a mine. All the aboveground holes possessed a mining motif to maintain the theme.

The final hole was a test of skill, which required the player to strike the ball over an undulating course and into a tube not much wider than the ball. Terry lined up the ball and struck it solidly. The ball rode the undulations and carried enough momentum to fly down the tube. A bell rang and the red light flashed, but instead of Terry's ball staying in the tube, it rolled back out of the tube and into the gutter trap.

"When you're on a streak, you're on a streak," he mumbled to himself.

Terry returned his putter to the ticket booth.

"Well done, you won a free pass," the attendant said.

"But the ball came back out."

"Well, the bell rang. That makes you a winner in my book." The attendant put a winner's pass on the counter. "You won a soda too. Sprite again?"

"That's good of you," Terry said, pocketing his winner's pass. "Thanks."

"You're welcome."

Terry took his soda and found a booth seat in the restaurant area. He scooped out a handful of ice from his soda and massaged it into his neck. His skin was hot and tight. He'd have to get used to putting on sun block. The sun rarely reached this sort of intensity on a regular basis in the UK, where the need for the stuff was for special occasions only.

"Do you mind if I join you?" The attendant slipped into the bench seat opposite Terry. "Because I don't think I've ever seen anyone as miserable as you walk through my doors."

There wasn't a lot Terry could say in reply. His face must have shown it.

"Sorry," the attendant apologized. "I suppose I was a bit insensitive there. What I meant to say is you look like you need to get something off your chest."

"Is this a service you offer to all your customers?"

"Nah," the attendant said, shaking his head. "Most of my clients haven't gotten past the Harry Potter stage yet. But you, you look like you know your ABCs."

"Finished learning them last week."

"There you go. See, I knew I could help. That's a fancy accent you've got yourself. What is it? English? Australian?"

"English."

"You've come a long way for a game of minigolf."

"Feels like it."

"So why are you here? I doubt you're scouting for PGA locations."

"No, I've just moved here."

"Cool, when did you arrive?"

"Yesterday."

"Yesterday. Wow, you did just arrive." The attendant slurped his soda. "You here on some business gig or something?"

"No. My wife's American."

"You don't sound too happy about it."

Terry had said *my wife* as if he was recounting how his dog had just died. "Yeah, well."

"Oh, I get it. That's the reason for the long face. Just found out she's no angel?"

"No, just haven't found her."

The attendant looked confused.

Terry told the attendant about Sarah's no show at SFO, his arrest, Pamela Dawson's lack of compassion, and Holman's reluctance to file a missing persons request. Although he wouldn't have guessed it, it felt good to share his problems with this stranger. It was a lot easier than if he'd confided in a friend. And in shedding a load, he was gaining an ally at last.

"Wow," the attendant managed after a long moment. "You've done well for being here"—he checked his watch—"less than twenty-four hours. You're the reason people have to buy insurance."

"Some people just have a knack, I suppose. I'm Terry Sheffield, by the way."

"I'm Oscar...Oscar Mayer." Oscar ground out his name like he was reciting a foreign language. "I own this rattrap."

"Pleased to make your acquaintance, Oscar Mayer." Terry offered his hand.

"The name doesn't mean anything to you?" Oscar said suspiciously, shaking Terry's hand.

"No." Terry sucked on his straw. "Should it?"

"You've never heard of Oscar Mayer?"

"You're the first I've met."

"Oh, I can see we're going to be good friends."

• • •

37

Around midday, Terry returned home with his new friend's telephone number and a healthy slice of optimism. Oscar was taking the day off from the Gold Rush tomorrow to act as a guide. Oscar's offer to help Terry any way he could was unbelievably kind, especially seeing as Terry had only known the guy for a couple of hours. He was overcome by Oscar's kindness. America wasn't such a bad place after all. He parked the Ford in his driveway.

As Terry got out of the car, a man pushing a lawn mower hailed him from across the street. Terry acknowledged the lawn mower man with a nod. The man switched off his mower and crossed the street.

"Mr. Sheffield, isn't it?" he asked.

"Yes," Terry replied.

The neighbor felt like trouble. Terry didn't know why he felt that way. Maybe it had something to do with the guy wearing both a belt and suspenders or the plastered-down comb-over he was sporting to cover a large bald spot.

"Noah Osbourne," lawn mower man said proffering a hand.

Terry shook it. "Terry Sheffield."

"What's that accent?"

Terry had the feeling this was going to become a recurring question. "English."

"New to the country?"

"Since yesterday."

"That is new." Osbourne nodded with approval. "Anyway, I'm the president of the Sutter Drive Neighborhood Watch Committee." Osbourne hooked his thumbs under his scarlet suspenders and twanged them. "We don't just cover Sutter Drive, you understand, but a number of neighboring streets."

"Right."

"But it began on Sutter Drive, hence the name."

Terry couldn't help staring at Osbourne's hair. Whatever goop he'd used to smarm it down with had turned his hair black.

This contrasted appallingly with the dusty-gray band of curls around the sides and back of his head. The clash of color and texture was most peculiar.

"When I saw you climbing over the fence yesterday, I had no option but to call the sheriff."

Osbourne waited a moment. Terry guessed he was waiting for a pat on the head or a medal for carrying out his civic duty so diligently. He'd be waiting a bloody long time, in Terry's estimation.

"Well, I wanted to let you know it was me who called the sheriff's department."

Terry didn't say anything.

"Sheriff Holman responds very quickly to calls coming from our neighborhood watch committee," Osbourne said, impressed with his own importance.

Terry still didn't reply, and Osbourne's face exhibited signs that he was realizing he wasn't welcome.

Breaking the silence, Terry said, "I was put in a cell."

"But it wasn't for long," Osbourne corrected, raising a finger. "You weren't in overnight or anything. I saw Deputy Pittman bring you back."

"I'd been in the country five hours, and I wound up in jail."

"A holding cell, actually."

Osborne's semantics failed to impress Terry, and he frowned.

"You understand how the situation looked. I had no choice."

"You could have asked me what I was doing."

Now it was Osbourne's turn to look unimpressed. "What? Ask you if you're a burglar and could you come down from that fence? No way. I'm retired, and I would like to remain retired for some considerable time to come."

Terry could see Osbourne's point, but he didn't want to admit it. Osbourne was one of those annoying people who needed to feel important, and being chairman of the neighborhood watch committee satisfied that need. Admitting Osbourne had a point would only fuel his desperation to be needed, but Terry felt sorry for the guy and caved.

"You might be right."

"Well, I wanted to come over and say sorry for the mix-up. We, the Sutter Drive Neighborhood Watch Committee, have your best interests at heart and would like to extend an invitation to you to join. We meet the second and fourth Tuesdays of the month. The meetings usually take place at my house, although we do like to rotate locations. Can I count on you being at our next meeting?"

"I'm sorry, no. I have some important issues I need to attend to before I consider anything else. So if you'll excuse me."

"Is it because of your wife?"

"Yes…yes, it is. How did you know?"

"Sheriff Holman alluded to something along those lines when he called me back to explain the misunderstanding."

"Have you met my wife?"

"Oh, yes," he said matter-of-factly, and then his manner changed. "She wasn't very nice to me, Mr. Sheffield."

Osbourne paused. Terry guessed he was after an apology. He wasn't getting one.

"Quite rude, in fact," Osbourne continued. "Saying she had no time for the neighborhood watch committee. But it hasn't stopped me from keeping an eye out for her and you."

Terry had wanted to dismiss Osbourne without giving him a second thought, but now he changed his mind. The guy might be an interfering busybody, but sometimes an interfering busybody could be most valuable.

"When was the last time you saw my wife?"

• • •

Some neighborhood watch chairman, Terry thought. Osbourne hadn't known anything useful. He wasn't the omniscient curtain twitcher he claimed to be. But one piece of information came out of the forty minutes he had detained Terry. Osbourne remembered seeing Sarah about a week ago, which tied in with the stack of unread mail Terry had discovered.

It wasn't much, but it was something Terry could throw Holman's way. He'd even toss in Osbourne's name so that Edenville's official and unofficial law-enforcement officers could share some personal time together. A mischievous smirk creased his mouth.

From his living room, Terry watched Osbourne fire up his lawn mower. Osbourne tried to make it look like he was tending to his garden and not watching his neighbors. Terry smiled and left him to his work.

He searched through Sarah's home office, hoping to find something that explained her disappearance. Sifting through her things left him queasy. It reminded him of when he and his mother had sorted through his grandmother's belongings after she died. But Sarah wasn't dead. He couldn't lose sight of that fact. Something had to be there to explain her absence.

Sarah's home office was pretty typical. She had arranged two desks in an L-shape with a PC on top. A couple of bookshelves lined one wall and file boxes filled the closet. The books didn't reveal anything beyond Sarah's reading taste. The files consisted of nothing but her assignments. His search would have been helped if Sarah had kept her office tidy. Nothing seemed to be in chronological order, and if Sarah put a book away the right way up, it was a miracle.

The computer looked to be the best option, and he fired it up. While he waited for the Dell to boot up, he stared at the walls. Post-it notes clung to the surface, each carrying an abbreviated snippet of information that only Sarah could understand. Framed newspaper articles hung on the walls—past glories— boasting a glittering career Sarah had carved out for herself. There weren't any Pulitzer prizes, but she had garnered a number

SIMON WOOD

of cover stories in a variety of newspapers and magazines. But only one framed picture interested him. It was a picture of them taken outside of the Luxor Las Vegas. The picture had been taken the day after their wedding.

He found it hard to hold back tears. The photo confirmed what he'd always known—Sarah did love him. She hadn't run out on him. She was in trouble and she needed help. The sheriff's insinuations were dead wrong. The photo blew all his doubt away. If Sarah didn't care, she wouldn't have a picture of him above her computer, where she could look at him every time she went to work.

The computer completed its boot up. He rummaged through Sarah's e-mail again but didn't find anything that would indicate she was planning a trip or going on the run. And no more of her friends or contacts had replied to his plea.

Terry turned his attention to the address book from the night before. Now came the tricky part. Whom to call? He didn't know one person from another, so he might as well start with the A's and work his way through. Just as with the e-mail he'd sent out the night before, he learned all over again how remote Sarah seemed from the people in her life. The people he got through to knew her, but not well. They were ex-coworkers, old college classmates, business contacts, and even ex-boyfriends. They mentioned being close at one point, but somewhere along the way they'd lost touch. That aspect worried him. He felt closer to Sarah than anyone he'd ever known, but did she feel the same way? In five years would she lose touch with him? Had she already?

Don't be a twat, he told himself. *Sarah's in trouble, and you're going to find her.*

He ran a highlighter over the last name and number he'd called. It was dark outside, and he hadn't come up with one useful lead. He wondered if all police work was as fruitless as this. If it was, no wonder so many crimes went unsolved. He closed the address book with the intention of repeating the same disheartening task tomorrow.

But after closing the address book, he changed his mind. He'd give it one more shot and dial one last number. He flipped to another page to dial the first number his eyes fell upon. He punched it in and put the phone to his ear. He didn't hear a dial tone. He heard silence, with the occasional hiss of static. It took a few seconds for Terry to realize it wasn't static he was hearing, but breathing. He'd picked up the phone to dial at the precise moment someone had called him.

"Hello," he said.

No one answered.

"Hello," he said again with no answer. "Is anybody there?"

The reply was more breathing—not heavy or strained, just the sound of someone calmly breathing in and out. Something Terry wasn't doing. Fear forced him to fight for breath like an asthmatic. He gripped the receiver more tightly.

"Hello," Terry said for the third time. "I know you're there."

He paused. He went to say hello again, but the caller interrupted him with a mocking laugh.

CHAPTER FIVE

The following morning, Oscar arrived with a toot of his horn. Terry checked his watch. It was exactly 9:00. He emptied his coffee cup into the sink and locked up the house.

"Morning to you," Oscar said, standing in front of his Toyota 4Runner.

"Right on time," Terry said. "I like that."

"Well, if I'm going to get you Americanized then we need to beat the rush. I thought we'd take my car."

"Thanks. I need to find a car of my own soon."

"Let me see what I can do," Oscar said, getting back into the 4Runner.

Terry climbed inside the SUV alongside Oscar and buckled himself in.

"So how was your night?" Oscar asked. "Any word on Sarah?"

The strange phone call Terry had received last night flashed in his mind, but he didn't share this with Oscar. They barely knew each other, and their burgeoning friendship wouldn't be helped if he threw sinister callers in along with his missing wife. The guy was going above and beyond the call of duty helping out a stranger, and Terry didn't want to spoil it by coming off crazy or paranoid.

"No, nothing."

"Don't lose heart. I have a feeling you'll be back with your wife in no time."

"I hope you're right. Where to first?"

"Somewhere we can get you baptized as an honorary American—Social Security office, then the DMV."

When Oscar explained the procedure for getting a Social Security number and driver's license, Terry was surprised that so much had to be done in person. He never had much to do with these government agencies in England. The UK equivalent of these documents had been dealt with by mail. The only time he'd come in contact with the UK's version of the DMV, the equally ominous DVLA, was when he took the test. He wished the US would adopt the same culture and save everybody time.

His encounter with the Social Security office wasn't too bad. The building was smaller than he expected, with an even smaller waiting room. A daytime soap played on an eighteen-inch TV in the corner. He filled in the appropriate forms and stood at the counter while his information was processed. The clerk told him he could expect his card in a couple of weeks.

"That was easy," Terry said, following Oscar back to his SUV.

"I'm easing you in nice and slow. Just wait until you get a load of the DMV. You'll be singing a different tune then."

The nearest DMV was some ways from the Social Security office, which meant a scenic drive across the county, giving Terry the chance to see more of his new surroundings. They bantered about the horrors that would await him when they reached the DMV.

"I want to ask you a personal question, and I don't want you to take it the wrong way, okay?"

Terry didn't know if he'd like what was coming, but he said okay.

"Have you contacted your family or friends back in England about what's happened?"

Terry fidgeted in his seat. He'd thought about it after Holman had released him, but he had decided against the idea. He shook his head.

"Can I ask why?"

Terry exhaled. "My friends and family didn't exactly approve of what Sarah and I were doing."

"Is that why you came to the US?"

"No. It wasn't a case of restless natives banging on the front door with pitchforks and flaming torches. People thought I was making a mistake marrying someone I'd met on holiday before I'd had a chance to get to know her. They were looking out for me, and I can understand that. What is it, one in three marriages fail?"

Oscar frowned. "Closer to one in two in the US."

With that remark, Terry got the feeling Oscar was on the losing side of that statistic. "Well, there you are. They just care."

Oscar was back on Solano Dam Road. He crossed the bridge spanning the dam and bore right with the road. The reservoir the dam held back was magnificent and millpond still.

"But if they care so much, why haven't you let them know that something's wrong?" Oscar asked. "They'd want to help, I'm sure."

Terry didn't want to answer this question. It was hard enough admitting the truth to himself, let alone to Oscar.

"Embarrassment," he admitted. "I'm embarrassed. If I tell everyone, then they would have been right all along. I know it's stupid and irrational, but I don't want everyone thinking, Look at what sad, stupid Terry got himself into."

"So you'd rather put your trust in strangers."

"Can you blame me?"

"Not really. It's a tough call either way."

Oscar changed the subject by turning into a Santa Rita County tour guide. He talked about the history of the dam and several other landmarks. Before long, Oscar was pulling into the DMV parking lot.

"Remember," Oscar said, "You gotta stay strong."

Although only 10:30, the DMV was a cattle market. Three security officers were herding errant strays into various roped-off lines for something or other. Terry was glad he had Oscar as his guide or he would have wasted a lot of time.

Oscar grabbed a copy of the California driving rules and regulations and handed it to Terry. "Read that. You'll need to know it for the written exam. Don't worry, you'll have plenty of time to read it."

Terry jumped through the DMV's hoops. In a battle of endurance, he waited in line to apply for his license then lined up to take the written test so that he could make an appointment for the driving test itself. It was early afternoon when they left.

"Thank God that's over," Terry said, pushing the door open.

"What did I tell you?" Oscar asked.

"It's on a par with your immigration department."

"When you get your license, whatever you do, don't let it expire or you'll have to do it all over again."

Oscar held the door open for a teenager, obviously coming in for her first license. She didn't acknowledge Oscar's chivalry. From the stricken look on her face, her mind was focused on one thing and one thing only—her test. Her mother thanked him on her daughter's behalf.

Oscar released the door then cried out. Somehow, he'd gotten his hand trapped between the closing doors. His hand was folded in half and his thumb flopped loosely against his palm at an unnatural angle. He cradled his hand to his chest.

The mother and daughter burst back out of the building at the commotion. The mother saw Oscar's damaged hand, blanched, and turned away. The daughter just stared.

"Jesus," Terry said. "Are you okay?"

"It's nothing," Oscar said, wincing. "It's dislocated, that's all. Happens all the time."

Without any fuss, Oscar snapped his thumb back into place with a wet click. Terry's stomach churned at the sound, and for a second he thought the mother was going to vomit.

"See, all fixed now. Nothing for anyone to worry about."

"I feel so responsible," the mother said. Although Oscar had demonstrated his hand was back to normal, her color wasn't returning.

"Don't be. It was my own stupid fault. My cuff got caught on the door handle."

Seeing there was nothing more to be done, the mother took Oscar's explanation as reason enough to leave. She apologized to him again and scurried back into the building dragging her daughter with her.

"Are you really okay?" Terry asked.

"Yeah, really. It tingles a bit, but honestly, it's okay."

"Can you drive?"

Oscar flexed his hand and winced. "It might be a better idea if you do."

Oscar fished out his keys and gave them to Terry. They got into the 4Runner and Terry started the engine.

"Do you want to see a doctor?"

"No, it's an old injury. There's nothing they can do." Oscar smiled. "C'mon, stop fussing and let's get something to eat."

Oscar directed Terry to drive to a small strip mall half a mile away. Terry pulled up in front of a sandwich shop. They got two made-to-order sandwiches, and Terry paid while Oscar found seats. As Terry brought their food over to the table and sat down, Oscar was still flexing his hand.

"Better?" Terry asked.

"Oh, yeah. Good as new."

"You said that was an old injury." Terry nodded at Oscar's hand. "What happened?"

"I used to be a welder, and a ten-inch pipe rolled off my bench onto my hand. The thumb joint was damaged, so it dislocates easily. But it does go back just as easily."

"Does it hurt?"

"No, not really. After the initial shock, it tingles like pins and needles."

"Well, it's an impressive party trick."

"Oh, yeah, a real icebreaker."

They unwrapped their bulging sandwiches and attacked them. Oscar mumbled through a mouthful of food that the sandwiches were good, and Terry grunted in the affirmative. Terry washed down his mouthful of food with his lemonade and wiped his mouth on a napkin.

"So if you were a welder, how come you own the Gold Rush?"

"I used to own a welding and fabrication company. I was doing really well, and I decided I wanted to retire early, so I sold the business. But I found retirement really boring, so when I saw the place up for sale, I bought it."

Oscar was holding something back. Terry could feel it. He didn't think Oscar was lying to him, but he was definitely leaving something out.

"So what is this job you're starting next week, Terry?" Oscar asked, diverting attention away from himself.

"I'm a scientist."

"Very cool. A real-life brainiac," Oscar said, perking up.

Terry shook his head. "Not really. I'm no Nobel Prize–winning, changing-life-as-we-know-it kind of scientist. Scientist is a very common term. I don't come up with the technology. I just prove whether it works or not. I'm no different than a car mechanic. It sounds fancy, that's all."

"Sounds very fancy compared to a guy who hands people rubber-headed golf clubs for a living."

They finished up their lunch, and Oscar drove back to Edenville. Their next stop was the bank. The Wells Fargo bank was an old stucco-clad building with a brick facade.

"I didn't know Wells Fargo was a real company. I thought it was a name made up for the movies."

Oscar laughed. "Oh, no, they're real enough."

They went inside and Oscar asked a bank teller for the manager.

"And can I say who's calling?" the woman asked.

"Yes, we have an appointment," Oscar said. "Terry Sheffield and Oscar Mayer."

"Oscar Mayer?" she asked with a smirk.

"Yes, Oscar Mayer," he replied with a frown.

The woman hid a grin behind a hand. "I'll get him for you."

"What is it with your name?" Terry asked.

"You really don't know?"

Terry shook his head.

Oscar eyed him for moment just in case Terry was messing with him. "Okay, I wish I could say it was a long story, but it isn't. It's the name of company that's famous for their hot dogs and bologna here. They even have a damn song about their bologna. Go in the supermarket and you'll see their stuff everywhere. It's not the most ideal situation to be constantly equated with kids' lunch food. As you can imagine, I took a lot of crap for it while growing up."

"Oh," Terry said after a moment. "I can see why that would bother you."

"Mmm," Oscar grunted. "They don't carry Oscar Mayer in England?"

"Nope."

"Maybe I should relocate."

When the bank manager appeared, he took them into his office and Terry opened an account, relieving himself of the wad of cash he'd brought over on the flight. Within thirty minutes, the bank manager presented Terry with a temporary checkbook, an ATM card, and an opening balance statement.

Rising to his feet, the manager asked, "Now, is there anything else I can do for you today, Mr. Sheffield?"

"Yes," Terry replied. "Could you tell me if my wife has an account at this bank?"

The bank manager chuckled. "Don't you know?"

"She's missing," Oscar said.

The bank manager stiffened. "Oh, I see."

Terry explained the situation. The bank manager nodded at the appropriate times and looked pained.

"Unfortunately, even if your wife does have an account with us, I can't divulge any details, even to you, unless it's a joint account. I hope you understand."

"Yes, I do. Can you check for a joint account?"

"Oh, yes." The bank manager typed away at his PC for a minute before shaking his head. "I'm afraid there aren't any accounts listing you as a joint holder. Maybe she has her account with another bank."

"You're probably right. Thanks for trying."

"Sorry that I couldn't help further. I hope you find her."

"So do I."

Terry and Oscar crossed the street and tried Edenville's other bank, the Solano Credit Union. Terry didn't have a joint account with them either.

Standing in front of the credit union, Oscar asked, "What do you want to do now? Talk to Holman?"

"No, I don't think so."

"Well, if you don't mind, can I take you home? Then I can get back to the Gold Rush before the after-school crowd starts."

"Of course not. You've helped me enough today."

On the short ride back to Sutter Drive, Terry found himself thinking about his mystery caller. He still didn't know if the call was a random prank or something more sinister. He hadn't intended on discussing the issue with Oscar, but he'd proved today he was a friend and someone he could trust.

"I want run something by you."

"Go for it."

"I got a weird phone call yesterday."

"And you'll be getting lots more once the telemarketers know you live in this country."

"I wish it had been a telemarketer."

"Oh," Oscar said. "What was the call?"

"I don't know. If I said it was an obscene call, I'd be exaggerating."

"Let me decide for you. What did they say?"

"They didn't say anything," Terry said and went on to explain about the caller who had laughed at him.

"Huh," Oscar said when Terry was finished. "Do you think it could have been Sarah?"

Terry shook his head. "No, this was a man's laugh."

"So who do you think this guy is?"

"Don't know."

"But you think it's related to Sarah's disappearing act?"

Terry nodded. "Yes."

"Have you told Holman?"

"No, I wasn't sure what I'd tell him. I don't think laughing at someone on the phone is a crime."

"Yeah, it's probably something to keep to yourself for now. But you can be certain of one thing."

"What's that?"

"If your caller was someone connected to Sarah's disappearance, he'll call again."

CHAPTER SIX

Terry's weekend passed without incident. The laughing caller didn't call and neither did Sarah. Holman was his only caller and he had little to say. Terry didn't see much point in sitting around the house driving himself crazy with worry, so he decided to go into Genavax on Monday, as scheduled.

At the reception desk, he asked for Pamela Dawson. When she arrived, she greeted him with the same offhand manner she'd used on the phone. She gave him a lightning-fast tour of the shared research, development, discovery, and testing labs punctuated with brief introductions to his new colleagues along the way. After the tour, Pamela dumped him with human resources.

Jenny Kuo, the human resources manager, greeted him with a broad grin, flashing a perfect set of white teeth, albeit one slightly too large for her mouth.

"You must be very excited to be working in a new country," she said. "I know I was."

Terry nodded, warming to her enthusiasm.

"Sorry to hear about your wife, though."

Jenny escorted Terry to her office and proceeded to march him through his terms and conditions and benefits package. The topic of his vacation allowance left a bruise. The ten vacation days were a far cry from the five-week entitlement he had enjoyed as the norm in England. Now he understood why American tour parties blasted through England as part of a five-day whirlwind tour of Europe. Jenny tried to soften the blow with personal days.

"Personal days, what's that?"

"It's your sick allowance for you and your family. If you have a sick family member to look after or need a mental health day, then take a day."

"Mental health day?"

"If work or life is getting you down, you can take a day away from it all—a mental health day." Jenny beamed, showing more healthy teeth.

Terry thought mental health days were a generous gesture, but they weren't going to make up for his loss of vacation days. He felt the need for a mental health day just thinking about it.

A review of Genavax's safety practices ate up the rest of the morning, and they broke for lunch. Jenny pointed out the staff cafeteria to Terry but excused herself from joining him. She had a lunch date elsewhere.

The lunchroom was a rectangle of duck's-egg-blue blandness. It was small for supporting the hundred or so Genavax employees, but after reviewing the menu, he saw why Genavax didn't require a larger lunchroom. Snack machines ran along one wall and seemed to be enjoying more fervent business.

Terry bought a tuna sandwich, a yogurt, and a carton of orange juice. He sat at a table by himself. He wasn't up to the awkward new-guy intros. He spread out his small meal and a newspaper he'd swiped from reception. He hoped this display wouldn't invite company.

His ploy worked for about five minutes.

"Dude, you the new guy?"

And you must be the surfer, Terry thought. The tie-dyed T-shirted and jeans-clad man was everything the brochure said a Californian surfer should be. His shaggy blond locks and miles of deep tan relayed a "Surf's up" attitude. The only problem was that the surfer dude was a little too old for the image. He was closer to forty than twenty.

"English, right?"

"Yeah, I'm English," Terry agreed.

"Cool. Very cool," he said nodding to himself. "They said a foreign guy was starting."

"I'm foreign, all right."

"Jeez, I'm being rude. Kyle Hemple." Kyle rubbed his palm on the back of his jeans and snapped out a hand.

Terry took it and shook. "Terry Sheffield."

"D'you mind if I chow down with you?" Kyle indicated to a vacant chair.

"Knock yourself out."

"Cool."

Kyle deposited his lunch onto the table—mainly fruit, which rolled across Terry's stolen newspaper. Apologizing, Kyle shepherded his lunch back to his side of the table. A wide-necked bottle containing a toxic-waste-green concoction caught Terry's eye. Kyle noticed him looking.

"Wheatgrass," he said, holding it up.

Kyle didn't say anything for a while. He just stared at Terry, smiling and bobbing his head.

Terry froze in the middle of a spoonful of yogurt. "What?" he asked.

"You're my first."

Terry struggled to hold back one of Kyle's grins. "First what?"

"You're my first English guy."

"Wow, really? I didn't feel a thing."

"Huh?"

Terry waved away his failed attempt at humor. "I hope it's a good experience."

"So far." Kyle bobbed his head again. "Just wanted to let you know I have nothing against you and the whole Civil War thing between our two fair nations. In the past. Forgotten."

"Don't you mean the War of Independence?"

"Same difference, dude. Peach?" He held out the fruit as a peace offering.

"Thanks," Terry said and took it, gracious in the honor of its meaning. He took a bite.

"The grapevine is humming with the news that your wife has gone AWOL. True?"

Suddenly, the peach developed a sour edge to it. "True."

"That sucks, man. I liked her."

"Excuse me?"

"A real looker, dude. You did well. I hope she's okay."

"What do you mean, you liked her?"

Kyle raised his hands in mock surrender. "Hey, man. Terry, dude, I wasn't trying to hit on her. I was just saying she's good-looking. Don't blow a gasket. Hey, you English are hot-blooded puppies."

Terry shook his head. "That's not what I meant. I haven't met anyone who's seen her since I came to America. I mean, do you know her? Have you seen her?"

"No. I just met her here once."

"When?"

"A couple of months back, I think. She came to check out the place or something. Oh, I remember, she brought in some paperwork."

Terry recalled Sarah had delivered the signed contract he'd mailed to her with some other documents. That was about six weeks ago, after final job negotiations.

"Did you speak to her?"

"I think I said hi, but that was about it. But she spoke to several of us. She came in here and had lunch. She was sounding out the joint to make sure the job was worth taking. She was cool."

Terry zoned out, taking a moment to get over his initial excitement at the notion of a recent sighting of Sarah. His disappointment at the false alarm took just as long to recover from.

When he tuned Kyle back in, he was an annoying buzzing in his head and he didn't understand what the sun-bronzed man was saying until after he had said it.

"Hey, back up a minute. What do you mean fuss? What did she do?"

"Dude, that's what I'm saying. It was so cool what she said to the Ice Maiden. I love your wife."

"The Ice Maiden?"

"Pamela Dawson. Your boss."

"What happened?"

"This was so sweet, you've gotta understand."

"I get it. What happened?"

"Well, Pam storms in, zeroing in on us jawing with your old lady. She's pissed and tells your wife"—Kyle snapped his fingers—"I forget her name."

"Sarah."

"Yeah, Sarah. Well, Pam tells Sarah she has no business being in here and asks her to leave. And Sarah gives it to her both barrels, man. It was cool."

This was like pulling teeth. Terry was losing his patience. "What did she say?"

Kyle's inane grin slipped a few inches. "Have to wait, dude. Lunch is over. Five-O."

"What?"

Kyle indicated with his eyes at the entrance. Pamela Dawson strode into the cafeteria accompanied by Luke Frazer—a tall, stick-thin man with a grey pallor whom Terry had met earlier. He was the lead scientist in the Quality Department and Pamela's right-hand man. She frowned in their direction. Kyle jumped to his feet, his chair scraping on the vinyl flooring.

"Hey, where you going? Finish your story."

"Later, man."

"Kyle," Terry whined.

"Don't worry, newbie. We'll talk. Stay cool."

• • •

Terry finished his first day at Genavax without getting the chance to press Kyle further. He drove home, frustration gnawing at him. What had Sarah fought over with Pamela? It certainly explained Pamela's lack of compassion toward Sarah's disappearance.

When Terry got home, he had a message waiting for him on the answering machine. He hit PLAY. It was a brief message from Sheriff Holman telling him to come see him if he got the message before seven. It was 6:20. Terry had just snatched up his keys to leave when the phone rang.

"Hello," Terry said.

"Hello to you." The caller was a man, his words slow and confused. It was obvious he wasn't expecting Terry to answer. "Is Sarah there?"

"No." The hairs on Terry's arms and neck bristled. Somehow, he didn't feel he was talking to a friend. "She's not here right now."

"Huh."

"Can I help you?"

"Who are you?"

"I'm Sarah's husband."

"Husband? I didn't know she was married."

"Are you a friend?"

"Mmm, more of an acquaintance."

"Can I tell her who called?" Terry asked, fishing for a name.

"When will she be back?"

"I'm not sure, but I don't think she'll be long." Maybe Terry was being paranoid, but the caller sounded like he was on a fishing expedition and Terry wasn't about to give up any information. "Can I get a number from you, er…?"

"I don't think you have any idea when she'll be coming back," the caller accused.

"Not to the exact minute, but…"

The caller had hung up.

• • •

Besides Holman, the sheriff's station was deserted when Terry walked in. He welcomed Terry with a smile.

"Mr. Sheffield, you got my message?"

"Yes." Terry stopped at the front desk and leaned on the counter. "Do you have any news?"

"Terry—I hope you don't mind me calling you Terry?"

Terry shook his head.

"What you have to understand, Terry, is that the first twenty-four hours are the most crucial of any missing persons investigation and with every hour that follows, the task becomes increasingly more difficult. Do you understand what I'm telling you?"

"Sheriff, can you get to the point?"

"Would you like a cup of coffee?"

"I don't want a coffee. I don't want a cookie. I've been in this country less than a week and my wife's been missing the whole time. I just want to know what the hell is going on. So please tell me."

"Mr. Sheffield, I understand your frustration. But let's keep things calm. Okay?"

Terry took a moment then nodded. "Okay. Sorry."

"Nothing to be sorry about. Okay, I've circulated her details with the local hospitals and morgues."

Terry's throat tightened. Air struggled to make it into his lungs.

"No one with your wife's name or fitting her description has been admitted."

Terry breathed easy again. "Good."

"But we don't know if she's remained local. In the time she's been missing, she could be a lot farther afield, so I'm spreading my search."

"She could be out of the country by now."

"No. That's something I do know. SFO, Oakland, San Jose, and Sacramento report not having had a Sarah Sheffield or

Morton go through their gates. So I'm going to assume she's not flying."

Holman had pacified Terry's fear to a certain extent. He'd wondered if the sheriff would do a proper job, but he seemed to be making all the right noises.

"I now have a copy of Sarah's driver's license, courtesy of the DMV, and I also know what car she drives."

"What is it?"

"A two-tone, white-and-gray Subaru Outback."

"She had a Toyota the last time I was here."

Holman nodded. "Well, I have something to look for now."

Holman proceeded to catalog a list of investigative dead ends, and Terry's heart sank. He was getting the feeling that Sarah would never be found.

"I'll keep trying, Terry, but you're going to have to be patient, unless you've got anything new for me to go on. Did you remember anything that could be of help?"

"Well, yes. A couple of strange things happened today."

"Oh, yeah?" Holman dragged a pad across the counter toward him and took a pen out of his shirt pocket.

"I started my new job."

"Where's that?"

"Genavax. Do you know it?"

"Uh-huh."

"At lunch, one of the guys said my wife had gotten into an argument with my new boss in the staff lunchroom about six weeks ago. It was very public and very heated."

"What was she doing there?"

"Dropping off my contract."

"So why was she in the staff lunchroom?"

"I don't know. I suppose she just stopped for something to eat."

"Okay." Holman scribbled notes. "What was the argument about?"

"Don't know. I never got that far."

"Hmm. So what are you saying?" Holman stopped writing and put his pen down. "That your new boss abducted your wife, is that it?"

That had been Terry's thought and it seemed like a good one in his head, but hearing Holman say it out loud, the thought sounded ridiculous. Obviously their confrontation meant something, but whether it had anything to do with Sarah's disappearance seemed unlikely. Terry let the idea go.

"I don't know what I'm suggesting," he conceded. "Just that it was odd. I shouldn't be listening to gossip, I suppose."

"Okay. And what's the second thing?"

"Yeah. A man called asking for Sarah."

"A friend?"

"I don't think so. He didn't know about us being married."

"So he might not be a close friend."

"This guy was peculiar."

"Peculiar, how?"

"He gave me the creeps. I don't know how to say it better."

"Okay. He wasn't a friend, so what's your guess?"

His guess was an ex-boyfriend, but his fear was a not-so-ex-boyfriend. He didn't have much stock in either theory. They were just products of a neurotic imagination.

"I wondered if he's involved with Sarah's disappearance."

"If he had abducted Sarah, he wouldn't be calling asking for her. Would he now?"

"I suppose not."

"Terry, listen to me. You're worried, and nobody can blame you, but stop trying to make three and two equal four. Let me do my job. Okay?"

Terry nodded.

"Let's put things in perspective," Holman said. "She's missing, but on the positive side, no news is good news. She's not in a hospital, so she's probably still okay."

Unless she's dead in a ditch and no one's found her yet, Terry thought but kept it to himself. If he didn't say it, maybe it wouldn't come true.

CHAPTER SEVEN

"I think it's dead, buddy," Oscar said.

"Huh?" Terry grunted.

Terry was standing over the Gold Rush's Dumpster. He stopped smashing the broom down on the overpacked Dumpster. The last trash bag that had gone on top of the others had burst from the repeated blows. Soda cups littered the trash enclosure, leaking out various soda-colored fluids. Strewn paper napkins turned the spill into a pulpy mess. It wasn't a pretty sight. He wiped away the sweat beading on his forehead in the evening heat.

"You killed that trash bag, all right."

"Sorry," Terry said.

"If I wanted a mindless thug to smash the joint up, I could have gotten someone doing community service," Oscar said without any rancor. "I thought a little evening work would keep you sane."

Since the weekend, Terry had been helping Oscar close up the Gold Rush, which meant emptying the trash, mopping out the toilets, sweeping the floors, and generally making the amusement center shipshape for a new day. The plan had worked up until tonight, but now Sarah and his sad situation was back on his mind. The innocent Dumpster had just gotten in the way.

"Sorry," Terry said again.

"Do you want get down from there before you do someone some damage?"

Terry hopped down from the Dumpster and helped Oscar pick up the spilled trash. Oscar held open a new trash bag he had tucked into a back pocket and Terry filled it. Oscar tied off the bag and tossed it against the side of the overstuffed Dumpster.

"Okay, let's get you inside and cool off."

Oscar walked Terry inside the Gold Rush and filled two cups from the soda fountain.

"Air hockey?" Oscar asked.

"Okay," Terry said.

Terry took the drinks over to the nearest air-hockey table and placed them on the edge while Oscar pumped a handful of quarters into the machine. With all the other arcade machines switched off, the hum of the air hissing through the holes in the metal plate was surprisingly loud. The puck popped out and Oscar guided it back toward him.

"Interesting mood swing you were having out there," Oscar said and faced off. "Wanna tell me about it?"

Terry blocked Oscar's shot. "It was nothing. Just relieving a little of the daily stress."

Oscar stopped the puck dead with his hand. "Terry, I know we haven't known each other long, but I know you weren't just venting. You were pissed off, and I think I know at whom."

"Can't we just play?"

"You saw Holman today, didn't you?"

Oscar fired the puck across the table. Terry didn't react fast enough to prevent it from disappearing into the mail slot of a goal in front of him. A new puck dropped onto the table. Neither of them made a grab for the plastic disc.

"Yeah. I wanted to see how he was getting on. I haven't heard anything from him."

Oscar tapped the puck over to Terry. "What did he say?"

"Not a lot. He doesn't seem to be any further forward than he was when I filed the report."

Terry hated badgering Holman like some lovesick teenager chasing after a girl. He knew how pathetic it looked. Holman's progress amounted to a "We're doing our best" and a pat on the head. Terry had stormed out before he lost his temper.

Terry was equally frustrated by how little else he'd learned about Sarah's encounter with Pamela. He'd become persona non grata at work, at least when it came to Kyle. He'd tried talking to him several times since their lunch meeting, and Kyle had practically run in the other direction.

If Terry were honest, he wasn't just angry with Holman or Kyle, but with himself. Cracks were appearing in his faith. Maybe Sarah hadn't been abducted. She'd left the house under her own accord, albeit in a hurry. A belief was forming and even though it didn't make sense, the belief grew—she'd run out on him. Suddenly, Holman's words trampled through his mind. "You don't seem to know squat about your wife." Terry was starting to think he was right. All he wanted was to be wrong.

"You know, he could be keeping things from you to protect you," Oscar suggested.

"I know, but I wish he wouldn't."

Oscar nodded.

"And in all honesty, I don't think he knows where she is," Terry said.

"Okay, Holman's getting nowhere while Sarah is slipping farther and farther into the shadows. So what are you going to do about it?"

Terry went to answer, but held himself in check. He noticed the effect Oscar was having on him. The frustration he'd taken out on the trash was gone. Oscar had reasoned it out of him. Terry's focus was on the constructive, not the destructive. He smiled and crouched over his goal with his hockey paddle ready to deflect any oncoming shots.

"I'll tell you what we're going to do," Terry said, "We're going to find her."

"Are we, now?" Oscar fired the puck across the table. "And how, exactly, are we going to achieve that?"

They spent the next half an hour knocking the puck back and forth, along with ideas for finding Sarah. They formulated a plan, deciding to pursue certain ideas and ditching others. The element Terry felt was most absent from Holman's investigation was awareness. He hadn't seen any appeals in the local newspapers or on television. Oscar scored the winning goal to seal the game. Terry slid his paddle across the table.

"We need to start our own milk carton campaign or something," Oscar said.

"What's that?" Terry asked.

"For years, they've been placing the pictures of missing kids on milk cartons and on junk mail flyers."

That was a neat idea. It wasn't one the police utilized in the UK. "Great, but wouldn't we have to go through Holman or something to do that?" Terry asked.

"Yeah, but I'm not suggesting that we put Sarah's face on a milk carton. We should do something similar, like a poster campaign. We'll run up a batch of flyers and get the stores to post them in their windows and nail them to power poles. How many times has a missing dog notice caught your eye?"

"Sarah, a missing dog?"

Oscar frowned. "Okay, bad choice of words, but you get my point."

"I'll agree with you, it's a nice idea, but that pretty much assumes that Sarah's still local."

"Granted, but we don't know anyone who has even seen Sarah in the last week. A flyer might just jog their memory. It's a start, don't you think?"

It was. Sarah's case seemed to have stagnated. Anything to get it going again was a good thing. If anyone came forward with even the slightest sighting, it would be good for his faith, if nothing else.

The next evening, Terry pulled into his garage and Oscar parked his SUV in the driveway. They'd had a good night. Out of the two hundred flyers they'd printed, maybe two dozen were left. Terry was overwhelmed by the willingness of most store managers to post his flyer in their windows and at the checkout stands. His hand throbbed from stapling the flyers to every power pole they came across.

Oscar locked the door on his 4Runner and brandished his depleted stack of flyers. "Do you want these?"

The two of them had divided Edenville into halves and regrouped at the Gold Rush before returning to Terry's house.

"Do you mind keeping them and handing them out at the Gold Rush?" Terry asked.

"Sure thing."

Terry examined the flyer on top of the pile he held. It was simple but effective. It was an eight-by-eleven sheet with a banner headline "MISSING—Have you seen this woman?" and a color photograph of Sarah he'd taken in Costa Rica. A short description and a phone number completed the flyer. He'd cobbled the affair together on his PC during his lunch hour, and Oscar had gotten them copied. Oscar had warned Terry not to expect every call to lead directly to Sarah and to expect a lot of crank calls. Terry wasn't bothered by crank calls. He welcomed them. If he was receiving calls, then Sarah's details were being seen; and if she were seen, then she would be recognized. He didn't care if he received a million calls, as long as one led to Sarah. He hoped to find the answering machine dripping with messages when he got inside. He removed the first flyer from his pile and gave the rest to Oscar.

"You can take these too, but I'll keep one, just in case someone asks."

"Good idea," Oscar said, taking the flyers. Both men knew Terry was keeping the flyer for quite different reasons. "I'll put these in the car."

Terry stopped him.

"Oscar"—Terry paused—"you know I have no way of expressing how grateful I am to you for all your help."

"Hey, pal. Don't go all misty on me." Oscar laughed. "I'm doing this as a friend, and there's no reason to thank a friend."

Terry stuck out his hand. "Sometimes it needs to be said."

Oscar shook Terry's hand and smiled. "I'll accept that."

"I'll get you a beer."

Oscar returned to his Toyota to put the remaining flyers back and Terry skirted his rental car to the door leading into the house. As Terry opened the door, Oscar stopped him.

"Terry," he said with trepidation.

"Yeah?"

Oscar didn't have to say anything more. A sheriff's cruiser slithered to a halt in front of the house. Its red-and-blue lights bathed the garage in alternating flashing colors. Sheriff Holman slid out from the Crown Victoria.

"Can I speak to you, Mr. Sheffield?" Holman asked. He glanced at Oscar and added, "In private."

"I'll go, Terry," Oscar said.

"No, stay," Terry said. "Sheriff, Oscar's a friend."

"Okay. Have it your way." Red light then blue light continued to whip Holman's back as he stood at the garage's entrance. "Can you tell me if you have any idea what Sarah was wearing when she went missing?"

"No. It's obvious from her closet that things are missing but what, I haven't a clue."

"Do you know if Mrs. Sheffield's shoe size is a six?"

"Sounds right."

"Do you know if she goes up to the reservoir?"

"Maybe. I don't know. Sheriff, I think we've already established that I have very little knowledge of my wife's life or movements, so stop pussyfooting around."

"Sheriff, this does seem a little over the top with the flashing lights and all, just to ask these petty questions," Oscar said.

"Who are you?" Holman asked. "A lawyer?"

"No, I'm Oscar Mayer."

Holman snorted. "And I'm the Pillsbury Doughboy."

"Can we move on?" Terry pleaded.

"Yes, Mr. Sheffield." Holman glared at Oscar. "I think we've found your wife, sir."

"Where? What did she say?" Terry's next question died on his lips. He'd been incredibly dense. He realized what all Holman's theatrics and silly-arse questions were about. His legs lost all strength and he collapsed into a sitting position on the steps.

"Mr. Sheffield, are you okay?"

"She's dead, isn't she?"

"Christ," Oscar muttered, raising a hand to his mouth.

"Mr. Sheffield, could you come with me?"

"She's dead, isn't she?" Terry repeated, this time more insistent.

"I need you to identify a body."

CHAPTER EIGHT

Six months earlier

"You'll protect me, won't you?" Sarah asked and pressed the crosswalk button.

"What do you mean?" Terry replied.

"During our vows you promised to protect me."

Terry might have said it, but the vows were just words from a bygone age. The only words that counted were "I do." Besides, it wasn't like their ceremony had been the kind most girls dream about anyway. There was no white dress, no jealous bridesmaids, no mother weeping tears of joy, and no friends still beered up from the bachelor party. No one did anything to embarrass them or ruin their day. Eloping didn't require any expensive or outlandish trappings. The ceremony had been carried out in a flat-roofed building that looked like a garden center thanks to its Astroturf carpeting and faux-stone walkway up to the altar. The minister did little to inspire authenticity, sporting an Elvis-style bouffant crispy from too much hairspray and silver from age. Terry wondered if he had an impersonation gig on the side. They were in Vegas, after all. Nevada sun rained through a skylight above the minister. Terry guessed that the skylight was meant to simulate the Lord's light illuminating everyone. Instead, the scorching heat burned them like bugs under a magnifying glass.

The ceremony had been fast, but what did they expect for a hundred bucks? Still, Terry wondered if the wedding vows had been read incorrectly. Although he hadn't attended many weddings, and hadn't taken much notice of what was being said at those times, the matter of saying "I do" came up a little too early in the proceedings for his liking. After the shock of having bound himself body and soul to Sarah for an eternity, everything else dissolved into a blur and the reverend's words were reduced to a low-level humming in Terry's ears.

The signal changed from DON'T WALK to WALK and they crossed Las Vegas Boulevard. Smiling, Terry answered, "I don't remember saying I would protect anybody."

"Well, you did, buddy boy, so you're stuck with me. You're my protector. What have you got to say about that?"

"How do we get this thing annulled?"

Sarah backhanded him across the stomach. The blow, although gentle, took him by surprise and winded him. He coughed once, shaking off the effects.

She carried on with the debate as they entered the Sahara. They sidestepped the gambling floor and went to the restaurant for their wedding breakfast. The hostess greeted them at the entrance and told them they could sit anywhere. The restaurant was as sparsely populated as the desert it was supposed to represent.

"So are you saying you wouldn't protect me?"

An Asian woman wandered among the tables brandishing Keno slips. Las Vegas couldn't afford to let a gambling chance slip by, even if you were eating. Terry couldn't imagine how much revenue was being lost while the patrons ate, used a restroom, or paused to breathe, but he supposed the casino owners did. They'd probably worked it out to the last penny.

"Why do you need me to protect you? Isn't that what the police are for?" Terry asked with a smile. "My protection extends as far as dialing 911."

Sarah frowned. Her face said it all. She wanted him to be serious, but he couldn't help teasing. A waitress came over and the newlyweds hastily ordered. The waitress was five years past the age for the length of the skirt she was wearing. When she turned to leave, Terry stopped her.

"Excuse me, miss. I hope you don't mind me asking, but are you married?"

She examined Terry quizzically for a moment, then held up her left hand, waggling her fingers to show off a simple gold band. "I don't wear this for looks."

"That's fantastic."

"What's it to you?" she asked.

Terry pointed to Sarah then himself. "We just got married."

"Congratulations," she said without much enthusiasm.

A Las Vegas marriage. It wasn't exactly original. She'd probably seen it a million times before.

"Thank you. We were discussing my role as my wife's protector, and I was wondering if you expect your husband to act as yours."

She gave Terry the once-over before turning to Sarah. "You landed yourself a real winner."

Sarah waited for the waitress to move out of earshot. "You'd better tip her big for that," she said with a smile that fought back a grin.

"Was I rude?"

She shook her head, the grin escaping its bonds. "No, you were a butt...and you still are."

"We've been married"—Terry checked his watch—"exactly twenty-two minutes and you're already calling me names. Are we on the rocks?"

Sarah's grin disappeared, replaced with a serious expression. She took his hand, squeezing it tight. "Be serious for a moment?"

"I am," he said grinning.

"I mean it," she said and gave his hand another tight squeeze.

"Okay, serious Terry now. What's up?"

"Would you be my protector, if it came down to it?"

Terry was concerned. His grin receded into the depths. "What's wrong?"

"My job can be invasive at times. To get a story, it sometimes means going the extra mile. It's not really dangerous—just risky—so I really need to know."

"You need to know if I'm the kind of guy that will look out for you?"

"Are you?"

Terry took Sarah's other hand in his and squeezed both of them just as tight as she'd squeezed his hands. "If you're wondering whether I would take a bullet for you, just be reassured you married your own personal Kevlar vest." Terry squeezed her hands again. "I don't need some tin pot, Las Vegas minister to tell me that I've got to protect you. I'm your protector already."

A tear ran down Sarah's cheek.

$$\bullet \quad \bullet \quad \bullet$$

Terry stared out the window, lost in his memory. "I'm sorry, Sarah," he said aloud, softly.

He and Oscar were in the back of Holman's cruiser barreling along a winding road.

Oscar turned. "What was that?"

"She asked me to protect her, and I didn't." Terry stared at a fixed point in the back of Holman's driver's seat. "I promised her."

"Promised what?" the sheriff asked into the rearview mirror.

"I said I would be there and would always look after her."

Terry drifted and wasn't aware of Oscar's comforting arm around his shoulders or Holman's question becoming a demand.

"When did you say this?"

"Sheriff, can we discuss this later?"

"No," was his blunt reply. "When did you say this?"

"On our wedding day."

Holman exhaled.

"Can we just get where we're supposed to be going?" Oscar asked.

"Where are we?" Terry asked, gazing out the window. The world sped by, stained red and blue by the cruiser's lights. It was familiar, but the car's speed and the night changed everything around.

"We're on Solano Dam Road, bud," Oscar answered.

"We're not in Edenville."

"That's right," Oscar said. "We're over by Lake Solano. Are you okay? You went a bit quiet on us for a while."

Holman sped past the sheer wall of concrete that was the Solano Dam. The man-made lake glistened oil-black in the moonlight. It felt malevolent under its nocturnal shroud.

"We're here," Holman said grimly.

The sheriff eased his cruiser off the road at a boat rental services and fishing supplies store called Marley's Cove. He drove across the parking lot to the access road leading to the lake. A series of sawhorses, a sheriff's deputy, and his cruiser blocked the road's entrance. Holman stopped his cruiser in front of the roadblock and rolled down his window. The deputy trotted over.

"Sheriff," the deputy said.

"Everybody here, Craig?"

"Yes, Sheriff. Coroner's here. Crime techs too. They're all doing their thing."

"Press?"

"Not yet. But I'll turn 'em away if they come."

"Thanks, Craig."

The deputy removed the sawhorses blocking Holman's way. The sheriff closed his window and drove on. The access road descended into a thick cover of redwoods lining either side of the road. The trees receded deep into the park, creating a dense canopy, which the moonlight penetrated with difficulty.

Blinding light spread out from the water's edge to cast long shadows where it hit the trees. The sheriff snapped down his sun visor and drove toward the light.

Terry wanted Holman to turn around. Let someone else identify the body. But he had to do this. It was the least he could do for Sarah now.

The road brought them out to a concrete boat ramp. A small jetty extended into the water with a hut at its end, but no boats or fishermen were around. In the distance, houseboats bobbed on the water like the lake was breathing.

Arc lights peered down from ten-foot standards. They illuminated the boat launch and the lakeside. Sheriff's department cruisers and vans were parked at odd angles to each other. A coroner's hearse was parked close to the water. Holman parked a safe distance from the fervor at the top of the boat ramp.

"C'mon, Mr. Sheffield," he said with genuine kindness in his voice.

Oscar helped Terry out of the Ford. Terry tottered, unable to find his feet, and Holman grabbed an arm. Both men guided him toward the cordoned-off area. Holman stopped ten feet from the outermost vehicle.

"Could you wait here a second?"

Terry nodded and Holman disappeared among the vehicles. When Holman reemerged, he beckoned to Terry and Oscar to join him. They threaded their way between the vehicles, peeling away the layers of privacy the sheriff's department had endeavored to create for the corpse. Terry stopped at the last vehicle that shielded him from the nightmare beyond. Oscar placed a hand on his shoulder.

"C'mon, pal. Let's do this thing."

Terry would willingly give ten years of his life for someone to replace him, but he couldn't foist this responsibility onto someone else. He had to see, had to know. He nodded and stepped around the vehicle.

A man in a paper jumpsuit and latex gloves finished covering with a sheet what was obviously a body. When he saw Terry, he stood up and tried to smile, but it came out as a facial twitch.

"Okay, Mr. Sheffield, this is Dr. Schovanek. He's the county coroner."

"Hello, Mr. Sheffield." Schovanek raised a hand in greeting. "Good of you to come out tonight."

Terry couldn't speak and nodded instead.

"Earlier this evening," Holman said, "fishermen trawled up a body, and I was wondering if you could tell me if you recognize the deceased. Is this your missing wife?"

Terry edged a step toward the shrouded body. His shoe came precariously close to the sheet. He drew his foot back, not wanting to touch death.

Schovanek crouched over the shrouded corpse. "I have to warn you that the deceased has been in the water for at least twenty-four hours. She's in bad shape. The fish were drawn to the blood."

Terry wanted the coroner to shut up. He didn't need to hear the details. He just needed to see Sarah—to end all the speculation and know whether she was dead or not.

"We're thinking the killer disposed of her here last night some time."

Killer? What killer? No one had mentioned murder. Holman had just said they'd discovered a body, not a victim. Terry turned to Holman. He was glaring at Schovanek. The coroner withered under the silent accusation.

"Murdered?" Shock dulled Terry's anger. "Why didn't you tell me?"

Holman exhaled and failed to maintain his eye contact with Terry. "I'm sorry, Mr. Sheffield. I should have been more clear."

Terry didn't have the words and shook his head.

"Um, is it okay that I show you the victim?" Schovanek asked.

Terry mumbled, "Yes, that's okay."

The coroner eased back the sheet, revealing the corpse's head and shoulders. Terry sagged. He didn't think he had anything left, but something kept him upright. He tried to tear his gaze away from the corpse, but he was compelled to look. The sheet covered her to preserve her modesty. From the way it clung to her body, it was obvious she was naked, except for a single shoed foot sticking out from one end. Schovanek brushed aside a tangle of hair to reveal an unhindered view of her face. Her face was full but not overweight. Immersed in the reservoir, the water must have bloated her body, making her doughy. The bleaching arc lights turned her skin whiter than white, deader than dead. But even under the harsh light, it was possible to see grays and purples tingeing her ivory complexion. Not that it mattered with the gash running across her throat. Her eyes stared far into the distance. Death had drained them of color as well as life.

"Mr. Sheffield, is this your wife?" Schovanek asked with all the compassion he could muster.

Holman sidled up to Terry. He spoke with compassion. "Mr. Sheffield, we need to know. I understand how traumatic this must be, but we do need confirmation. Is this Sarah?"

"It's not her. It's not Sarah."

"Mr. Sheffield, now, are you sure? The water has distorted the body."

"Yes. It's not Sarah. Did you check for the birthmark her right hip?"

Schovanek checked. "No birthmark."

The look on Holman's face said everything. If he didn't have Sarah Sheffield lying violated before him, then who did he have?

"What's happened to her mouth?" Terry asked.

"Her tongue's been cut out." Schovanek realized he'd said too much and winced, wishing he could take back his words.

Holman shot the coroner another scolding look. Schovanek frowned in apology.

"Jesus Christ," Oscar murmured.

"Before or after?" Terry asked.

"Before or after what?" Schovanek asked dumbly.

"Was her tongue cut out before or after she was killed?"

"Christ, Terry," Oscar said. "You don't need to know that."

"I do," Terry said. "Before or after?"

Schovanek glanced at Holman before replying, seeking approval. He got it and replied, "Before."

Terry shook off the morbidness and allowed himself to feel a weight lift. Sarah wasn't dead—she was alive. She was still out there somewhere, waiting to be found. Relief washed over him, and as much as he tried to hide it, a smile kept taking over his face.

Was it wrong? Terry thought. *Wrong to feel this good in the presence of a murdered woman?* He knew he was staring at some other poor son of a bitch's nightmare, but he couldn't feel guilty. He was thankful for too much. He'd been given a second chance. He hadn't failed Sarah. He still had time to be her protector.

"Thank you, Mr. Sheffield. I'll have someone take you home," Holman said.

Oscar came over and rested a hand on Terry's shoulder. "Thank God it wasn't her."

"Sorry, Sheriff. I wish I could have helped more."

Holman nodded and guided Terry away from the corpse. "Not a problem. I'm just glad it isn't your wife. Unfortunately, she is somebody's wife or daughter."

"The question is, who is she?" Terry asked.

Oscar said something, and Terry realized Oscar wasn't with them. He'd remained rooted to the spot, still staring at the corpse while Schovanek covered the body again.

"Mr. Mayer, please," Holman said, gesturing for him to leave.

"What did you say, Oscar?" Terry asked.

"I can pretty much say this woman is married and has two children."

"What are you saying, Mr. Mayer?" Schovanek asked.

"I know who this woman is."

CHAPTER NINE

"Mr. Mayer, you know this woman?"

Holman had a good poker face. At first glance, he didn't react to Oscar's claim, but Terry thought he caught the widening of the sheriff's eyes.

"It wasn't until Terry said it wasn't Sarah that I realized who it is. To me that looks like Alicia Hyams."

"Who?" Terry asked.

"Do you know her, Mr. Mayer?"

"No."

"Then what makes you think it's Alicia Hyams?"

"I don't. Not for sure. But the description, it seems to match. Don't you think?"

Holman went silent contemplating Oscar's proposition.

"Deputy Pittman, these two need a ride back to Mr. Sheffield's home," Holman said after a long moment.

"Who is Alicia Hyams?" Terry asked.

"Alicia Hyams? Ask your friend. He seems to have all the answers." A hint of irritation crept into Holman's tone.

"This way," Deputy Pittman ordered, pointing to a cruiser.

They rode home in silence. There was so much Terry wanted to ask Oscar, but not in front of the grim-faced deputy. Oscar had stung the cops with his observation. They'd screwed up. They should have recognized Alicia Hyams without Oscar's intervention. Mercifully, the ride came to an end. Terry thanked Deputy Pittman for the lift.

Terry got Oscar inside his house before asking, "Who is Alicia Hyams?"

"You promised me a beer," Oscar said, sounding tired.

"It was where I was heading." Terry opened the refrigerator and liberated two bottles from a half-opened cardboard case. He popped the tops with the bottle opener built into the fridge door and handed one to Oscar.

"You don't watch much TV, do you?" Oscar gulped from the bottle.

"My mind has been on other things."

"Alicia Hyams was headline news about a week or so ago. And she will be again if that body turns out to be her."

Terry fell into a seat at the dining table. "What do you mean?"

"She disappeared about the time you arrived."

Alicia Hyams's circumstances had an all too familiar ring to them. Tonight's events had the makings of a dress rehearsal for the real thing. Next time, Holman's call would lead to Sarah's body. Terry emptied his beer in one long pull.

"She disappeared?" Terry echoed.

Oscar realized what he had said. "Oh, don't get that idea. This is something completely different. Alicia was swiped from the outlet mall in Vacaville on the afternoon of the thirteenth. Mall security found her car unlocked with the keys in the ignition and her purse on the passenger seat."

"How do we know that's different?" Terry jumped up and went for another beer. "We don't know what the hell happened to Sarah. The circumstances could be identical."

Terry cracked open two more beers. He returned to Oscar, setting down a second bottle next to his first with a bang. Oscar frowned at the second bottle.

"You're not being realistic," Oscar insisted.

"How am I not being realistic?" Terry demanded.

"You're jumping to conclusions to find some meaning for what's happening. Whether you like it or not, Terry, you're too close to the problem."

"The problem?" Terry spat. "Sarah's a problem?"

Oscar remained unfazed by Terry's hostility. "Yes, Sarah is a problem. For you."

Terry snorted and took his frustration into the living room, with the beer as backup, and paced the room. What did Oscar know? It was easy for him to tell him what was what, because none of this mattered. He wasn't at the middle of this hell.

"You can't think without her," Oscar continued. "You're upset and overwhelmed. Everything has been turned upside-down since the moment you stepped off the plane."

"You think you know the answers to my problems, don't you? Sherlock-sodding-Holmes."

"Now you're just being an asshole."

Terry cursed and wiped a hand chilled from holding the beer across his brow. Oscar was right. He was being an asshole. He kept stumbling from one self-invented nightmare to another. It was time to stop. He put the bottle on the coffee table.

"Yeah, you're right. I'm sorry," he said.

"Good. I've broken through at last." Oscar smiled. "Now sit down and shut up."

Terry did as he was told and relaxed into an easy chair. Oscar repositioned himself at the dining table, sitting back-to-front, straddling the seat and resting his arms on the chair back.

"Comfortable?" Oscar inquired.

"Yes. Terry Sheffield has resumed normality. Apologizes for any technical difficulties experienced. Okay, why is Sarah's disappearance different from Alicia Hyams's?"

"Because Sarah's car is missing, along with her clothes and other belongings. If she'd been abducted, then her stuff would still be here."

Terry couldn't fault his friend's logic.

"That means Sarah went somewhere."

"But where?"

"That's not the interesting point."

"What is?"

"She chose not to tell you about it."

That silenced Terry. His wife had chosen to disappear, not telling him in the bargain. It was embarrassing. He was such a fool. What kind of woman had he married?

"The question is, why?" Terry managed after a minute.

"She could be protecting you."

"From what?"

"I don't know. Maybe it's something to do with her work. It could be a story she's been working on."

"But she would have at least given me a clue."

"Who says she hasn't? You might not have seen it yet. She wasn't at the airport, and you assumed foul play. She might have left you a note somewhere explaining everything, but you've been too busy trying to see abductors at every turn to find it."

"You might have a point," Terry conceded.

"Yeah, and I'm sorry to say it's a point you'll have to consider alone. I need to go home."

Terry thanked Oscar and saw him out. He dumped the beer bottles in the sink, pouring the remaining contents down the drain. It wasn't late, but the evening's ordeal had eroded him, so he called it a night.

• • •

He woke up late for work, having turned the alarm clock off after the first ring. The clock announced that it was after nine. He groaned and wrestled himself out of bed. There was no way he was going into work today. He called Pamela to use one of his mental health days. She reacted as he expected.

"You're taking a mental health day already?" she asked in an accusatory tone.

"I am entitled."

"Yes, but you've been with Genavax less than a week."

He cut Pamela's lecture short. "The sheriff called me out to a crime scene last night. They thought they'd found my wife."

"And had they?" Her tone softened.

"No. They found somebody else."

Terry heard Pamela inhale to say something, but she didn't. It was a few seconds before she spoke again. "When you say found, what do you mean?"

"They found a body," Terry admitted with a sigh.

"And it wasn't your wife?"

"No." Images of Alicia Hyams's mutilated corpse threw themselves at his mind's eye, her face fish-belly white, except for the black gash across the throat. "It was somebody else."

"Was it that woman they found in the lake?"

"Yes."

"That's terrible. I hope you're okay."

Pamela's sudden show of concern confused Terry. She was so coldhearted before, but now she was the total opposite. He wondered if her hard exterior was all a front to prove her managerial toughness. But something in her manner didn't ring true. She was trying too hard. He tried to make his excuses, but she was having none of it, continuing to ask question after question.

"Did she look like your wife?"

"A bit, I suppose. It was difficult to tell."

"But there was a resemblance?"

"I don't know."

"There had to be or the sheriff wouldn't have called you out."

"You're probably right."

"She had to be a dead ringer for your wife." Pamela's statement seemed to be said more to herself than to Terry.

Terry didn't know what the hell she was getting at, but he didn't like it. Her morbid curiosity with Alicia Hyams looking like Sarah bordered on the distasteful. Kyle's recollection of the fight in the lunchroom between Pamela and Sarah came to mind. His thoughts were leading him to places he didn't want to visit, and he was thankful when the doorbell rang.

"I've got to go, Pamela. Someone's at the door."

"Okay. Take it easy and we'll see you tomorrow. Take care, now."

Pamela's concern felt insincere, and he was more than happy to hang up on her.

He opened the door to stare face to face with Sarah's likeness, but not Sarah herself. Pressed against the screen door was one of his flyers. It had been ripped off something. There were ragged edges where the corners should have been. Holman was the glue that held the poster in place.

"Morning, Sheriff."

"I keep finding these things everywhere I go. Anything to do with you?" Holman demanded.

"Come in."

Terry stood back to let the sheriff in. Holman crumpled the flyer, shoved it in his jacket pocket, and came inside. Terry couldn't understand how the sheriff could wear his county-issued windbreaker. It was far too hot. Maybe he was used to the California heat. He wasn't breaking a sweat. To him, it probably felt chilly. Holman closed the front door, letting the screen door slam.

"Coffee, Sheriff?"

"No, thanks," he growled.

"Suit yourself." Terry ignored the sheriff's hostility and measured out fresh grounds into the coffeemaker. "What can I do for you?"

"You can stop getting in the way of my job."

Terry poured a pot of water into the coffeemaker and switched on the machine to brew. "I didn't know I was."

Holman grunted like an angry bull. He retrieved the crumpled flyer and flattened it out on the breakfast bar. He rapped a finger on Sarah's reproduced face. "You don't see anything wrong with this?"

Terry crossed his arms. "No, not really."

"Well, let me set you straight. This is wrong. It gets in the way. It's a distraction. It doesn't help me find your wife, Mr. Sheffield."

"Well, it helps me. It makes me feel like I'm doing something useful to help find Sarah."

"You did something useful. You contacted me. You don't have to do anything more. That's what I'm employed to do. All you've got to do is sit around and wait for me to bring her home."

"Sit around?" Terry said. "You've got to be joking. Last night you showed me a murdered woman you thought was Sarah. Is that the kind of door-to-door service you're offering?" Terry didn't give Holman a chance to defend himself and plowed on. "If it is, there's no way I'm going to sit around waiting for you or anyone else to do their job."

"I made a mistake. I'm sorry. I understand how distressing it must have been."

"You have no idea," Terry said sharply.

Terry and Holman locked stares, each trying to make the other understand the gravity of their position. Terry waited for someone to shout, "End of round one. Fighters back to their corners."

Holman was granite. Terry found it difficult to tell if the sheriff was seething and keeping it bottled up or if he'd simply gone offline. The coffeemaker gurgled.

"Truce," Holman said after a long moment.

Terry nodded. "Sorry. I didn't mean to get out of my pram."

"Huh?"

"I didn't mean to lose my temper," Terry said, correcting his obscure English euphemism.

"I'm sorry too." Holman started to say something else but changed his mind and smiled.

"Can I get you that cup of coffee?"

"Sure."

Holman drew back a chair and sat at the dining table. Terry pulled out two mugs and poured the coffee.

"Milk? Sugar?" Terry asked.

The sheriff shook his head. "No on both counts."

Terry added creamer to his coffee and brought the steaming mugs over to where Holman was sitting.

"There you go," Terry said, setting down the mug in front of Holman.

"Thanks." Picking up his mug, he blew at the vapor trailing off the surface and sipped it. "You make good coffee."

"With no wife, I get a lot of practice."

The sheriff cracked a smile. "Well, let's see what I can do to change that."

"Have you found out anything new?"

Holman shook his head. "No. Since the discovery of Alicia Hyams, your wife's case has lost some of its urgency."

"Lost some of its urgency? You mean it's relegated to second-division status."

But Holman already had his hands up in surrender. "Yes, the cold, honest truth of the matter is that your wife's case isn't as important as it was yesterday. I have a missing person, but I also have a murdered woman. Now, honestly, which do you think is going to be at the top of my list of priorities?"

Terry didn't respond.

"But it doesn't mean that I'm not going to do anything about your wife."

"So you're sure it's Alicia Hyams?"

"Yes. Mr. Hyams, her husband, made a formal identification early this morning."

Poor bastard, Terry thought. He knew exactly how the man was feeling. Of course, he'd been taken to the brink, but Alicia Hyams's husband had been pushed over it.

"What happens with Sarah?"

"This afternoon I will be holding a press conference with Mr. Hyams and we'll make an appeal for witnesses to come forward. I spoke to the media about doing a similar appeal for your wife, but I need your approval."

"There's nothing to approve," Terry said. "When?"

"Monday at eleven. I want to put the weekend between your wife's case and Alicia Hyams's. I don't want anyone getting confused."

"Do you think it will help?"

"I'm hoping so. We need something to kick-start the investigation. This could be the tonic we've been looking for." Holman checked his watch. "I'd better be going."

"Yes. Of course."

Holman gulped the remainder of his coffee. Terry didn't know how the man did it. The brew was far too hot for him to sip, let alone gulp.

Holman got up to leave. Terry followed him to the door. Although twenty years Terry's senior, Holman carried himself with the confidence of a man who could handle all situations. Terry couldn't help admiring him. He darted around Holman to open the door for him.

"I want to say thanks, Sheriff," Terry said, offering his hand. "You don't have an easy task, and people like me don't make it any easier."

Holman took Terry's hand and crushed it. "You're just trying to do your best for your wife. It's totally understandable."

"Well, I'll speak to you Monday."

Letting himself out, Holman agreed and pushed the screen door to one side. He went to let it go, but stopped.

"And Mr. Sheffield, no more flyers."

"Okay. Do you want me to take them down?"

The sheriff shook his head. "No need."

Terry imagined that Holman had sent his deputies out to remove them already. "Why?"

"How many calls have you received because of them?"

"None so far."

"And you won't."

"It's been less than a day. Give it a chance."

"Trust me, Mr. Sheffield, flyers like yours rarely have an impact."

The instant Terry closed the door, the phone rang. Knowing his luck, it was probably someone responding to one of his flyers. Picking up the phone, he watched Holman drive away.

"Hello," Terry answered.

"Oh, you don't sound like Sarah," the caller said, sounding surprised.

"I'm not."

The caller was male, but he didn't sound like Terry's mystery caller. This guy didn't have the malevolent streak the mystery caller possessed.

"Goddamn it, have I dialed the wrong number again?"

Who is this clown? Terry thought.

"I'm always dialing wrong numbers. I should use speed dial, but I can never work the damn thing out, and no one ever has the time to do it for me."

This definitely wasn't Terry's mystery caller.

"You wanted to speak to Sarah Sheffield?" Terry asked, interrupting the caller's speech on his technical ineptitude.

"No, Sarah Morton. I have dialed the wrong number. Dammit. Sorry to have disturbed you. Have a nice day."

"No, you haven't," Terry said before the caller hung up. "Sarah's my wife."

"Married? She's not married." The caller paused. Somewhere the penny dropped. "Oh, yeah. She eloped some months ago with some English guy."

"I know. I am some English guy."

"Of course you are." He laughed at his foolishness. "Put her on the phone?"

"She's not here."

"Tell her I called, then."

"You don't understand. She's missing."

That stumped him. And it shut him up, which was a blessing in itself. Terry had only been on the phone for a couple of minutes, but the caller already had his head buzzing.

"How long?"

"Don't know. A week maybe," Terry said. "Who is this?"

"I'm Marcus Beasley, Sarah's editor."

Finally, someone who knew Sarah. He hoped his luck was changing.

"When was the last time you spoke to Sarah, Mr. Beasley?"

"Marcus, please. And it would have been over a week ago. That was why I was calling. She's got a deadline to meet, and I haven't seen hide nor hair of her. And unlike in the movies, we don't hold the front page for the star reporter."

"Marcus, she's been missing for over a week. Her car's gone. So are some of her clothes. I don't think she's holding out on you."

"Oh," Marcus squeaked, suitably silenced.

"I think she's in trouble. Do you have any idea where she could be?"

"I don't. Sorry, what's your name?"

"Terry Sheffield."

"She still uses Sarah Morton."

Terry understood from a continuity standpoint that it made sense for Sarah to stick to her maiden name when it came to her work, but he couldn't help wonder if it was sign of her limited commitment to their marriage. "I know."

"Not important anyway."

"Not really."

"Sorry, Terry, I don't know where she could be. She never says. She always plays her cards close to her vest, if you know what I mean."

He didn't really. Sarah seemed to be so open, but he'd only known the vacation Sarah, not the day-to-day Sarah. It made him wonder what he really knew about her. The more he learned about her, the more he felt he'd fallen for the wrong version of her. Maybe she was a driven, uncaring person. He sagged and sat on the floor with his back against the front door.

"Do you know what she was working on?" Terry asked.

"A couple of things."

"Anything dangerous?"

"Dangerous? This is *California Now*, not the *Washington Post*."

"How about…"

"I'm gonna have to put you on hold a moment, Terry. I've got another call. It might be Sarah."

It was a nice thought, but Beasley wasn't fooling anyone.

"I'll be back in a second, but I might cut you off. I don't always get this right."

What a muppet, Terry thought and smiled.

"Here goes."

There was a click then music. Terry was on hold. But just as quickly, Beasley was back.

"Terry, you there?"

"I'm here."

"Good, I didn't screw it up. Look, I need to take this call, but why don't you come into the office Monday. Say around seven p.m. Sound good?"

"Sounds great."

"Good. Do you know where we are?"

"No."

Beasley offloaded Terry onto a receptionist who gave him a San Francisco address. The address meant nothing to Terry, but the receptionist assured him it was a popular locale and whizzed off a staccato list of directions. He hung up happy to have a starting point at last but disappointed that he would have to wait.

Terry shook off his disappointment and drove to Genavax. He stopped in at Jenny Kuo's office to explain that he would be taking a second mental health day because of Holman's planned press conference. Jenny was just as understanding as he expected. He repeated the exercise with Pamela Dawson. She was more than accommodating and just as saccharin as she had been on the phone earlier. He smiled, making his excuses and escaping before her verbal molasses could bog him down.

He was determined to talk to Kyle Hemple, but this wasn't the time. He left and went in search of a cell phone. He needed something that would work as a pocket guide to operating in America. He bought the latest smartphone and went for a late lunch. While he ate, he familiarized himself with his phone and downloaded various apps he thought he might need. By the time he was connected to the world, it was late afternoon. He drove back to Genavax and waited for Kyle to leave for the day.

Kyle was one of the first to leave Genavax. Terry unpeeled himself from the Ford Focus. The Central Valley's heat had turned the Ford into a greenhouse. Even with the windows down, there was no relief. As he slipped from the car, his T-shirt clung to his back. Terry jogged over to Kyle as he stood by his Toyota Land Cruiser.

"Kyle, wait up."

Kyle craned his neck and grinned when he spotted Terry. "Dude. I didn't think you were in today."

"I wasn't. Can we talk?"

"What about?" Suspicion fluttered behind Kyle's eyes.

"Not here. Let's go somewhere."

"Sorry, man. I don't have the time."

"I only need a few minutes. C'mon, Kyle. I won't keep you long, I promise."

Kyle came close and kept his voice hushed. "I don't have the time to talk about what you want to talk about."

What the hell was going on at Genavax? Kyle's fear wasn't a good sign, especially when there was a possible connection to Sarah and her disappearance. "Kyle, you don't know what I want to talk about."

"I'm sorry, Terry." Kyle brushed past him, jamming his car key into the sun-bleached Toyota's door. "No."

Terry snatched Kyle's arm as he went to dive into the Land Cruiser. His gaze bore into the aging surfer's eyes. "Kyle, if you know what's happened to my wife, you can't remain quiet about it."

"You don't know what you're asking."

"Kyle, please."

Kyle shook his head. "I'm making a big mistake talking to you, but follow me."

Terry followed Kyle's SUV. He expected to drive into town and find a bar or restaurant, but Kyle joined the freeway and exited at some nowhere rural county road. They followed the highway for five miles, flanked by open fields. Kyle made a right onto a gravel road leading to an abandoned airstrip. They parked on the worn and barely legible numbers at the end of the runway.

He couldn't have found a quieter place, Terry thought, getting out of the Focus. "Is this really necessary?"

"You wanted to talk, didn't you?"

Kyle stuffed his hands in his pockets and walked on the dashed line running down the center of the runway. The tarmac was pitted and missing in places. Wild grasses grew in clumps in the cracks. Terry fell in next to Kyle.

"I used to skydive here," Kyle said. "That was years ago. I don't do it anymore. When the dive club left, the airport closed. But I still like to come here when I want to think."

There was a touch of the Zen master about Kyle that Terry wouldn't have credited him with possessing.

"Kyle, what is it you're not telling me? And what does it have to do with Sarah?"

"I told you about the bust up between Pamela and your wife, yeah?"

"That was as far as you got. You didn't say the reason."

"Sarah had done a little digging into Genavax's performance."

"Into its finances, I know. I told her to do that. I've been bitten by biotech startups who have nothing but a couple of months of rent in the bank and very little else."

"From what I gather, she went further than that. I think she found a few wrinkles where there shouldn't have been any."

"What wrinkles?"

"Irregularities."

"Spit it out, Kyle."

"Jesus, man." He flashed Terry his best whipped-puppy look.

Terry softened. "Just tell me, Kyle. Please. It could be important."

"She alluded that some of Genavax's breakthroughs came as a bit of a surprise. Results had been better than expected and Genavax was on the fast track to success."

"What was her point?"

"Don't know."

"Did she think it was because of falsified data or industrial espionage? What?"

"Dude, I don't know." Kyle's stride quickened. "I'm just telling you what she said. I don't know what she meant. I just know it pissed off Pam."

"But you work at Genavax. You must know something."

"I don't. I keep my head down and do my work. Personally, I don't care what Genavax gets up to as long as its checks don't bounce."

"Where did Sarah get her info?"

"Don't know."

Kyle's speed outpaced Terry's. Terry hooked one of his arms to slow him down. Kyle wasn't getting off that easily. "You do know something."

Kyle spun around, pivoting in Terry's grasp. "Don't ask, don't tell. That's the code I use. I know nothing. Get it?"

Terry knew Kyle was lying. He knew more than he was letting on, but it wasn't the time to press him any further. If he treated the situation right, he might get Kyle to break his silence.

"I get it."

"You push too hard. You're as bad as your wife. Dude, when we're back at Genavax and you see me, don't talk to me. Got that?"

"Did someone talk to you after we had lunch?"

Kyle tugged on his arm in Terry's grip.

"Did someone threaten you?"

Kyle glared instead of answering him, but it was all the answer Terry needed. There was something very wrong at Genavax.

Terry nodded and released Kyle's arm.

Kyle turned and stormed off back to his Toyota. Terry watched him, giving the man his space.

Terry waited until the only evidence of Kyle's presence was the dust kicked up from his tires before trudging back to the Focus. On the drive home, he listened to the drone of the car engine, not thinking about Kyle, Sarah, or the cloud that blighted his life. He put his brain into stasis and left it there. Autopilot got him to Sutter Drive.

Turning onto his street, he spotted an unfamiliar car pulling into his driveway. He didn't know anyone with an old model Honda Accord. Out of instinct, he thumbed the garage door remote.

As the door retracted, Terry's visitor blew out of the driveway, reversing at high speed, and straight at Terry. They both slammed on their brakes and the Accord came treacherously close to front-ending Terry. The Honda driver snatched a forward gear and roared off.

Terry tried to seize a glance of the driver, but the Honda sped off into the distance too rapidly for him to see anything.

Terry didn't give chase. A numbing chill had swept over him. The replacement battery for the garage door opener was still in its packaging by his foot, thrown there by the force of his braking. He hadn't opened the garage door—the Accord driver had.

CHAPTER TEN

"Thank you for attending the press conference this morning," Holman said to the assembled media representatives.

The group consisted of two dozen reporters from the local television affiliates, their technicians, and a handful of local newspaper journalists. The building wasn't large enough to hold them all, so Holman held the press conference in the parking lot, using the side of the building as a backdrop.

Terry sat on Holman's left, behind two picnic tables squeezed together. A Santa Rita County Sheriff's Department flag was draped over the edge of the tables to hide their legs and feet from view. Two blowups of Sarah's face hung on the wall behind Terry and Holman. The photographs helped hide the municipal building's weathered stucco. Fingers laced, Terry stared at the picnic table's surface, examining its grain and avoiding the media vultures with microphones and tape recorders outstretched.

"Your support is greatly appreciated." Holman glanced at his notes. "Sarah Sheffield has been missing for a minimum of eleven days. It has been hard to ascertain the exact date she disappeared due to the lack of corroborative sightings. However, signs are that she left her home of her own accord. A bag was packed and the car was taken—a 2009 white-and-gray Subaru Outback, license number 6NHS374. There is no sign of a robbery or the use of force.

However, the amount of clothing taken suggests that Mrs. Sheffield didn't intend to be away for such a significant length of time. Also, there has been no active use of her credit cards. Mrs. Sheffield is a journalist and writes under her maiden name, Sarah Morton. So we are appealing to anyone who might have seen Sarah"—Holman held up an eight-by-ten photo of her—"to call our special hotline, 1-800-HELP-NOW. Now, I would like to give Mrs. Sheffield's husband, Terry Sheffield, a minute to make an appeal."

Terry looked up from the table and stared into the expectant faces. He tried to speak, but his throat seized. He coughed and apologized. "Thanks, Sheriff Holman, and thanks to everyone for coming."

He took a moment to make eye contact with those assembled. A pretty Asian American reporter smiled, as if to will him on with his difficult task. He didn't want to smile back with the cameras filming. This wasn't the time to be smiling.

Terry didn't have a set speech, but Holman had told him not to worry about what he said. He was there as window dressing, no more than an investigative prop to garner pity from the public. Holman called it his "abandoned puppy tactic."

"If anyone has seen Sarah, or even thinks they've seen her, please call the sheriff's 1-800 number. You have a picture of her, please use it. Get her face out there. I've come to this country to start a new life with my wife, to live the American dream—please help me do that." Terry shifted in his seat. "And Sarah, if you're watching, please call. Even if it's just to tell me that you're okay. Just call, please. That's all I've got to say."

Holman patted Terry on the shoulder. He forced a thin smile and nodded approvingly.

"Thanks, Mr. Sheffield," Holman said before addressing the media. "I will accept a few questions."

One reporter leaped to his feet. "Is there any connection between Sarah Sheffield's disappearance and the murder of Alicia Hyams?"

Terry turned to Holman. He wanted to know the answer to that question too.

Holman cleared his throat. "There is no reason to link the two cases together. The circumstances are completely different. Mrs. Hyams was abducted. Mrs. Sheffield left her home of her own free will. Any resemblance between these cases is purely coincidental."

From the look on the sheriff's face, he'd been hoping this subject wouldn't be raised. Terry wondered if it was because there was a connection or because he didn't want wild speculation making the headlines. Terry hoped it was the latter.

"Are there any new developments in the Hyams case?" another reporter asked.

"I'm not willing to discuss that case at this time. We're here to discuss Sarah Sheffield. Now, are there any other questions?"

Terry had to credit Holman's superior crowd-control techniques. He made his point felt. His granite stare was enough to get proceedings back on the right track. He fielded a couple of questions linked to Sarah's disappearance and dealt with them efficiently.

A lull followed, and Holman brought the conference to a close. He thanked everyone and that was it. No one dillydallied. As soon as Holman stood, the media people wrapped up shop.

"Thanks, Mr. Sheffield," Holman said, shaking Terry's hand. "You did very well. I think we got our point across. We should receive some calls from this."

"I hope so, Sheriff."

"I'll call if I hear anything."

Deputy Pittman tugged on the county sheriff's flag and it came away from the tables. Holman snapped up the chairs he and Terry had been sitting on. It was all over.

Feeling surplus to requirements, Terry returned to his car. He wormed his way between the journalists and tiptoed over cable feeds coiled on the ground like spilled intestines. He sidestepped a sound engineer checking his recording and overheard a snippet of conversation he wasn't meant to hear.

"This has all the hallmarks of one of Sarah Morton's classic setups."

Terry whirled to see who had made the remark. It was the reporter who had asked if there was a connection between Sarah and Alicia Hyams. He was slouched against his news van's passenger door smoking a cigarette. He was speaking to his cameraman, who sat on the side door's sill, hunched over his camera as he ejected the tape. The reporter hadn't known Terry was close, and the cameraman's frantic gesture to put a lid on it was too late.

"What did you say?"

The reporter spun on his heel. He looked as if he'd been pricked with a needle, but he recovered and the look disappeared as quickly as it had come. He whipped the cigarette behind his back and flashed his toothiest grin. "Excuse me?" he asked, denial plastered poorly across his face.

"I heard what you said. How is this one of Sarah Morton's classic setups?"

The reporter fluffed a response.

"The sheriff's over there. Do you want me to get him so you can explain to both of us?"

The reporter dropped the act. The game-show-host grin disappeared and the cigarette came back out. "Okay. Okay, what do you want to know?"

"I want to know what you meant."

The reporter took a deep drag on his cigarette and exhaled, blowing thick smoke over his shoulder before stubbing the butt out on the ground with his foot. "Ramon, I'm gonna take fifteen and have a cup of coffee with Mr. Sheffield."

A shared parking lot separated the sheriff's office and the Java House. The reporter stopped in front of the coffeehouse and jerked a thumb at it.

"This place good?"

"Don't know. I've never been here before."

"It'll do. They're people after my own heart," he said and tapped a sign on the door.

The sign was the Starbucks logo with a red circle over it and a red diagonal slash bisecting the Starbucks name. The reporter opened the door for Terry and they went in.

The Java House had only two customers. Behind the counter a willowy college-age girl with hair dyed so red it was copper-colored responded immediately.

"Welcome to the Java House. Can I take your order?"

"Yeah," the reporter said. "I'll take a low-fat latte and a…" He pointed at Terry to answer for himself.

"Make it two." He didn't want a low-fat latte, but he couldn't be bothered to contend with the endless menu board behind the girl's head.

The copper-headed girl rang up the order on the cash register. "They'll be just a minute, okay?" she said.

"Can you bring them over?" the reporter asked and paid.

"Sure thing."

They seated themselves at a table by the window. The morning heat radiated through the glass, penetrating the carefully air-conditioned environment.

"I'm Tom Degrasse, by the way," the reporter said and held out a hand. "Sorry about earlier."

Terry shook. "Forget it."

"Yeah, well. It was uncalled for."

"Do you know Sarah?"

"Most of us here today do. Our paths have crossed covering the same stories."

All smiles, Copperhead came over with the lattes. She placed them in front of Terry and Degrasse. "Thanks for not choosing Starbucks."

Degrasse grinned. "Don't you love small-town businesses? They really know how to stick it to corporate America."

"Yeah, that's great. What makes you think Sarah's pulled some stunt?"

Degrasse sucked the foam off the top of his latte, making a mess of his face. He wiped the froth ring from around his mouth with a napkin. "Stunt. That's an interesting word. I think that's a strong word."

"Okay, to use your vernacular, a classic setup."

Degrasse smiled wryly and licked his lips. "Okay, maybe I was a little harsh with my earlier outburst. I was irritated to see so many people gathered together in her name."

"Why?"

"Sarah is a determined woman. When she locks onto a juicy story, she doesn't back down. She'll do anything to get that front page and everything goes on the back burner. From what the sheriff said, I doubt she's missing."

"So you think she's just out following a story and damn the rest of us," Terry accused.

Degrasse held up his hands in surrender. "Hey, don't shoot the messenger. I'm just telling you like it is."

"And what makes you such an expert?"

"Personal experience."

"What experience?"

"A few years back, when Sarah worked for *The Sacramento Bee*, everybody wanted an exclusive with the lieutenant governor's wife. She'd just blown the whistle on her husband's involvement in a crooked construction deal on a new state prison. Sarah announced the time and location for a fake press conference. We guppies took the bait and turned up to an empty room while Sarah had a one-on-one with the lieutenant governor's wife."

It was a shitty thing to do to her competition, but Terry wasn't sure if what Sarah had done was unethical or not. It didn't sound like anything out of the ordinary for the media. It wasn't as if they were as pure as the driven snow. How many times had the tabloids made an outrageous claim only to end up paying out in the civil courts? But that wasn't what bugged him. He didn't want to hear that Sarah was ruthless.

"So you think Sarah's manipulating the situation?"

"She could be, but I don't know."

"Okay, let's say she is. What are all the theatrics for?"

"I honestly don't know, Terry. There isn't anything big on the books right now."

"Except Alicia Hyams," Terry suggested and sipped his latte.

"Already been there. I can't see her angle. If there is one, it's all Sarah's. None of us are chasing the same bone."

Ramon rapped on the window, startling both of them. "Tom, we've gotta roll, man," the cameraman shouted, muffled by the thick glazing.

"I'll be two minutes."

Ramon examined Terry quizzically. "Okay, Tom. Two minutes. Don't make it twenty," he said and then left.

"I've got to go." Degrasse stood. "All differences aside, I hope she comes back."

"So do I."

"Give her my regards."

"Will she want them?"

The TV reporter laughed. "I doubt it, but give them anyway."

Degrasse fished out his business card and offered it to Terry. Terry stood, took the card, and shook Degrasse's hand.

"Terry, I can see you love Sarah, so don't take this the wrong way."

Terry guessed he would.

"I don't know how you two hooked up, but how much do you really know about your wife?"

"People keep asking me that."

"Haven't you wondered why?"

Terry said nothing.

"Don't let her break your heart."

• • •

Terry entered an anonymous office building in the shadow of the Transamerica Pyramid. The lobby felt like a wasteland, dark and quiet. He half expected tumbleweeds to cross his path as he approached the reception desk. It was a few minutes after seven and the working day was over for most people. The night security guard looked up.

"Marcus Beasley, please," Terry said. "I'm Terry Sheffield."

"Is he expecting you?" the guard asked punching a number into the phone.

"Yes."

The guard nodded and spoke into the phone. "Mr. Beasley, I have Terry Sheffield here to see you." He listened to the reply. "Okay, I'll send him up."

The guard hung up and pointed to the elevators to the right of Terry. "Take the elevator to the twelfth floor. Mr. Beasley will be waiting for you."

"Thanks."

Terry crossed the lobby to the elevators and pressed the up button.

The guard called out, "Don't keep him too long. We have a hard enough job getting him out of here most nights."

Terry smiled and nodded. "Workaholic, is he?"

"You better believe it. He's the first to arrive and last to leave. Whatever you do, don't take the job. You'll never see your family."

The elevator pinged and the door slid open. "I'll bear that in mind," Terry said, stepping into the car.

The elevator doors opened onto the twelfth floor. The drone of vacuum cleaners working in the distance greeted Terry, but Marcus Beasley didn't. He spotted an office directory on a wall opposite the elevator and was scanning for *California Now* when his name was called. A short, dumpy man wearing thick glasses trotted toward him and shot out a stubby arm.

"Marcus Beasley, editor in chief of *California Now.*"

"Hi," Terry said, his body vibrating from the little man's jackhammer handshake.

"You found the place okay?"

"Oh, yes," Terry lied. He'd found San Francisco easily enough, but couldn't negotiate the streets. Despite the GPS on his phone, he was forever trying to make turns onto one-way streets from the wrong direction. In the end, he found a parking meter, parked, and hailed a cab.

"Good. This way."

Beasley escorted Terry along a corridor and into an office suite. It was smaller than Terry expected for a glossy magazine. He was expecting reams of reporters running around with press tickets poking out of their hatbands, but was sorely disappointed. Beasley must have spotted Terry's look.

"Not what you were expecting?" Beasley asked. He negotiated a path around the cubicles.

"No, not really."

"For a periodical to survive these days, you don't need much. The magazine can be typeset on a computer. Writers are all subcontracted, as is the printing. There's no need to saddle a magazine with so much overhead."

"Very slick," Terry said.

"Coffee?"

Terry shook his head.

"Sorry, you're English. You'd prefer tea. Would you like a cup?"

"No thanks. Never liked the stuff."

"You're English and you don't drink tea?" Beasley exclaimed. "Did you leave England or were you run out?"

Terry laughed.

"Well, I'm glad you don't want any. I don't have any anyway. I don't know why I do that. I'm always offering things I can't supply," Beasley babbled. "Must be the reporter in me, always committing to a deadline I can never meet. Anyhoo, here's me."

Terry followed Beasley into a corner office with great views of other skyscrapers' twelfth floors. The editor squeezed into a threadbare executive chair, which was out of place with the rest of the modern office suite. Sinking into his seat, Beasley smiled as if he was luxuriating in a hot bath. It was obvious why that chair was part of the office.

"You're here, so I can guess Sarah hasn't called."

"Correct."

Beasley inhaled thoughtfully. "Very strange."

"You're her boss. Do you think her disappearance has anything to do with her job?"

"Have you ever read *California Now*?"

"No."

"We're a checkout-stand glossy, somewhere between *TV Guide* and *Woman's World*. We do family-oriented pieces for the family-oriented reader. We don't get to uncover the Watergate tapes. Hell, we wouldn't even bother."

Terry frowned.

"Hoping to find a connection?"

Terry sighed. "Well, yes. I thought she'd gotten into trouble with a story. Are you sure she's not working on something dangerous?"

"I'm sure. As far as I know, she was working on a couple of human-interest pieces. An all-female America's Cup team had just returned, and the San Diego Zoo was celebrating the birth of a pair of polar bears."

"Not life-and-death stuff, then."

"No. Sorry. Do you want to see her desk?"

"She has one here?" Terry asked, surprised.

"Most freelancers like to work from home, but we keep desks open for anyone who likes to use our facilities, and Sarah did."

"Yes, I'd like to see it."

Beasley stood and his expression sagged. He wasn't happy to have left the comfort of his chair. He led Terry to a messy cubicle strewn with paper, unopened mail, and notes and photos pinned to the walls. The pictures corresponded with the stories Beasley had mentioned.

"Can I look through her things?"

"I'll leave you alone."

Terry sifted through the mess. He didn't find anything of any value, just a mishmash of internal memos, shorthand notes, contact names and numbers. Beasley returned after ten minutes.

"Find anything?"

"Not really." Terry held up a wad of Post-it notes. "Can I take these?"

"If you think they'll help."

"Thanks."

Beasley leaned against a partition wall. It sagged under his weight. "Sarah wasn't exclusive to me. She was freelance. She might have been working on something for someone else."

"Do you know who?"

"Could be anyone. It all depends on who bites."

"She mentioned that she used to work for the *San Francisco Chronicle* and the *Examiner*. Could she be working for one of them?"

"Possible. Come to think of it, Sarah did offer me something."

"What?"

"She intimated she'd stumbled onto something hot. Something that would blow my socks off, but I told her I was an old man and I didn't need my socks blown off anymore."

"Did she say what it was?"

Beasley shook his head. "No. She's cagey when she wants to be. If I wasn't biting, she wasn't telling. Is there anything else I can help you with?"

"Actually, you can. I was speaking to Tom Degrasse earlier today."

"That pampered poodle? What did he have to say?"

"He suggested that Sarah's disappearance was part of a scam to break a big story."

Beasley mulled over the notion. He sniffed before speaking. "Sarah is a journalist and a damn fine one at that. She writes features for me, but it's not where her heart is. She's an investigative journalist. She wants to discover the next Jack Abramoff scandal, and she'll do her damnedest to find it."

Terry left Beasley's office with a hollow feeling that had little to do with his grumbling stomach. He needed some food inside him, but decided not to eat in San Francisco, not relishing getting lost in the unfamiliar city. He took a cab back to his car and retraced his way to the Bay Bridge.

Approaching the Edenville turnoff, Terry wasn't in the mood to cook for himself, so he drove on to the next exit, which serviced the Greenview Mall. The mall had a food court to suit all tastes. Terry picked a Thai place. He settled into a two-person booth and tucked into his cashew chicken with jasmine rice and a 7UP. He didn't get far.

"Terry Sheffield?" a blond man asked.

Terry nodded with a mouthful of food.

"Can I join you?"

Terry swallowed. "Do I know you?"

The man sat down, unfolded a sheet of paper, and placed it in front of Terry. "No, but I know her."

Terry stared at Sarah on one of his own flyers. He had been hoping for a moment like this. He had expected to be elated, but instead, his food soured in his stomach. He pushed his meal to one side and picked up the flyer.

Gazing at Sarah's image, he said, "How do you know who I am?"

"I just saw you on the evening news. I was in a Walgreens yesterday, and I saw the flyer. I picked one up, and I was going to call you tonight; then I saw you sitting here."

The guy was chipper, delighted to have found Terry. It was a shame Terry couldn't summon up that same feeling.

"Where are my manners? My name's Jake."

"Nice to meet you, Jake. So you've seen Sarah?"

"No, I worked with her. I was helping her with a story."

"Are you a journalist?"

"No, nothing like that. I helped her with research and stuff," Jake said. "So have you heard from her? Sarah, I mean."

Terry gave him a look.

"Duh! Obvious."

"Yeah, well," Terry said, shrugging his shoulders.

"But she hasn't called or left a message?"

"No. If she had, I wouldn't be searching for her."

"Yeah, right."

Terry wasn't sure if Jake was as dumb as he made out. If he was, he couldn't see him being much help to Sarah's research. He wondered if this guy really knew Sarah.

"Why did you want to get in contact?"

"Just reaching out. I liked working for Sarah and I want to help find her. If you need someone to ask questions, chase down sightings, I'm your guy."

Help sounded good to Terry. With Oscar, he was a team of two. A team of three wasn't much better, but if he could build a grass roots team working to find Sarah, he stood a chance of finding her.

"Do you think her disappearance has anything to do with the story we were working on?" Jake asked. "Because if it does, then I should be looking over my own shoulder. What do you think?"

The question took Terry by surprise. Sarah's work had the potential for drawing trouble. "I don't know much about Sarah's work. What story were you working on together? Was it Genavax?"

Terry regretted mentioning Genavax the second he had said it. Holman's warning about cranks rang loud in his head. It occurred to him that this guy could be anyone. He needed Jake to give him information, not the other way around.

"Nah," Jake said, shaking his head. "Our story wasn't anything heavy. It must be something else. She was working on a lot of things. Have you found any of her notes?"

"No. I haven't found anything."

"Look, if you do find them, I'd be happy to look them over."

"Thanks." Jake seemed well-meaning enough, but Terry wasn't sure he trusted him.

"Got any ideas about what made her disappear?" Jake asked.

"None."

"So you haven't seen Sarah, heard from her, found any of her notes, and you don't know what stories she'd been working on that could have led to her disappearance, right?"

"Right," Terry said warily.

"It's a stumper, all right." Jake checked his watch and jumped to his feet."Well, I've gotta go."

Terry tried to stop him. "Can I get a number?"

Jake screwed up his face. "I'm really late, and I don't have a pen."

"I do."

"I don't have time. Sorry."

Don't have time, Terry thought. *What was this guy playing at?*

"I'll call you." He brandished the flyer. "We'll talk real soon, Terry."

Jake darted off, swallowed by the evening shoppers. Terry didn't know what to make of his new acquaintance. He took another stab at his meal, but the food wasn't that great and his appetite had made a discreet exit. He dumped the chicken and rice into the nearest trash can but kept his soda.

"Hey there, pal."

Terry turned to find Oscar walking toward him with shopping bags in each hand. Terry smiled, but Oscar didn't.

"Who was that you were talking to?"

Terry didn't like the suspicious tone in Oscar's voice, and he tried to lighten it. "What, jealous?"

"I'm serious, Terry. Who was that you were talking to?"

"His name's Jake. He said he worked with Sarah, but he was kind of odd. I'm not sure who he was."

Oscar didn't look convinced. Shoppers leaving the food court brushed by them.

"Oscar, what's up?"

"I don't know what he told you, but I doubt he worked with Sarah."

"So you don't think his name's Jake?"

"His name's Jake, all right. Jake Holman."

"Jake Holman," Terry said slowly. "Sheriff Holman's son?"

"The one and only."

CHAPTER ELEVEN

Terry let himself into his house with Holman still on his mind. The sheriff had sent his son to spy on him. What the hell was that all about? Did Holman think he was hiding something? Terry thought they were past that stage, especially after Holman had gone to all the trouble of organizing a press conference. This had to be some plan to try to trip him up. He remembered some quotation about catching more flies with honey than vinegar. The answering machine blinked a red number one at him. He hit play.

"Terry, it's Marcus Beasley. I forgot to mention something. Why I didn't remember it when you were here earlier, I don't know. It must have something to do with getting old—or just the workload. You wouldn't believe the long hours I spend here. It's more than a full-time job."

Terry smiled. He could see why Sarah liked working for Beasley. *C'mon, Marcus, get to the point.*

"Sarah told me once that she keeps a file box or some such with all of her notes on the hot stories. She never keeps them in the office or anywhere they could be poached. I don't know if that helps. But if you find anything, let me know."

Jake Holman had mentioned something about Sarah's notes, and now Beasley had. There had to be something in it. That something galvanized him into action.

He started with Sarah's home office. He pulled the room apart. He emptied out drawers and unloaded the closet. The floor was awash with discarded storage boxes, their contents eviscerated. Only after he had gutted the room did he realize that if Sarah wanted to keep something hidden, the last place she would hide it would be her office.

The house didn't have a full attic. The roof's pitch was shallow, but it did have enough space to store a file box. Using a ladder and flashlight he found in the garage, he climbed into the crawl space. It was a nice thought, but no good. The flashlight beam uncovered fiberglass insulation and roof joists, but that was all.

Terry moved the search into the garage. He put himself into Sarah's mind. If he wanted to hide something, where would he put it? He popped open old paint cans. He found a box marked "Christmas Decorations" and hoped it was a lie, but the contents were true to their labeling. The toolbox would have been a good place, but Sarah wasn't using it.

Every smart hiding place resulted in disappointment. The toilet tank held only water. Bedroom closets and a chest of drawers contained clothes. No matter which room he tore apart, it was how it should be. Standing in the living room with the couch upside-down, he lost faith in the quest.

He hoped Beasley hadn't been wrong. The house was a bomb site. Every room was overturned, and he had nothing to show for it. Then he spotted it.

The coat closet by the front door had a floor panel. The panel gave access to the crawl space under the house. There was another access panel in the smallest of the three bedrooms and he'd already opened that one. He'd even gone into the crawl space, but he hadn't checked every corner of the building. He yanked the panel up.

Terry didn't have to go down into crawl space again with all the cobwebs and dirt. Sitting on the dirt below was a metal file box. He reached down and snatched it up. It was locked, but he didn't have time to find the key. He grabbed the screwdriver from the garage and jimmied it open, snapping the lock.

Papers tumbled onto the floor. Terry gathered them up. He cleared a space on the dining table by wiping an arm across the surface, sending everything onto the carpet. He sat and examined his find.

His discovery was a jumble. Dropping the contents on the floor had decimated any order the notes were in. It would take painstaking patience to get it all back in order—patience he didn't have. He was too excited. He wanted the answer to leap out at him, but good sense took over and he persevered. He examined every scrap of paper, but it didn't mean a thing. Some of it was in shorthand—a foreign language to him. That could be easily deciphered. Beasley or someone would help him out. But that wasn't the problem. If her non-shorthand notes were anything to go by, it wouldn't make any sense to anyone anyway. These were Sarah's notes, for Sarah to understand. The reason for her disappearance might be contained among the sheets of paper in his hand, but it meant nothing without Sarah to explain it all. As depressing as his task seemed, he plowed on.

Fatigue seeped in and he could barely keep his eyes open, but as something started to trickle from Sarah's notes, the drive to keep going filled him. A thread was developing. He kept coming across the names of four women. None of them seemed very special. They had led unremarkable lives. In fact, they seemed to be pillars of their respective communities in various parts of California, Nevada, and Oregon. Nothing seemed to point to anything that would have made the information worth hiding from would-be news poachers.

Terry continued to sift through the information hoping to find a nugget worth its weight in gold. After another hour of sifting, dawn crept over the horizon, bathing the dining area in peach-colored light, and Terry didn't think that nugget was going to present itself. He was ready to call it a night—a day now—when a fifth woman's name appeared on a list with the other four. He hadn't found any other notes on the fifth woman, but he didn't need to find any. He knew her already.

"Alicia Hyams," he murmured to himself.

. . .

Terry needed sleep, but he went into work. He couldn't afford to take a third personal day. Besides, he didn't want to be at home right now. After last night's discovery, he needed distance, a chance to think things through. Not that he was in any condition to think about anything. It felt as if mice had been scurrying around inside his head, and one of them had taken a crap somewhere small and inaccessible. He was physically shattered too. His mental battering had filtered through to his body. He seemed to be coated in a layer of sludge that showering couldn't remove.

He sneaked into the lab ten minutes late. If he was expecting Pamela Dawson to be all sweetness and light, he was wrong. She was the Ice Maiden again. Actually, he was glad about the return to normality. Nice didn't suit her too well. He went to his bench, feeling her searching stare burning holes in his back. He guessed there would be a closed-door visit to her office, and there was. It was nothing too vicious—just slightly menacing. Genavax was sympathetic to his situation, but the company wasn't about to let him slack off at the expense of others, blah, blah, blah. Returning to his bench, he descended into a work mode that kept him busy, but not especially focused.

Terry made it through to lunchtime and sat in the staff lunchroom in a daze. Returning to work, he bumped into Kyle Hemple. Kyle wasn't happy to see him and blanked him. He'd certainly lost an ally.

Terry checked his watch and was glad to see the day coming to an end. His cell-culture samples were completed and needed storing in the freezer. It was a walk-in affair with a six-inch lip inside the door to prevent spills from escaping. Putting his samples on a bench, he eased back the meat locker-style door.

A blanket of arctic air smothered him, taking his breath away and crystallizing the blood in his veins. The freezer was kept at a soul-numbing minus thirty degrees Celsius. It wasn't cryogenically cold, but it didn't feel far off.

He didn't like the freezer—nobody did. It was dangerous, and everyone was extra careful when entering the damn thing. According to the company grapevine, it had been expensive to construct, and engineers had pored over the design to ensure the refrigerant and the insulation were state of the art to guarantee Genavax didn't run up a monstrous utility bill. So much effort went into this single aim that the safety-release handle inside the freezer was of secondary importance. A couple of years ago, a person had gotten trapped inside when the safety-release button failed with near-tragic consequences. If the door closed while someone was inside, the poor bastard would have about thirty to forty minutes before hypothermia killed him. The trapped person's only hope was that someone heard him screaming and thumping on the door. After the near-fatal incident, Genavax took swift action to remedy the situation. Taking no chances, it made a door wedge from a packing case. So the lives of Genavax's employees rested on a fifty-cent chunk of wood. Terry jammed the wedge under the crack of the door with his foot.

He snatched up his samples. He tried not to, but he breathed in. His lungs burned as if icicles were forming on them. His actions were swift. He didn't want to be stuck inside the yeti's jockstrap any longer than necessary.

The freezer was filled with shelf after shelf of microtiter trays arranged on mobile racks similar to a baker's cart of loaves of freshly baked bread. Each cart was labeled with a project name and number, and each rack was labeled with the particular sample ID. Terry made sure that he knew which rack was set aside for his test runs. With the skill of a well-practiced waiter, he slid batch 243 onto rack 243.

The tray snagged on something. Terry retracted it and dropped to his knees to clear the blockage. He breathed in and the arctic python constricted his chest. Glancing through the narrow slit between trays, Terry saw his problem immediately. There was a tray, half the size of his, already on his rack. He couldn't quite reach it, so he pulled the cart clear of the others and removed the tray from the back.

Terry would have returned the tray to its rightful place, but the labeling and the tray size weren't like any of Genavax's other projects.

"What are you doing?"

Terry turned to find Luke Frazer standing in the doorway. He was Pamela Dawson's right-hand man—so much so, some said he was perched on her middle finger.

"Do you know how long you've been in here?" he barked. "The temperature has risen ten degrees. You should be in and out in less than a minute. And what are you doing with that?"

Terry was shivering, and he hoped it didn't look like he was quaking in his boots. His wavering voice didn't help matters.

"I found a rack in the wrong place. I was trying to refile it."

"Let me see," Frazer said, barging into the freezer.

Frazer snatched the tray out of Terry's hands and gave it a cursory glance. He tried to give the impression that he didn't know what he was holding and that he had used his superior knowledge to solve the mystery, but it was obvious he recognized the rogue samples immediately.

"I'll deal with this," he said, looking down his aquiline nose.

Strangely, he didn't seem to be affected by the extreme cold. No wonder he was dubbed Frosty Frazer, a nickname that went hand in hand with Pamela's Ice Maiden persona.

"What are you waiting for?"

"Nothing."

"Then rack your test and get out before you ruin everything this company is working toward."

If he weren't so damn cold, then maybe Terry would have argued. Instead, he picked up his tray and slid it easily into rack 243. As he left the cold for what seemed to be the tropical heat of the lab, Frazer stopped him.

"Sheffield, if I were you, I wouldn't poke my nose into business that didn't have anything to do with me. Your wife did that and look what happened to her."

• • •

Oscar's 4Runner followed Terry's Ford Focus into his driveway. Terry parked inside the garage and Oscar left his SUV outside. Hopping out, Oscar didn't look too happy with Terry's request to meet him after work.

"What's so important that you couldn't talk over the phone?" he asked as he entered the garage, the door closing behind him. "I do have a business to run."

"After I left you at the mall, I had a message from Sarah's editor. He said Sarah kept a private lockbox with her stories she didn't want anyone to find."

"And you found it?"

"Yes. And I think Sarah's in real danger."

Terry fiddled for the key to the door from the garage to the house. He didn't normally lock it, but after last night's discovery and the run in with the Honda, he wasn't taking any chances. Excitement made him all fingers and thumbs.

"Hey, why all the security?" Oscar asked.

Terry told him about the Honda with the garage opener.

"But what if this person has keys to the house too?"

"No one's managed to get into the house yet," Terry remarked.

"Have you been to Holman about any of this?"

"No, not yet. I wanted to run it by you to make sure I'm not blowing things out of proportion."

Terry found the key and stuck it in the lock. As he swung the door open, he knew something was wrong.

"Jeez," Oscar said. "Did we have an earthquake?"

Terry stepped inside, with Oscar close behind. Oscar shook his head at the carnage of last night's search. Terry cast his eye over the scene and his feeling intensified—something wasn't right. This wasn't how he had left his home this morning.

"You've been robbed, pal." Oscar brushed past Terry. "I'll call the cops."

"No...don't."

"Why?"

"I did this."

Oscar snorted. "Why?"

"I was searching."

Terry answered Oscar's questions, but his focus wasn't on his friend. His mind was recounting his last actions before leaving for work. He'd done enough tidying to make a bed to sleep on and a shower to bathe in. He hadn't bothered with breakfast, but what had made him late was packing Sarah's notes into the box file and replacing it in the crawl space. Terry went to check the rooms.

"Hey, where are you going, Terry?" Oscar asked.

"Something's wrong."

"I know. You're a crappy homemaker," Oscar said. Terry disappeared into a bedroom and Oscar had to raise his voice to be heard. "I would guess you were never in the military."

He caught up with Terry in Sarah's office.

"What is wrong with you? You're like a dog on a bone hunt."

"Someone's been here. I can feel it."

Oscar blocked Terry's path and gestured with his hands. "It's hard to tell with your talents as a cleaner."

"I know."

"Okay, what's been changed?"

"Nothing," Terry said after a long moment.

"You're losing me, man."

Terry brushed past Oscar and walked back into the living room. "Something's not right."

"You're telling me. You need to Febreze this place. It smells like dirt in here."

That was it—the air. Terry raced to the closet by the front door. It was half open. When he left this morning it had been closed. Sliding the door back, he fell to his knees. The floor panel was to one side, exposing the house to the musty dirt scent of the crawl space.

"The box is gone," Terry said.

• • •

Oscar hefted an easy chair back onto its feet. "Alicia Hyams's name was on the list?"

Terry busied himself with the task of returning everything to its rightful place in the attempt to turn his refugee camp back into a home. "It was the last of the five names."

"And who were the others?" Oscar turned his attention to the kitchen.

"They were like Alicia Hyams—ordinary people."

"Not that ordinary. Alicia Hyams was murdered."

"That's what worries me."

"You think the other four women could be dead too?" Oscar hefted a stack of plates into an overhead cupboard.

"Yeah."

"And that Sarah could be the sixth?"

"Yeah." Terry fell silent. The admission scared him.

Standing with a mug in each hand, Oscar asked, "Why didn't you take the box straight to Holman?"

Terry shrugged. "I wanted an honest opinion. I wanted to see if you would see what I saw. You, I trust. Holman might not be straight with me."

Oscar nodded and hung the mugs on the mug tree. "Okay, let's take this step by step. You're worried that the list was a list of victims."

Terry nodded and slotted the couch cushions back into place.

"Did you find any obituary notices for any of these women?"

"No."

"Hmm."

"What does that mean?"

"Just a thought."

"Go on."

"You're not going to like it."

"There's not a lot I do like hearing these days. You'd better just tell me."

"Okay," Oscar said, frowning. "Sarah was long gone before you arrived, which makes it nearly three weeks."

"Yeah."

"And Alicia Hyams was snatched the week you arrived."

"So?"

"So Sarah compiled that list before Alicia Hyams was a headline."

Terry nodded. It was an interesting point and a frightening one. Had Sarah known what was going to happen to Alicia Hyams before it happened and been powerless to save her?

"I'm finished in here," Oscar said. "Where next?"

"Sarah's office."

They shifted their attentions to stacking the papers and files in their rightful places, although Terry was guessing where everything went. He hadn't taken any notice when he'd been pulling everything off the shelves.

"Okay, Alicia Hyams hadn't been kidnapped at the time Sarah made the list, and let's assume the other women aren't dead," Terry said. "What does that prove?"

"I don't know," Oscar said, shrugging.

"But what if the other women are dead?"

"I don't know."

"See. You don't know. Anything could have happened."

"You're right, I don't know, but it doesn't mean we have to assume the worst. For all we know, the women on Sarah's list might be old college buddies," Oscar said.

"But she kept their information hidden. What does that tell you?"

"Okay, but consider this. Alicia Hyams's murder may have nothing to do with Sarah's disappearance. It could be purely coincidental."

"Is it likely?" Terry asked.

"Maybe, maybe not, but we can't nail our colors to any particular cause. Not right now. There's so much we don't know. You can't just write Sarah off as dead."

"I'm not trying to write her off, I just don't know what to think."

"Then don't try. You'll only drive yourself crazy."

"I know." Terry jumped up. "But it's hard not to. My wife is missing. She has a murdered woman's name in her files. Why wouldn't I think she's heading for the same fate?"

"I suppose you're right." Oscar pulled up Sarah's office chair and sat. "There is something we can do that might help."

"What's that?"

"Talk to the women on the list."

"We can't talk to Alicia Hyams."

"No, but we can speak to her family."

Terry frowned.

"Don't look like that," Oscar snapped, but he wasn't angry. He was more like a football coach trying to rally his players before the big game. "Do you want to find Sarah?"

"Yes."

"Good," Oscar said. "Were these other woman local?"

"No, not really. One was in Oregon. Another was from Nevada. Alicia Hyams and two others were from California."

"Okay, so we've got a lot of dialing to do. It's interesting that these women aren't geographically close. It might give some credibility to the fact that Alicia Hyams's death isn't linked to Sarah's disappearance."

Terry tried to stop Oscar from his stream of consciousness, but he continued to reel off theories and ideas, making connections then dismissing them. Eventually, Terry made himself heard.

"Oscar, listen. Please."

"What?"

"There's one problem."

"What's that?"

"I can't remember their names. Alicia Hyams is the only name I remember."

Oscar frowned.

"I didn't try to memorize them," Terry explained. "I didn't think I was going to have to."

• • •

The next afternoon, Terry wheeled out his shopping cart from the Raley's supermarket. As he pushed his cart back to his car, he tried to recall the names on Sarah's list. He was loading the Ford's trunk with paper sacks when a familiar voice called him.

Terry turned. "Hello, Jake."

"You remember me, then?"

"It's hard not to remember the sheriff's son. Have you come to do a bit more spying?"

"Terry," he moaned.

"Go tell your dad that if he wants to ask me something, then he should ask it himself."

Jake grabbed Terry's shopping cart. "It's not like that!"

Terry noticed they were attracting glances from shoppers and staff leaving the supermarket.

Jake relaxed. "I am Ray Holman's son." He removed one of Terry's sacks and put it in the trunk. "But I'm not a spy...not for him."

Terry put the last two bags in the trunk and closed it. "Okay, you're not a spy, then what are you?"

"The prodigal son." His smile was crooked. "Except my dad wasn't that pleased to see me. No fatted calf waiting on the barbecue."

Terry didn't know whether to believe Jake or not. It wasn't beyond the realm of possibility, but this could be a well-rehearsed sob story to sucker him for the second time. Terry decided to give Jake enough rope to be his own hangman.

"Did you walk or drive?" Terry asked.

"This is America. No one walks."

"Have you eaten?"

"No."

"C'mon," Terry said and pointed at a McDonald's.

Jake chose a meal deal. Terry, not being much of a fan of fast food, settled for a coffee. He normally wouldn't have chosen McDonald's, but he didn't want waste too much time on Jake. He wanted to hear what he had to say and move on. Terry paid and took their food to a booth away from everyone else. Jake tugged the wrapper off his Big Mac and bit into the sandwich. Terry sipped his coffee. What it lacked in flavor, it made up for in temperature. He pushed it to one side to let its nuclear core cool off.

"Do you really know my wife?"

Chewing, Jake nodded. He swallowed and raised two fingers. "Scout's honor."

"I was never a Scout."

Jake frowned and dropped his burger on the tray. He sucked on his Coke. "Okay, I admit it. I misled you. I didn't tell you my pop was the sheriff. Guilty as charged. Can we move on?"

"That depends. Why wouldn't you be spying for your dad?"

"A long story." He stuffed about half a dozen fries into his mouth at once. "But I won't bore you with the details. Let's just say I disappointed him. I didn't grow up the way he would have liked."

Terry thought the way Jake ate was interesting. He kept his food on the tray. Personally, Terry couldn't stand to eat off a tray. It was too restrictive, but not for Jake. He hugged his tray with his arms, forming a barrier around his meal. Terry decided Jake's school days must have been tough.

"You said you were the prodigal son. Have you been away for a while?"

"Yeah, it's hard growing up as the sheriff's son. Everyone thinks you're snitching to him. So when I had my first chance, I left. I've moved around over the years."

"Why have you come back?"

"My mom died a few months back. Cancer."

"I'm sorry."

"Yeah, well." He shrugged. "What are you gonna do?"

"You came back for the funeral?"

"Yeah, and I decided to stick around. I got quite nostalgic coming home."

"How did you hook up with Sarah?"

"Our paths crossed on a story. She needed information and I provided it."

"When was that?"

Jake scrunched up his face. "Two or three months ago. Then again a few weeks ago."

"I see."

A cloud fell over Jake's face. "Hey, are you pissed at me because I spent time with Sarah?"

"Should I be?"

"Don't you trust her?"

"Yes, but you brought the subject up."

Jake exhaled. "This is getting screwed up. I came to help you. Now you're suspecting me of all kinds of crap, and I'm trying to guess your thoughts."

"Funny, that's what I was thinking."

Jake smiled.

Terry sipped his coffee. It was now at a temperature fit for human consumption. "So what do you want to do?"

"Start again from the top." Jake shoveled in more of his food. "Hi, my name's Jake Holman. I'm Sheriff Ray Holman's son. We do not get along. I know your wife, Sarah. I've worked with her. No, I don't know where she is. No, nothing funny happened between the sheets when you weren't around. And no, I'm not working for my father. Anything else you want to know?"

One question did spring to Terry's mind. It had finally dawned on him why Jake protected his food the way he did. "Did you serve time in prison?"

That sent a flare into the air. Jake thrust his tray with the food on it straight at Terry. Terry snatched up his coffee before the tray could spray it all over him, but it didn't stop him from getting a lap full of fries.

"Screw you!" Jake jabbed a threatening finger in Terry's face. "I tried to help you."

He leapt to his feet and stormed out. Terry watched him go and noticed no one was talking. He turned to see all eyes centered on him.

"I think he wanted a Happy Meal."

Terry helped a McDonald's employee clean up the mess before driving home. Obviously, he'd struck a raw nerve. But thoughts of Jake Holman evaporated when he arrived home. Two cruisers from the county sheriff's department filled his driveway.

Neighbors, eager for developments, surveyed events from their front yards. Terry parked, blocking in the cruisers.

Deputy Pittman was on the porch. She scowled, but didn't attempt to stop him from entering. He brushed by her.

"Mr. Sheffield, glad you could make it. Sorry about the door."

Terry glanced back at the door. Splintered wood hung from the door frame close to the dead bolt.

"We have a warrant." Holman slapped a tri-folded wad of papers against Terry's chest.

Terry examined the paperwork, but the words meant nothing. "What the hell is going on?"

A deputy Terry didn't recognize came into the living room from the direction of the bedrooms and dropped to his knees in front of the crawl space hatch where Sarah's lockbox had been fastened to the underside. At least they wouldn't find Sarah's notes.

"Mr. Sheffield, we have reason to believe your wife isn't missing but hiding out here," said Holman.

Terry laughed. "And where did that cock-and-bull story come from?"

Holman's answer was interrupted by the deputy who had the crawl space hatch turned over. The lockbox was still missing, but a small Ziploc bag was in its place. Inside it was a woman's wallet and a pair of earrings.

"Sheriff Holman, I think those are the earrings Alicia Hyams's husband described."

"And that looks like her wallet," Holman added.

The deputy opened the bag, fished inside for the wallet, and opened it. "It's hers."

"Oh, come on," Terry said. "What the hell is going on here?"

"That's what I'm hoping you can tell me, Mr. Sheffield." Holman spun Terry around. "I think you'd better come with me. You've got a lot of explaining to do."

CHAPTER TWELVE

Terry was calm now, at peace and alone in the interview room. He was in the same room they'd put him in him when he had been arrested for breaking and entering into his own home. He kicked off his shoes and leaned back in his chair, awaiting Holman's next move.

He'd been ready to explode when Deputy Pittman dumped him in there. He was being screwed. He wanted Holman, and he wanted a bloody explanation. But Holman was conspicuous by his absence, and Pittman had confined him to the room. That had been hours ago.

With the quiet of the interview room to cool his temper, he wondered what Holman had planned for him. If his intention was to let Terry stew in the hope that he would be easy to break during the interrogation, then the sheriff's scheme had backfired. He'd given Terry too much time. His white-hot rage had cooled, and he was content to stare at the ceiling, listening to the hum of the fluorescent lights while trying to piece events together.

Who could have placed Alicia Hyams's wallet and earrings at his house? Her killer. He would have had access to her possessions. This was an obvious point, but it begged the question, why plant her belongings on him? What was his connection to the killer? Sarah. The thought sent his stomach into free fall. Although he didn't want to admit it, Sarah and the killer were linked in some inexplicable way. She must have been on to the killer. It was the only explanation. The next question didn't bear contemplating. The repercussions were too alarming. How did the killer get into his home to plant the items? There were no signs of forced entry. He could have picked the locks, but the visit from the Honda driver who had opened the garage with the garage-door opener said otherwise. That meant the killer had a way into his home. And that meant only one thing. He'd abducted Sarah.

Terry couldn't breathe in the windowless room. He'd been banking on the notion Sarah was on the run, but how else could the killer have obtained the garage-door opener? He couldn't delude himself anymore. Sarah was a hostage. It explained how the killer could just walk into his home, steal Sarah's confidential notes, plant the wallet and earrings, and make off with no one noticing. It chilled him to think about it.

Another chilling thought rocked Terry. If the killer had access to their home, he could still come and go as he pleased. When he got out, he'd change the locks—if he got out.

Terry tried to think practical thoughts—get released, then change the locks—but these thoughts were swallowed up by his fears for Sarah. If Alicia Hyams's murder was a guide, then the killer didn't plan on keeping Sarah hostage forever. She could be dead in days, if she wasn't already. He tried to ignore that inevitable outcome. He couldn't lose hope that she was still out there, not free, but alive.

But the killer wasn't the only one who could have planted the evidence. Holman could have done it. Hadn't that been Terry's knee-jerk response when the deputy produced the wallet and earrings? But how likely was it that Holman was corrupt? Out of the hundreds of thousands of cops in the country, how many were bent? There was probably a decent number jaded by their careers, but corrupt? Terry couldn't imagine there being many. However, he couldn't escape the fact that the sheriff's department had found Alicia Hyams's body. Who said they hadn't found her belongings at the lake? Holman might have planted the evidence to set him up or to push him into confessing. The fact that Holman's son had tried to pump him for information didn't help Terry dismiss the idea.

"The earrings," he said, sitting up.

Taking himself back to the reservoir, he tried to remember if Alicia Hyams had been wearing earrings. He remembered the bright lights, the lapping of the water against the boat ramp and her corpse, but not the earrings. She might have been wearing them, but he wasn't sure. It wasn't something he had taken notice of at the time. He jumped to his feet.

He paced the interview room like a caged animal. Alicia Hyams's face filled his mind. With sickening detail, he recalled her naked body covered by a sheet, her silt-clogged hair, her white-white face, and her bloodless lips, but he just couldn't remember if she'd been wearing earrings or not. He cursed and sat back down.

A key clicked in the lock and the door opened. Terry stood. Holman and Deputy Pittman stood in the doorway. Holman had the keys in his hand. Deputy Pittman rested a hand on her holstered weapon.

"Ready to talk?" the sheriff asked.

"Yes," Terry answered.

"Let's get the proceedings started, then," Holman said.

Terry nodded, finding it hard not to show his contempt.

"Good."

Deputy Pittman closed the door, leaving Holman and Terry by themselves. Holman indicated for Terry to sit. Terry sat. Holman chose to stand, leaning against the wall.

"Where to begin?" Holman asked.

"With my phone call. Aren't I entitled to one?"

"And legal representation," the sheriff said. "But that would apply to someone under arrest, and you're not under arrest. You're just helping us with our investigation."

"So I can leave, then?" Terry stood to leave.

"If you want." Holman slid into the interrogator's chair opposite Terry. "But I wouldn't recommend it. You would be forcing my hand, and that would just complicate matters."

Terry stared at Holman. He searched the sheriff's face, looking for something to show him what the man was thinking. Holman had to be a good poker player. He wasn't giving anything away. Terry knew Holman was playing with him. If he walked, Holman would say he was running because he had something to hide. If he stayed, Holman would badger him until he had something to pin on him. He didn't have any options. Terry sat back down.

"Good man," Holman cooed. "I'm glad you decided to display some sense. Would you like to have a lawyer present?"

Terry shook his head. "Innocent people don't need lawyers."

"You know I've got you," Holman said. "So why don't you tell me why you killed Alicia Hyams?"

"Sheriff, you haven't got a thing and you know it."

Holman opened up the file he'd brought with him. He held up two evidence bags. One held Alicia Hyams's wallet, the other her earrings. "I think these will do for starters. Physical evidence. You can't ask for better."

"I've never seen them and I didn't hide them."

"And I suppose you still believe in Santa Claus."

"Sheriff, can't you see you're being played?"

"And you're the one who's doing the playing."

"Can I ask how I came to find you with a search warrant at my home?" Terry asked.

"We had an anonymous tip."

"That was convenient." Terry crossed his arms. "And I suppose this anonymous tip said you'd find personal effects belonging to Alicia Hyams under my floorboards."

SIMON WOOD

"No."

Terry was puzzled. It wasn't the answer he'd been expecting. "So what was the warrant for?"

"Our tip said you and your wife were wasting police time. Sarah was at the house all along and if we checked, we'd find her and the Subaru."

Terry thought of eagle-eye Osbourne, the Grand Pooh-Bah of the Sutter Drive Neighborhood Watch. But Osbourne wasn't the secretive type. He would have wanted his identity known.

"But you didn't find Sarah, and you didn't find her car. Instead, you just so happened to find damning evidence on an unsolved murder. Don't you think that casts some doubt on your anonymous caller?"

"Can you explain this?" Holman tossed another evidence bag at him.

Terry picked up the bag. His breath froze in his chest. It was Sarah's list.

"Where did you find it?" Terry mumbled.

"In the garage. Did you misplace it?"

The garage, he thought. The killer must have dropped it on the way out. He couldn't afford to blow this opportunity. He had to remember the names. He read and reread the names to himself, frantically trying to commit the names and locations to memory.

Holman jerked the sheet of paper back.

"Who are these women?"

Terry recited silently to himself, "Hope Maclean, Delano, California. Judith Stein, Medford, Oregon. Myda Perez, Carson City, Nevada. Christy Richmond, Anaheim, California. And Alicia Hyams, Sacramento, California."

"Well?" Holman prompted.

Terry looked up and Holman snatched the bag away from him.

"What is Alicia Hyams's name doing on that list?" Holman demanded.

"I don't know."

"And who are other women on the list?"

"I don't know."

Terry didn't want to think about his answers to Holman. He was still committing the names to memory. He ran the names and places through his head again and again. They were sticking. He just hoped they stayed long enough for him to write them down.

"Is this your writing?" Holman tapped urgently on the list.

"No."

"Whose is it?"

"Sarah's."

Holman picked up the list and examined it himself, as if Terry's mention of Sarah's name enabled the sheriff to recognize her writing. Holding the bag at the corner, he asked, "Why'd she make this list, and why's Alicia Hyams's name on it?"

"I don't know."

"Have you seen this list before?"

"Yes."

"When?"

"A couple of days ago. Her editor told me she kept her research hidden in a box. I found it." "What was in the box?"

"Notes. They didn't mean much."

"Where are the notes now?"

"Where you found the earrings and wallet."

"They're gone? That's convenient."

"Like your anonymous caller."

Holman leaned back in his chair and rested his hands on his stomach. "Is there something you want to say about the anonymous caller?"

"He didn't sound something like your son, Jake, did he?"

Holman stiffened. "What?"

"Your son, Jake. How long has he been on the payroll?"

Holman's jaw muscles tightened. "I don't know what you're talking about."

"Your son introduced himself to me as one of Sarah's researchers. He said he'd picked up one of my flyers after seeing me on television. How dumb do you think I am? Did you think I wouldn't find out? Christ, you've got some balls, Sheriff."

Holman lost his cool. He leaped to his feet and leaned over his desk, his hands supporting his weight. "My son has nothing to do with my investigation."

"Oh, no?" Terry liked seeing the sheriff on his back foot. "I think it's funny that Sarah's private documents were stolen from my house and replaced with physical evidence. And all this has happened after your son tried to befriend me."

Holman's hands curled into fists. "My son does not work for the Santa Rita County Sheriff's Department."

There was a knock at the door. "Sheriff," Deputy Pittman called through the windowpane.

"Not now, Pittman," Holman shouted.

"Sheriff," Deputy Pittman said again, opening the door.

"Pittman, I'm in the middle of an interrogation."

"Sheriff, Mr. Sheffield's lawyer's here."

"My lawyer?" Terry said. "I don't have a lawyer."

Holman glared.

"You do now," she said opening the door wide. "And he wants to talk to you."

Standing behind Deputy Pittman, next to Oscar, was a man Terry had never seen before.

• • •

In the chill evening air outside the sheriff's department, Terry and Oscar made their farewells to Jonathan Schreiber, the lawyer Oscar had hired. He'd been very efficient, citing an endless stream of legal mumbo jumbo to force Holman to release Terry. All told, it took less than half an hour to go from Holman's overheated interview room to Edenville's cold streets.

But Terry wasn't free. He hadn't been charged, but there was a question mark over his head. Holman could and probably would come for him again when he'd built a case he could pin on him. Alicia Hyams's possessions being in his house didn't amount to much, but that would change if Holman found something more damning. Terry would have to prove he was innocent before someone else could prove him guilty.

Schreiber waved good-bye from inside his Lexus and drove into the night. Terry waited until the lawyer was a pair of taillights in the distance before speaking.

"Thanks," he said. "I owe you big time."

"That you do." Oscar smiled. "I expect a card on every one of my birthdays," he said, wagging a scolding finger.

Terry smiled back. "You'll get one, have no fear. Christmas too."

"Dude, I'm Jewish."

"Chanukah, then." Terry's laces were still undone from kicking his shoes off in the interview room. He bent to tie them. "Is the lawyer expensive?"

"Oh, yeah. Schreiber is good."

"I'll pay you back."

"Don't worry about it. I know you're good for it."

Terry was humbled. Oscar's kindness left him speechless. He had no idea how he was going to make it up to his American friend. "Oscar, I don't know what to say."

"Say you'll put me in your will."

"Oscar, consider it done. You don't know what this means to me."

"You getting misty on me again?"

"Oh, shut up," Terry said. "What now?"

"When was the last time you played a round of minigolf?"

Terry sucked in a breath. "Has to be days."

"Let's go, then."

Getting into Oscar's 4Runner, a thought struck Terry. "Hey, how did you know I'd been arrested?"

"Because you're famous."

A chill seeped into his bones and it had nothing to do with the cold air. "What do you mean?"

"Your face was all over the TV today."

• • •

"So how are you doing?" Oscar asked, taking his golf ball out of the cup.

"All right, I suppose." Terry shrugged. "You know." He took his second shot, overhitting it, and the ball missed the hole by six feet.

Oscar nodded.

Terry took his third shot and missed. His fourth made the grade.

They wandered over to the castle hole. Oscar teed off, his first stroke missing the doorway and falling into the gutter.

"You know your head's not out of the noose, don't you?" Oscar said. "Holman isn't going to be deterred."

Terry nodded and took his shot. His ball went straight through the doorway. "But I know I'm innocent."

"But do you know who isn't?"

"No."

"Then to prove you're innocent, we have to find Alicia Hyams's killer."

They walked down the steps to where the castle had spat out their golf balls. Because Terry's ball had gone through the castle doorway, his was closer to the hole than Oscar's. Oscar went to take his second shot. Terry stopped him.

"Why are you helping me?"

Oscar straightened and rested on his club. "Don't you want me to?"

"Of course I do. I'm damn lucky to have you, but why put yourself through all that trouble? You hardly know me. I could be lying through my teeth. For all you know, you might be my next victim."

Oscar examined Terry for a long moment.

"Because you're not a killer." Oscar hunched over his ball and positioned his club.

"Still doesn't explain why you're helping me."

Oscar straightened and smiled. "Are you trying to put me off my stroke?"

"No," Terry said, smiling back.

"So you want to know?"

"Yes."

"Okay, then. I suppose I'm helping you as a penance."

"A penance?"

"I didn't help someone once. They needed me, and I wasn't there for them."

"Would things have been different if you'd gotten involved?"

Oscar inhaled deeply. "Hard to say. But that's not the point. The point is I didn't try."

"Who was it?"

"Another time." Sadness tinged Oscar's smile. He tapped the ball and made the putt. "When this is over, maybe."

Terry let the matter drop. He could see it was personal, and painful. Oscar would tell him when the time was right. Terry took his shot and holed the putt, equaling Oscar's feat.

They wandered over to the next hole. The Gold Rush's floodlights created multiple shadows. Squat dwarfs and skinny giants, black as night, clung to the soles of their shoes, changing shape with every step they took. Oscar lined up his shot but didn't take it.

"What did Holman have on you?"

"Didn't the news tell you?"

"Holman made no comment other than they had a warrant and discovered physical evidence." Oscar blasted his first shot through the metal corkscrew.

"They found Alicia Hyams's wallet and earrings."

"Where?"

"Under the floor in my closet where Sarah's files were hidden."

"Shit." Oscar waited for Terry to take his first putt. "How did Holman come to look there?"

"He says he got an anonymous phone call saying Sarah wasn't missing, that she was at the house. He got a warrant and searched the place. He didn't find Sarah, but he just so happened to find Alicia Hyams's earrings and wallet."

"That's convenient."

"Isn't it just."

"The killer must be staying local."

"Maybe."

Oscar took his second shot. "What does that mean?"

"How do we know Holman received an anonymous call?"

"You think he made it up?"

Terry shrugged and took his stroke.

"That's a big accusation, man."

"He sent his son to spy on me, didn't he?"

"Did he admit that?"

Terry shook his head. "He says he didn't, but he did. It stands to reason. I don't believe in that kind of coincidence."

"Okay, I'll grant you that Holman sent Jake on a fact-finding mission, but that doesn't mean he planted evidence."

"Do you remember if Alicia Hyams was wearing earrings when we saw her?"

Oscar frowned and shook his head. "It was the last thing I was looking at."

Terry sorely wished he could remember that simple fact. It would confirm or deny a lot of his suspicions.

"I think you're barking up the wrong tree with that one, pal. Holman's been sheriff here longer than dirt. There's never been a hint of him being anything but honest."

"It was just a thought. I'm just looking for something to explain this."

Oscar sank his putt. "You're way off. I wouldn't bandy that theory around. Holman is well liked. If he gets wind of that, I don't think an army of Schreibers will be able to sweet-talk you out of jail. Anyway, there are other candidates."

Terry's third shot went wild. There was too much emotion behind the stroke. The ball bounced over the concrete boundary and rolled into one of the Gold Rush's man-made ponds. "Like who?"

"Deep Throat, your mystery caller. He and Holman's anonymous tipper could be one and the same."

Fishing his ball out of the shallow water and shaking it dry, Terry said, "He hasn't called me in a while."

"Maybe he doesn't have to. He knows where you live. He knows who you are. What more does he need?"

"Doesn't mean anything." Terry made a drop shot back onto the nylon-carpeted green. "Maybe the guy was just an obscene-phone-caller. Maybe he's had his fun and moved on to greener pastures."

"Yeah, true, but what if Deep Throat is the Honda driver? He doesn't have to call when he has access to your house."

"He will now. I'm changing the locks. And getting a new garage-door opener."

"But you're locking the proverbial barn door after the horse has bolted. If he took Sarah's lockbox, he probably got all the information he needed from the house. You won't see him again."

"That still doesn't explain who 'him' is."

"Who else has an ax to grind?" Oscar asked.

Pamela Dawson and Frosty Frazer sprang to mind. "There's my boss and her sidekick."

"Okay, what about them?"

Terry recounted their weird behavior, Sarah's bust up with Pamela, and Kyle Hemple's gossip. "I've got to admit the general atmosphere is one of fear. Everyone seems frightened of their own shadow."

"Okay, we'll add this pair to the mix, but they're hardly leading candidates."

Terry knew Oscar was right. No one stuck out. He was trying to make the puzzle fit, regardless of whether he had to use a sledgehammer to do it. He made his putt and his ball joined Oscar's in the hole.

Leading off on the next green, Oscar said, "Where do we go from here? We know you didn't do it. How do we go about proving who did? Hot damn. Hole in one."

Terry tossed a scrap of paper at the celebrating Oscar.

"What's this?"

"Our starting point. Sarah's list of names."

"I thought you said it was stolen."

"Holman found it during his search. Whoever stole it must have dropped it."

"And you stole it from Holman?"

Terry shook his head. The moment Schreiber had jumped in to bail him out, Terry had snatched a burglary prevention flyer and seized a pen from his lawyer to scribble the five names and locations Sarah had written before he could forget them. "It's a copy."

"What do you want to do?"

"Find out if these women are alive. See if they know each other. See if they know Sarah."

Oscar checked his watch. "This game is taking forever. Let's go."

"Can you give me a ride home?"

A troubled look crossed Oscar's face. "You'd better crash at my house."

"TV people?"

"They probably know you're out and about."

"Okay. Can you give me a ride into work tomorrow?"

"You gonna go in?"

"Why not? It should be interesting."

$$\bullet \quad \bullet \quad \bullet$$

From the receptionist to the CEO, their faces said it all. Their expressions shrieked, "How come a murderer is allowed to walk the streets?" Terry possessed the power of the grim reaper. No one made eye contact or acknowledged him. No one wanted to be his next victim. Terry carried on as normal, trying his best to ignore their stares. He wasn't bothered. Their reaction was only to be expected. He did have a suspected murder rap hanging over his head. It was hardly a career-advancing qualification.

Entering the lab, Terry realized why he was handling the situation so well. He was innocent. Proving his innocence was a different matter, but he was innocent and no one could shake that. Simply, he was prepared. Nothing could harm him. He got as far as sitting down before Pamela Dawson called him into her office.

Here goes, he thought.

"Yes, Pamela," he said, entering her office.

"Close the door, please."

Pamela's office wasn't a real office—it was a lot of Plexiglas and very little insulation. Any affairs that needed to be conducted privately couldn't be. It was all on show. As he closed the door, he noticed his colleagues focusing on Pam and him and not their work. He smiled to show them he was aware of them.

"On second thought, let's take this to one of the conference rooms," Pamela said.

Business at Genavax had begun early, and all the conference rooms were busy except for the boardroom. It was more dramatic than they needed, but beggars couldn't be choosers. Pamela flicked on the lights.

"Please, sit."

Terry did, but Pamela didn't. She stood stiffly, occasionally shifting her weight from one foot to the other in a birdlike fashion.

"I won't pretend that I haven't heard, Terry." Her tone was terse.

"I don't expect you to."

"Terry, as far as I know, unless you can correct me, you were questioned as a suspect in Alicia Hyams's murder."

"That's correct."

"You've placed Genavax in a very embarrassing position."

Embarrassing, Terry thought. He was potentially facing a murder trial. He felt his predicament trumped Genavax's. He straightened in his seat.

"I've mentioned before that Genavax went to a lot of trouble to hire you." Pamela cut a groove in the carpet, pacing ten or twelve feet in one direction only to reverse. She reminded Terry of a carnival duck shoot, with the targets passing back and forth. "Frankly, we've been disappointed. We are not seeing the return on the time and effort invested in you. First of all, you've demonstrated absenteeism."

"My wife is missing, and I took personal days. They are allowed in my contract."

But Pamela wasn't listening to him and plowed on, oblivious to his justification. "You've also interfered with the progress of other projects."

"What projects?"

"Luke Frazer found you in the freezer playing with a set of samples."

"No, he didn't. The wrong rack was stored on my shelf. I was trying to relocate it."

She stopped pacing and raised a hand to silence him. "None of that is important. The murder investigation is."

"It's not like I've been charged," Terry said.

"Regardless, you've put everyone here in an uncomfortable position. We have the company's image to consider."

"Am I fired?"

She hesitated. "That hasn't been decided. But I don't want to raise your hopes."

"What the hell happened to innocent until proven guilty?"

"It has nothing to do with innocence. It's about perception."

"Perception! What exactly is your perception of the situation?"

She snorted. "The perception is, if you haven't heard, that you came to this country and abducted and killed Alicia Hyams."

"And I did all this with the consent of my wife, I suppose?"

Pamela shrugged. "Well, there are two theories on that one."

"Like what?"

"One is that your wife discovered your crime and ran away, and the second is she's dead somewhere, killed in a similar fashion to Alicia Hyams."

"What a load of bollocks," Terry said, leaping to his feet.

Pamela stiffened, taking a step backward.

"Talk sense for a moment. How could I have abducted Alicia Hyams? She was abducted between two and three p.m. on the thirteenth. At that time, I was in an airport shuttle on my way to my house."

Terry froze, trapped in the moment. He rewound what he'd just said and picked through events as he recalled them. Adrenaline-driven euphoria overrevved his brain, clouding his logic, messing with his puzzle. He stared at the ground to concentrate his focus.

"What are you saying?"

He needed a moment to think, to check his mental facts. Yes, he was right. He'd been in an airport shuttle with a bunch of witnesses when Alicia Hyams was taken. Holman had been so focused on the stash of Alicia's personal items and the list of names that he'd found in the crawl space at Terry's house, he hadn't even tried to verify Terry's whereabouts before Schreiber had sprung him. Terry should have realized it earlier, but he'd been too emotional, too wrapped up in the turmoil to keep a level head. But he was levelheaded now.

"What I'm saying is there's no way I could have done it, and you just gave me the proof." Terry pounced on the phone on the desk and dialed Oscar's cell number.

"Gold Rush," Oscar answered.

"Oscar, call Schreiber. Tell him to meet me at Sheriff Holman's. I have the world's greatest alibi." He slammed the phone down with more energy than he intended, making Pamela jump. "Yes!" he shouted with delight.

He raced for the door.

"Where are you going?" Pamela demanded.

"I'm going to prove what I knew and you should have believed."

CHAPTER THIRTEEN

Hours after blowing Holman's case apart, Terry and Oscar were being loud. The restaurant's mood music had been turned up twice to compensate, but they didn't care who heard them. Alcohol dictated the volume.

Schreiber stood. "I'll leave you guys to celebrate alone. My ride's here, and I have other clients to defend. Enjoy." He reached for his wallet.

"No way," Terry said. "Dinner is on me. You did me proud."

"I'm not sure I did anything. I think you proved yourself innocent."

"Maybe, but you cut through the red tape. That's something I never could have done."

"Okay. I accept your hospitality." He stretched to shake Terry's hand, then Oscar's. "Stay out of trouble, guys. I hope we don't have to do business again." He smiled. "I'm one businessman who doesn't hope for repeat business."

"Good luck to you, counselor," Oscar slurred at Schreiber's retreating form.

He waved as he left the restaurant.

"Good man," Oscar said.

"That he is," Terry agreed.

Their waitress returned.

"Shall I bring you your bill?"

She was all smiles and politeness, but her question seemed more like a request.

"We haven't finished yet," Terry said. "Have we?"

"No, we haven't," Oscar said emphatically. He waggled an empty bottle that once held a moderately expensive Californian Chardonnay. "Can you bring us another bottle of this?"

"Actually, you've been disturbing the other customers. If I do bring you another bottle, you have to promise to be quiet."

"Sorry, but we're celebrating," Terry said. "If we've been obnoxious, I apologize. We'll do better to respect everybody else."

The waitress, Becki, according to her name badge, smiled and nodded, accepting Terry's apology and promise. He found his accent worked wonders. Surprisingly, a couple of coworkers and store clerks had described it as exotic. He didn't understand it himself. He considered his accent plain, but he did find that it defused situations. Americans, regardless of color, creed, or background, changed their opinion of him when they found out he was English and not American. His accent was perceived as a hallmark of honesty and dependability. He was accepted in more places than a platinum credit card. If Oscar had said the same thing to the waitress, they'd probably be leaving, so he wasn't going to knock it. Becki relieved Oscar of the empty bottle.

In the bar, someone turned up the television. The news-anchor's voice penetrated the background music, and Oscar blew Terry's bridge mending.

"Hey, buddy." He leaped from his chair. "Turn that up."

Oscar lurched toward the bar. Terry shrugged apologetically at Becki and followed his friend. He wanted to see the news as much as Oscar did.

The female anchor went into the lead story. Oscar clutched the bar rail, grinning like a kid on Christmas morning. Terry joined Oscar. He ignored the glances they were drawing.

"Turn it up another notch," Oscar urged.

The bartender shrugged and hit the volume button.

"Dramatic events unfolded today in the murder investigation of Alicia Hyams and the disappearance of Bay Area journalist Sarah Sheffield. This report from Tom Degrasse."

The smooth and professional Tom Degrasse didn't have a cigarette in his hand for his report. He was standing outside the sheriff's department. It was a recording from earlier in the day, after Holman had dropped all interest in Terry as a suspect, at Schreiber's insistence. Terry's lawyer had demanded an immediate press release be made to clear Terry's name.

"I'm outside the Santa Rita County Sheriff's Department in Edenville where there's been a new twist in the Alicia Hyams murder case. Less than twenty-four hours ago, Terry Sheffield, a British citizen, now a resident in the United States, was questioned in connection with Mrs. Hyams's murder after personal effects belonging to the deceased were found at his home. Interestingly, Mr. Sheffield's wife, Sarah, has been missing for over three weeks, which has raised suspicions of his involvement in that case. But all that changed this morning."

Degrasse's report cut to another recording of Holman making a statement to an assembled group of reporters. Holman's name filled the bottom of the screen.

"I would like to reiterate that due to irrefutable evidence, Terry Sheffield has been eliminated as a suspect in the murder of Alicia Hyams."

Terry and Oscar cheered.

A wave of questions struck Holman, which he didn't respond to until the cacophony of voices burned itself out. One voice made it through with its question.

"Sheriff Holman, can you tell us what evidence has come to light?"

Holman looked uneasy, but he answered. "It's an issue of timing. At the time of Alicia Hyams's abduction, Terry Sheffield was entering the US. We have corroboration from airport immigration."

"Who's trying to cover up their screwup?" Terry said to the television. "I was in your office, not the airport, when Alicia Hyams was kidnapped."

"But do you suspect foul play in the disappearance of Sarah Sheffield?" the reporter demanded, following up her previous question.

"There is no evidence of foul play."

Another slew of questions ensued.

"Do you have another suspect, Sheriff?"

"Is Alicia Hyams's murder in any way connected to Sarah Sheffield's disappearance?"

"What is your next course of action?"

Holman shouted the questions down with his commanding voice. "All I'm willing to say is that I can categorically state that Terry Sheffield is not responsible for Alicia Hyams's death."

Holman turned his back on the reporters. The camera tracked him returning into his offices.

"Categorically," Terry said, chewing the word over. "Does that mean without a doubt?"

"I think it does, man," Oscar replied.

The report cut back to Tom Degrasse. "Sheriff Holman and Mr. Sheffield declined to comment further, but Mr. Sheffield's lawyer, Jonathan Schreiber, made a statement on his behalf."

Schreiber appeared on the screen. "Terry expressed his supreme pleasure at being eliminated from the sheriff's investigations."

"Hell, yeah," Oscar seconded.

"Amen to that," Terry said.

"He is also grateful to Sheriff Holman for his statement today."

"Are you?" Oscar asked.

Terry shrugged. "I'm grateful he let me go."

"Terry wishes to be left to resume his life in the US and hopes Sheriff Holman's investigations lead to a speedy capture of Alicia Hyams's murderer and the return of his wife. Thank you."

The report cut back to Tom Degrasse to sum up. "There you have it. Authorities are no closer to finding Alicia Hyams's killer than a week ago. Let's hope developments are swift and forthcoming. This is Tom Degrasse reporting for KTAH, San Francisco. Now, back to the studio."

Oscar slapped Terry on the back. "Well done, buddy."

"God, I'll never get tired of watching that."

"I know I will," a familiar voice said from behind them.

Terry and Oscar whirled to find Holman standing there. He looked ready to burst.

Terry sighed. "Okay, we've been loud, but we haven't done anything wrong."

"You're not here to arrest him again, are you?" Oscar asked.

Holman glared at Oscar.

"What do you want, Sheriff?" Terry asked.

"I was passing by and saw you two whooping like monkeys at feeding time, so I wanted to make sure you weren't being a nuisance."

Becki came forward with their check in an American Express bill holder. "No nuisance here," she said. "They were just settling up."

"Thanks," Terry said, but not for bringing the bill.

"As long as they weren't causing trouble."

"No trouble," she said with a smile.

Holman grunted.

"Anything else, Sheriff?" Terry asked.

"Not for tonight. But we are far from finished, Sheffield. You can count on that."

Terry, Oscar, Becki, and the rest of the patrons in the restaurant watched Holman leave. No one spoke until the doors closed.

"Becki, you've earned an excellent tip," Oscar said, handing her his Visa card.

She went to charge Oscar's card. Terry waited for her to be out of earshot before speaking. "Did you smell alcohol?"

"I thought that was us."

"It was, but we weren't the only ones."

"So?"

"It doesn't seem like him. Don't you think it's a bit reckless to be drunk on duty?"

"He's had a bad day. Totally understandable. We have a good day—we drink to celebrate. We have a bad day—we drink to commiserate. What else is alcohol for?"

For burying guilt, Terry thought.

• • •

Another day, another dollar and a different attitude. That was how Genavax welcomed Terry the following day. Condemned by a TV jury the day before, he was the conquering hero today. Colleagues either congratulated him, shook his hand, slapped him on the back, offered him a sympathetic ear if he needed it, or, the most touching of all, apologized for prejudging him. Today he was "The Man," as Kirk from shipping had said.

If attitudes were changing, his needed to change too. He had to buckle down and get on with his work and for good reason. In part, he needed this job. Sarah was missing and there was a mortgage to pay. It would be nice if there were a home for her to come home to. More important, Sarah had discovered something that had Pamela spooked, and if it was connected to her disappearance, he needed to figure out what it was. He couldn't do that if Genavax gave him his marching orders. So for now, he'd be a good worker bee.

Jenny Kuo stopped him in the corridor. She asked if he was okay and gave him a card with a 1-800 number to a counseling line. He remembered her mentioning the service at his induction.

"It's free and confidential," she said. "Nobody from Genavax will know what is discussed. They are trained in stress management."

"Thanks, Jenny," he said, holding the card up.

"Will you use it?"

He smiled. "Probably not. I have a good friend who's been supportive. But I appreciate the offer."

"There's no stigma in using it. Even things built Ford tough need a tune-up now and again."

He liked her attempt at not attacking his masculinity. It was cute. "The thought hadn't crossed my mind."

"Okay. I'll leave it up to you, then."

He wondered if Jenny's insistence was because no one had ever chosen to use the service. He felt he should use it just to placate her desire to be an excellent human resources manager. He thanked her and pocketed the card.

The lab was harmonious in its support. Even Frosty Frazer mumbled his congratulations, as did Pamela Dawson. Terry went into her office and closed the door.

"May I have a quick word?" he asked.

"If you must." She crossed her arms over her flat chest.

"I know my Genavax career hasn't gotten off to a flying start."

Pamela grunted.

"But I want to change that. I've never been fired, and I've never had a bad reference. I'm a good worker, and I'll prove to you that you haven't made a mistake by hiring me."

Pamela looked as if she'd heard this speech a thousand times before from a thousand people who were one excuse away from being fired. Terry carried on regardless.

"I'm determined to make it work at Genavax. I will make up the time I've missed. You'll see a change."

"I appreciate your saying so," she said. "Let's hope you can turn things around. If that's all, we'd better get back to our work."

SIMON WOOD

And that was what Terry did. He put his head down and bea-
vered away. He stopped for a short lunch break and carried on
through to five and beyond.

Everyone pretty much vamoosed at or just after five, with
two exceptions—Frosty Frazer and Pamela. They were disciples
of the Genavax faith and believers in the corporate grail, always
first to arrive and last to leave. But Terry knocked them from
their thrones. They disappeared around six thirty. He stayed
strong long after seven.

That was the state of play until Thursday.

• • •

His phone rang. "Terry Sheffield."

"Terry, it's Frank from security. Have the Ice Maiden and
Frosty gone?"

"Yeah, about ten minutes ago."

"Can you come to reception? There's a package that needs
signing for."

"Sure thing."

A skinny FedEx delivery driver was in the reception area
with Frank. He held a refrigerated container, looking relieved to
see Terry.

"Man, you just saved my ass."

"Have I?"

"Yeah, I screwed up. I should have been here a couple of hours
ago, but I missed the package in the truck. In twenty minutes,
the refrigerant runs out and FedEx is liable if this shipment's no
good." He handed the container off to Terry. He exhaled as he did
so, glad to be rid of his burden.

Terry checked the expiration date on the container. The
driver had made it by the skin of his teeth.

"Can you sign for it?"

"Sure," Terry said, putting the container down and taking the clipboard.

"I didn't want to sign for it," Frank said, "just in case it was damaged."

"Oh, that's fine. I'll get this straight into the fridge for tonight and let Pamela sort it out in the morning. No harm done."

"Cool," the driver said.

Terry handed the clipboard back. "Dodged a bullet there, mate."

"More than you know. Screw up on these runs and you get assigned the gang-territory routes."

"Well, you lucked out this time," Frank added.

"FedEx, when it absolutely, positively has to be there, right?" The driver saluted. "Have a good night, guys."

"Take it easy." Frank let the driver out and locked the door behind him. "You gonna call it a night now?"

"I think so. I'll just take care of this."

"Good, make it an early one for a change…if you can call six forty-five early."

"Just trying to make a good impression."

"Don't be too eager to please. Working too hard never did anyone any good."

Letting the lab doors swing shut behind him, Terry examined the container. He checked the documentation under the plastic envelope. The medical samples were addressed to Pamela.

Terry started jotting out a note for Pamela. He glanced at the sender's information to see if it was one of their regular suppliers. It wasn't. The package was from the Nevada State University Children's Research Hospital. He was sure Genavax wasn't working on any projects with any children's hospital. An uneasy sensation washed over him.

"What does Genavax need with a children's hospital?" he murmured to himself.

CHAPTER FOURTEEN

Terry sat at his dining table. He stared at the phone number on the scrap of paper he held in one hand. The phone was a lead weight in the other. This was one number he wished he didn't have to call.

"Are you going to call him?" Oscar asked.

"Yes, I am."

"Well, you don't look like it. I went to a lot of trouble for that number. It cost me a couple of Giants tickets."

Terry frowned.

"Do you want to find Sarah?"

"Of course I do," Terry said.

"Then call."

Terry hesitated.

Oscar held out his hand. "I'll do it if you want."

That was the easy way out. He should make the call. Sarah was his wife. Terry punched in the number and waited for someone to pick up. The wimp inside was still hoping for an answering machine when a man answered the phone.

"Mr. Hyams?"

"Yes." The man sounded tired, drained of all spirit.

"You don't know me. My name is Terry."

Oscar smiled and patted Terry encouragingly on the back.

"If you're a reporter I don't want to talk to you. Please leave my family in peace. Let us grieve."

"Mr. Hyams, I'm not a reporter," Terry said quickly, before Hyams had the chance to hang up. "I'm a worried husband. My wife went missing at the same time as yours."

"Who is this?"

"Terry Sheffield, Mr. Hyams."

"You son of a bitch. You've got some nerve calling me. Why they let you go, I'll never understand."

"Because I'm innocent."

"Yeah, you're innocent like every other scumbag on death row. I'm putting the phone down, and I'm calling the cops."

"Mr. Hyams, don't."

"Give me one good reason why I shouldn't."

"Because I think your wife was talking to mine."

"What?"

"Your wife's name was on a list of five names my wife had in her files."

Terry's answer took the heat out of Hyams. "Who else was on the list?"

"Four other women." He read out their names from his scribbled list. "Do they mean anything to you?"

"No."

"Did my wife ever call Alicia?"

"I don't think so."

"She might not have called herself Sarah Sheffield. She might have called herself Sarah Morton."

"No, I haven't heard of your wife."

Leaning back in his chair, Terry sighed. He was tired of the dead ends. He was wasting his time again.

"Does he know anything?" Oscar whispered.

Terry shook his head. Oscar frowned.

"I should be getting back to my kids," Hyams said.

"One last question, Mr. Hyams."

"Yes."

"Was your wife ever in the news or anything? Did she make the headlines? It can be for anything, from bake sale to federal witness."

Silence intervened.

"Mr. Hyams?"

"Yes, Alicia did make the headlines." Hyams sounded a hundred years old.

"How did she make the headlines?"

"A few years back, Chris, our little boy, was in day care. Alicia suspected that the day-care manager's husband was molesting the children."

"Was he?"

"The cops found magazines. The kids confirmed Alicia's suspicions. The cops built a case from there. They prosecuted, and the guy went to prison. The city closed the center, and his wife moved away."

Terry could tell Hyams was holding something back. It was in his tone. The story was far from over. "What else?"

More silence ensued before Hyams answered.

"Pedophiles aren't too well liked in prison. He eventually killed himself."

Terry was silent. He still felt the story wasn't complete. He let silence draw the truth out.

"A few months after his suicide, the real story came out."

"He wasn't a pedophile?"

"No, he was innocent. The kids had been playing doctor and one of them was a little too knowledgeable, a little too worldly. He'd said all the right things. Alicia believed what the kids had said."

"What about the magazines?"

"They were *Playboy*s. The cops used them to get a confession."

"Poor bastard."

"Alicia wasn't a bad woman," Hyams pleaded. "She wasn't vindictive. She had only the best intentions. She didn't deserve to die." A sob slipped out.

What a mess, Terry thought. He couldn't help but feel for the innocent man who'd taken his life. But if he'd been in Alicia Hyams's position, would he have acted any differently? He doubted it. It was a nasty collision of events where there were bound to be casualties.

"Could we speak in person? You might be able to help me further."

"I'm not sure. I'm stretched very thin."

"How about the weekend? Any time would be good with me."

"I don't know. I've got to go."

"I'll call tomorrow, perhaps?"

But Hyams had already hung up.

"That sounded serious," Oscar said. "What was that about?"

"About seeing bad guys that aren't really there. I have a really bad feeling about Sarah's list. I need to find out who these women are."

Terry went into Sarah's bedroom office and fired up her computer. He launched Google on the computer and his finger froze over the keyboard.

Oscar pulled up a chair next to him. "What's wrong?"

Cyber trails, he thought. These days, you were what you typed. Sarah had wiped her browser history, and maybe he shouldn't start one that could compromise either of them further down the road. If Holman came after him again looking for evidence of his involvement in this, a questionable search-engine history would fit the bill.

"I don't think it would be a smart idea to do this search on my home computer. Are there any cyber cafés around?"

"Cyber cafés? This is Edenville. Y2K hasn't caught up to us yet."

Terry grinned.

"There are a couple of Wi-Fi hotspots kicking around, or there's the library. They have terminals."

"The library sounds good. I just want something that Holman can't trace back to me."

. . .

The library smelled of musty books, as all libraries do. The odor hung in the air, eating the oxygen and the life from the room. Terry wondered if there was a universal air *un*-freshener that came free with every state-owned library.

They checked in at the front desk, and the librarian escorted them to a bank of six PCs next to the reference section. They were set up like phone booths with a partition to provide privacy. Only two of the six computers were in use, by a couple of kids doing their homework. Terry and Oscar sat next to each other.

"The library will be closing in an hour, gentlemen."

Terry moved a stack of paper to one side and discovered that his predecessor had been accessing porn sites. The booth was strewn with printed downloads of a lot of very naked women. The time stamps were only minutes old. He admired the guy's nerve and smiled as he pulled his list of names out of his jeans pocket. He picked up one of the printouts, turned it over, and wrote two of the names on Sarah's list, then handed it to Oscar.

"See what you can find out on these two."

Oscar took the sheet, turned it over, and leered at the open-legged centerfold. "What have you been up to?"

Terry cracked a smile. "Try the other side."

"Not sure I want to."

"Remember, we've only got an hour."

"Okay."

Terry googled Hope Maclean's name. Proving the World Wide Web was more chaff than wheat, Google threw back over a quarter of a million hits in half a second. He was looking at thousands of Hope Macleans and any one of them could be Sarah's Hope.

He refined his search by punching in the names of all five women on Sarah's list and got no hits. Sometimes, dealing with the Internet felt like talking to an inept translator. If you didn't speak its language just the way it had learned it, you were wasting your time.

He started over, this time incorporating the only other piece of information he knew about the women—a city.

He retyped Hope Maclean's name and added Delano to the search. He still got back over two thousand hits, but the first page of results were all connected to the same topic—city government embezzlement. According to the reports, the mayor of Delano and several members of the city council managed to funnel three-quarters of a million dollars of city redevelopment funds into their own bank accounts. Hope Maclean had been Delano's city clerk when she discovered the scheme and reported it to the state. An investigation followed, leading to arrests of everyone involved. Terry printed the most in-depth stories for reference.

It sounded like the kind of story Sarah would cover, but Terry didn't find her byline on any of the pieces. As sordid as the tale was, he failed to see the significance of it. The piece had failed to break the gravitational pull of the local newspapers and TV, and it wasn't even current. The events had taken place in 2007.

Why did you make Sarah's list, Hope? he thought.

He opened a new page and googled Judith Stein and Medford. Just as with Hope Maclean, the search kicked back a common story on the first page of hits. In 2009, Judith Stein revealed a scam at a nursing home. Her mother was a resident, and Judith found the staff wasn't administering her medication. Judith also discovered the staff was abusing the residents and stealing Social Security checks. Again, the story was significant, but not earth-shattering.

Just to confirm, he plugged in Alicia Hyams's name and got the news stories to back up her husband's account.

Switching among open windows, he examined the three stories and saw a pattern. Each of these women had exposed a crime or misconduct. Was this the connection Sarah had seen?

"Have you found anything out?" Terry asked.

Oscar leaned around the partition. "Yeah. You?"

Terry nodded.

"Tell me what you've got."

"All these women have a small claim to fame as whistleblowers. Hope Maclean was a city clerk who discovered that half the city council was embezzling funds, and Judith Stein uncovered elder abuse at a nursing home. What have you got?"

"Juicy stuff, like you. In 2010, Myda Perez was a nurse who turned in a hospital physician for a series of botched procedures resulting in one death and two people left in a vegetative state. And in 2011, Christy Richmond was a prostitute who beat a felony charge by blowing the whistle on a vice squad that ran a stable of hookers."

"A stable of hookers," Terry echoed. "What a delightful turn of phrase you have there."

Oscar grinned. "What would you call them?"

"Anyway, I checked out Alicia Hyams too. She voiced her fears about the pedophilia in 2006. The guy was convicted in 2007 and committed suicide the following year. The truth only came out last year that one of the kids had made the whole thing up."

"Was it her kid?"

"No, a kid called Johnny Masterson. He was the one who liked to play doctor."

"How old was this Johnny?"

"Four."

"So how did the pedophile accusation start?"

"Alicia started kicking up a fuss and word was getting around the day care. She quizzed her boy, and he pointed her in Johnny's direction. Apparently, little Johnny had been told by his parents to be wary of strange men who might touch children. So he pointed the finger at the day-care manager's husband."

Oscar exhaled. "Imagine if you got accused of something like that and you knew you didn't do it. Nobody would listen to you. Everyone would convict first."

Terry didn't say anything. He didn't have to imagine. He'd been accused of a crime he hadn't committed. It was an experience he never wanted to repeat.

Oscar's expression turned grim. "I found out something else about these women and it's not good."

Terry's stomach tightened. "What is it?"

"Myda Perez was murdered a year after the scandal, and no one has seen Christy Richmond since she testified against the cops."

It was coincidence, Terry told himself. Murders happened. Prostitutes disappeared. It is the world we live in. But as much as he wanted to believe in coincidence, he knew he was lying to himself.

He turned back to his computer and added the word "dead" to Hope Maclean's search field. The results listing changed and the headlines for the top results reported Hope Maclean's murder. Oscar was saying something, but Terry could only hear the rushing of his own blood in his ears.

He pulled up Judith Stein's page and repeated this pattern. The results changed, but the answer was the same. Judith Stein was dead too.

"I think all these women are dead, Oscar. First they went missing, then they were killed. Now, Sarah's missing. I'm scared. I'm really scared."

"Shit. You don't know that for sure. Christy Richmond is just missing."

"You're right, we don't. So clear your weekend."

"Why?"

"We're going on a road trip. We're going to these cities, and we're going to find out as much as we can about these women and how they died."

CHAPTER FIFTEEN

"What is it?" Terry asked, unsure of what Oscar had brought him.

"It's a car."

"I know, but what is it?"

Oscar sighed. "Don't you know a classic when you see it?"

"Not really."

"Classic cars aren't all Jags, Aston Martins, and Rolls-Royces. This country produces its own fair share of desirable machines."

"It does?"

Oscar frowned. "Are you going out of your way to hurt my feelings?"

Terry smiled. "Okay, what am I looking at?"

"A Chevy Monte Carlo," Oscar announced proudly. "'85 vintage."

It didn't look like the playground of the rich and famous inspired it. The car was huge with precious little styling. Close to eighteen feet long, it was a slab-sided hunk of steel. Despite its size, it had only two doors, giving it an acre of hood and a trunk big enough to store a family. The black paint job made it look as aggressive as hell.

"It's…er…lovely."

"Don't be like that. Don't knock it until you've driven it." Oscar tossed Terry the keys.

Examining the keys, Terry said, "Do we have time for this? I thought you wanted to get this road trip underway. We've got a lot of miles to cover."

"You'll want to test drive it first, won't you?"

"Why?"

"It's yours."

"Mine?"

"You've been moaning about the rental charges and how you needed your own car. Well, I got you one."

Terry stared at his keys then the car.

"Try it. You won't regret it."

Terry frowned. "Where'd it come from?"

"It's my nephew's. He's going to college, and it's either an education or the car. The car goes."

"How much?"

"Two grand," Oscar said. "Put your eyebrows down. That paint job alone is worth it. And that engine is custom."

Terry wasn't convinced. The car wasn't him. It was so American.

"Are you getting all English on me?"

"What's that mean?"

"All quiet and disapproving."

"No."

"Then get in."

Terry gunned the engine. The Monte Carlo roared with the unmistakable rumble of a V-8. He thrust the selector into reverse, and the car trundled off the driveway and into the street.

"Can you feel that power?" Oscar jerked his eyebrows. "That's V-8 power."

Terry selected drive and hit the gas. The nose of the car rose and the acceleration thrust Terry deep into his seat. In the rearview mirror, he saw over five hundred miles' worth of tire tread seared to the asphalt in two greasy streaks.

"Steady on, Andretti. There's a lot of power under that hood."

Terry winked at Oscar. "I know."

Terry thrashed the Chevy around the neighborhood too fast and reckless, but it was a test drive, so what the hell?

"What do you think?" Oscar asked, as Terry pulled into his driveway.

The Monte Carlo was Detroit gold—big, bold, and bad. Big enough for a family of eight, it only had seats for five. The engine was raw, all power with no refinement. It had more horsepower than the chassis could handle. The car wallowed in the bends. It wavered on the straights. It was everything the Motor City promised and more. Terry loved it.

"I'll take it."

Fifteen minutes later, they were on I-80 heading toward Sacramento. In the trunk were two changes of clothes for each of them. On the backseat was a cooler full of cold sodas. Between the front seats were notes, names, addresses, and Terry's smartphone. If everything went according to plan, they would rack up more than a thousand miles over the weekend and return with answers.

"What's our first stop? Alicia Hyams's husband?" Oscar shouted over the engine and wind noise. The windows were open because the air-conditioning wasn't powerful enough for the job—a fact Oscar had neglected to mention.

Terry shook his head. "No. I tried to call him back last night to arrange a time and place to meet. The phone number has been disconnected."

"Do you think someone got to him?"

"Yes—us. I think we brought up too many bad memories."

"Where to, then?"

"I've never been to Oregon."

Once Sacramento had become a speck in the rearview mirror, the drive to Medford descended into the realms of the tedious. As they took turns driving, the gaps between towns stretched and there was little to occupy Terry's mind. I-5 seemed an endless asphalt ribbon. He found himself looking forward to seeing the next exit sign for something to stimulate his mind. As Redding retreated into the south, his thoughts drifted to Oscar and the barrier he'd put up at the Gold Rush.

"After Schreiber had gotten Holman off my back, you said you were helping me as a penance."

Oscar stiffened and his hands gripped the wheel until his knuckles shone white. Terry wondered if he should let the matter drop but decided to keep pressing.

"You said you let someone down. Who was that?"

Oscar fidgeted in his seat, adjusting his hands on the wheel. He kept his gaze fixed on the road and didn't reply. Terry was going to press the matter further when Oscar finally spoke.

"My son." His voice dropped to a whisper. He still didn't look at Terry. "You're my penance for what I didn't do for my son."

"What didn't you do?"

"Don't ask any more questions, please. Just let me tell it, okay? I want to tell you, and I'm going to, but I need to do it my way."

"Sure."

It took Oscar another fifteen miles to compose what he wanted to say and in that time, Terry didn't speak.

"A few years back, Julia, my wife, and I were suffering the effects of a teenage son going through puberty. Daniel was doing the usual teenage stuff. Staying out late, being monosyllabic with his responses and disrespectful. Nothing out of the ordinary. Then as he turned sixteen, we noticed a quantum shift. It took us a few months before we realized it was drugs. Maybe if we'd been more honest with ourselves we'd have seen the signs earlier. Can you pass me a soda from the cooler?"

"Sure." Terry reached over and pulled out a Coke. He opened the can before handing it to Oscar. "There you go."

Oscar made eye contact. The sadness Terry saw shook him. He realized it was the same kind of sadness he was feeling for Sarah.

"I guess I was an absent father," Oscar said. "My welding firm was doing well, so, essentially, Julia raised Daniel. I don't know if that had anything to do with it, but I do wonder. Anyway, we couldn't ignore his drug habit once his health took a nosedive and things started disappearing around the house. We confronted him and told him what lay in store for him if he continued down the junkie road. Not surprisingly, he didn't react the way we wanted. We had a massive fight."

Terry waited for more, but Oscar had stalled. He was tearing himself apart with his story, and Terry felt nothing but guilt for bringing the subject up. Oscar sniffed and wiped his tearless eyes before continuing.

"Daniel ran away that night, and we haven't seen him since. That was nearly four years ago."

"I'm sorry, Oscar."

"Obviously, in true locking the gate after the horse has bolted style, I sold the business to spend more time at home. But once Daniel had gone, Julia didn't want me home. Within six months, we were separated and began divorce proceedings. Once I was on my own, I didn't want to go back into welding, so I bought the Gold Rush. Do you want to know the stupid thing? I bought the Gold Rush because Daniel liked to play minigolf as a kid. I suppose I'm hoping he'll walk in one day and want to play with his old dad. Isn't that stupid?"

"No, not really."

"Do you mind driving for a while?"

Oscar eased the Monte Carlo onto the shoulder and they swapped places. For the rest of the drive, they didn't speak. Arriving in Judith Stein's hometown of Medford, they looked up the location of the Shady Oaks Nursing Home on Terry's phone and followed the GPS directions. Terry pulled up opposite the address. The nursing home was still there but with a new name and a fresh lick of paint to hide the past. The home now had the fancier name of Creek View Assisted Living Facility.

"Judith Stein left her mark," Oscar said, pointing at the sign. "Hmm."

"So what do you want to do?" Oscar asked.

"Go in." Terry said.

"And say what? Do you remember Judith Stein, the woman who brought you people to your knees?"

Oscar made a good point, but the long drive had given Terry plenty of time to formulate a plan. "Can you act?"

Terry made a U-turn and pulled into Creek View's parking lot. As they entered the facility's foyer, the pungent stink of industrial-strength air freshener slapped them across the face. Terry choked and glanced at Oscar. He wrinkled his nose in agreement. They were attended to immediately. A Joan Rivers type, small and painfully thin, with tight skin and sharp features, appeared from an office behind the reception desk. She looked so well preserved that she would probably take a thousand years to decompose.

"Hi, I'm Marge Kenny. Welcome to the Creek View Assisted Living Facility. How may I help you?"

Terry stepped forward. "Hi, my name is Blair Anthony. I'm interested in this facility as a possible home for my father."

"Would you like a tour?" She held out a hand to Terry.

Marge's hand was cold and fragile to the touch. "Yes, I would. Thanks," Terry said.

Offering her hand to Oscar, she asked, "And you are?"

"Harry Johnson," Terry replied for Oscar. Oscar smiled and nodded.

"Pleased to meet you, Harry." Marge handed them each a glossy brochure. "Here's some literature with our rates and finance plans, but we can discuss that at the end of the tour."

Marge led the way into Creek View's day room, a large lounge with a patio overlooking a small, well-tended garden. Residents populated about half of the room. They whiled away their lives playing board games, watching TV, or staring out the window. Marge smiled and offered a greeting to anyone who looked their way, while reciting some meaningless details about the facility. Terry made the pretense of listening. She didn't dwell and led them into the garden, making sure she shut the French doors behind her.

"I don't like to ask these questions in front of the other residents. Can I ask a few questions about your father?"

"Please do."

"What condition is your father in?" Her smile was pained as she showed her concern. "Does he have any special needs?"

Terry hemmed and hawed. "Dad's okay. He's a little forgetful. He has high blood pressure and doesn't see too well these days. Generally, he's not the firecracker he used to be."

Marge smiled agreeably. "I understand. Shall we?"

Marge moved the tour to the exercise room and gym. She made a big play of the facility's attention to the physical as well as the mental. The equipment looked almost new.

She showed them a typical apartment. It didn't look like much of an apartment to Terry, more like a college dorm room with a disability bathroom attached and without the colorful posters.

Terry's own mortality seeped into him like a winter chill. Was this his future? Would he end up in a ten-by-ten box, with the only luxury being a stainless-steel rail next to the toilet? He hoped not. If he ever needed the encouragement to make sure he was self-sufficient in his twilight years, this was it.

Marge ushered them through the kitchen facilities, medical clinic, and pharmacy. She brought the well-practiced tour to a close back in the foyer.

"Come into my office, won't you?" They all sat. "Can I ask what brought you to Creek View?"

"My father has reached a point in his life where he needs supervision, and I thought it would be good to bring him home."

"Your father is from Medford?" Marge said cocking her head.

"No, but he's an Oregon boy."

"You don't sound like you're from here."

Terry smiled a disarming smile. "I was born in Portland. My dad is American and my mum is English. They split. He came back and I stayed with my mum in England. But when Mum died a couple of years back, I came to the US to be close to Dad."

Terry's slick answer was impressive, even to him.

"And Harry, are you a relation?"

"No, I'm a friend," Oscar replied.

"Harry's an Oregon boy too, and when I said I was driving up to the Beaver State from California, he jumped at the chance to show me around. Isn't that right, Harry?"

"Sure is, Blair. Never miss the chance to come home."

"And your father is in California at the moment?"

"Yes."

The story sounded convincing enough, and Marge launched into a pricing schedule that made Terry's toes curl. No wonder they offered financing options. Oscar stopped her in her tracks.

"I remember some trouble with a nursing home around here. It must be some years back. Something to do with abuse and withholding medication."

Marge tried to maintain a smile, but it cracked under some serious pressure. She got up, closed her office door, and leaned against it.

"I won't lie to you, this was the facility with the dark history. But let me assure you that none of the staff or management who worked here then work here now."

"Were the allegations true?" Terry asked.

Marge returned to her desk, taking time to formulate her response. "I'm not sure whether everything alleged was true. You must understand, I wasn't here then."

Terry nodded. "But that doesn't answer my question. I'm thinking of placing my father here."

Marge pulled her chair closer to her desk and lowered her voice. "I believe there was an abuse of trust."

"That's appalling," Terry said.

"Very sad," Oscar agreed.

"But nothing was ever proven."

"Why?" Terry asked.

"The woman who made the allegations disappeared. About nine months later, they found her washed up on the beach in Cape Sebastian State Park. What she was doing out there, no one ever knew. Accident, some said. Others said suicide. I don't think we'll ever know. Either way, the police could never say one way or the other. She'd been in the water the whole time and she was pretty badly decomposed. So badly, her tongue was missing. Eaten out, they believe."

Marge's words dissolved into a gurgle in Terry's ears. He'd been ready to leap in with another probing question, but Judith Stein's missing tongue silenced him. Alicia Hyams's tongue had been cut out. What if the coroner had been wrong about Judith, and too presumptuous with his conclusion? With severe decomposition, it was understandable if the examiner had missed that her tongue had been cut out. He felt Oscar's gaze burning into him, but he couldn't look at his friend. The implications were too explosive.

Terry inhaled when he and Oscar walked out of Marge's facility. He was glad to breathe fresh air again and not the sickly, perfumed stench of recycled air breathed many, many times before. Marge called out her farewells. Striding across the parking lot, Oscar waved good-bye. Terry kept on walking, his hand tightening around the glossy brochures, his sweat bonding them to his flesh.

Getting into the Monte Carlo, Oscar said, "Christ, Terry. Her tongue was missing. That's too much of a coincidence."

"I'm afraid that the deaths of the women on Sarah's list may be connected after all."

Medford's city limits loomed. Terry's foot was planted on the gas. He wanted out. The place was tainted. He felt that if he stayed too long, the tragedy that claimed Judith Stein would claim him too.

"What do you want to do?" Oscar asked.

"I want to know if Myda Perez's tongue was cut out. The news stories didn't go into any real details about her murder."

"It's after four. We won't get into Nevada until late tonight. Let's get a room, get something to eat, and plan our next step."

They registered at a motel close to the California state border. Oscar took over the driving duties and found a steak house for an early dinner. They were ahead of the evening rush, but they caught the early-bird, senior-savings hour. Watching weak jaws and bad dentures chew tough steak reminded Terry of life at Creek View. His appetite had been poor to start with and it evaporated altogether as he thought again about Judith's fate.

"C'mon, Terry, snap out of it," Oscar said. "I know what you're thinking."

"Do you?"

"You're thinking that if Judith Stein and Alicia Hyams had their tongues cut out, then how long is it before we find Sarah in the same condition? Am I close?"

"Too close. But what if I'm right?"

"We'll cross that bridge when we come to it."

• • •

The following morning, they hit the road early with a freshly stocked ice chest on the Monte Carlo's backseat. Terry wasn't consumed with the sense of adventure he'd felt setting out the day before. He insisted on driving, wanting the distraction.

The Chevy crossed the Nevada state line at midday and entered Carson City sometime after one. Terry gassed up the Monte, as he was coming to call it.

"Where do you want to go first?" Oscar asked, looking up directions in Terry's phone. "We can check out the hospital Myda worked at when she blew the whistle on that doctor. It's not far." Terry left the pump feeding the Chevy's greedy belly and scoured the car for his notes. Myda Perez hadn't been married. She had lived with her mother, also named Myda. None of the news articles mentioned an address, but one featured a picture of her, with her mother, standing on the porch of their home. The house number 3325 was clearly visible in the shot.

"Let's leave the hospital for the moment. Hand me the phone, I want to find Myda's family," Terry said.

Terry pulled up a phone directory for Carson City and looked up Myda Perez. They were two M. Perez's listed, but only one lived at 3325 North Saratoga Way. He punched the address into his phone and Oscar took the wheel. Twenty minutes later, Oscar made a right onto North Saratoga Way. It was a quiet street filled with fifties tract homes, many with recent additions or complete makeovers. He slowed to a crawl and they scanned for house numbers.

"I see it," Oscar announced and sped up.

Oscar stopped the Monte. Terry compared the house against the newspaper photo. It was a perfect match.

"Showtime," Oscar said, opening his door.

Terry followed Oscar across the road with his notes under his arm.

Oscar rang the doorbell. Nothing happened. He glanced at Terry. Terry shrugged and Oscar tried the doorbell again.

This time, movement came from inside.

"Sounds hopeful," Oscar remarked.

It was several minutes before the door was answered. The senior Myda Perez opened it as far as the security chain allowed.

"Myda Perez?" he asked. "Can I ask you a few questions about your daughter?"

That was enough to set the old woman off. She launched into a tirade of Spanish.

"*¿Puedo preguntarle acerca de su hija?*" Oscar asked in a polite and calming tone. "*¿Cómo fue que murió?*"

Oscar's valiant attempt to ask how her daughter had died only inflamed the situation. Mrs. Perez slammed the door and the security chain came off. A moment later, the door flew open. She blasted them with explosive Spanish, shoving them back with her walker.

Both Terry and Oscar took two steps back. They tried to calm the woman with disarming gestures, but nothing was going to placate her.

"Mrs. Perez, we mean you no harm," Terry pleaded.

They were so focused on Myda's distraught mother, they didn't see their attacker. A blur body-slammed Oscar. He collided with Terry and both men crashed into the garage's stucco wall, sending Terry's notes flying.

Their tackler was a powerfully built Hispanic man in his twenties. He towered over them. "Get the hell out of here. Leave this woman alone. Can't you see she's not well? Whatever you're selling, she don't want it."

Terry managed the beginning of an apology and an explanation before the tackler turned his attentions to Myda Perez. He countered her rapid-fire Spanish with a barrage of his own, continually switching from Spanish to English and back.

"Abuelita Perez, it is okay. It's cool." The man gripped her walker and steered it toward the house. He cooed comforting words, telling her everything would be okay and he would take care of it.

He guided her back inside and closed the door. Terry and Oscar tottered to their feet. Seeing them still there, the man's face blackened.

"You still here?" he demanded. "Didn't I tell you scumbags that we're not interested in what you're selling?"

"We're not selling anything," Terry managed, backing away.

"Then what do you want?"

"We wanted to find out how her daughter died," Terry said. "Do you know what happened to Myda?"

"Yes."

"Can we speak to you? I promise not to take more than five minutes of your time."

The man hesitated, weighing up the request, before saying, "C'mon."

His name was Javier Rivera. He was a Ford dealership mechanic and the younger Myda's godson. He walked them over to his front yard, five houses away on the opposite side of the street.

"Your five minutes start now."

Terry explained everything he and Oscar had unearthed. He showed Javier Sarah's list of names and the news articles he'd printed from the library. He handed him Myda's article last. Tears welled in the young man's eyes.

"You know that son of a bitch she turned in is still practicing medicine. She proved he'd screwed up, killing a man and turning those kids into vegetables. What a joke."

"I thought the doctor lost his license," Oscar said.

"He lost his Nevada license. He's in the Midwest somewhere, probably killing more innocent people."

Terry asked the vital question. "How did Myda die?"

"Dr. McKethen was finished. After the last hearing was over and the medical board ruled against him, we thought it was over. But things turned nasty."

"How?" Oscar asked.

"Doctors are their own little club. Myda was dumped on at work. Every kind of crappy job, she got it. She was a charge nurse, man, and she had to slop out bedpans."

"They decided she'd sold them out," Terry suggested.

"She was a nurse, not a doctor. She wasn't one of them. Unless you have a string of letters after your name, you're nothing."

"But they saw her as a squealer," Oscar suggested.

"Yeah," Javier agreed. "Even her friends."

"How long did this go on for?" Oscar asked.

"A couple of months. She found herself on the graveyard shift all the time, so when she didn't come home that night, we didn't know anything was wrong."

"When was she found?" Terry asked.

"A week later, a hundred feet from the highway. A traveling salesman stopped for a leak and found he was going on Myda's half-buried body." Javier wiped away a tear. "He pissed on her body, man."

"Christ, I'm sorry," Terry said.

"Her throat was slit and her tongue was cut out." Javier sniffed and ran a hand across his nose. His eyes were red. "They never pinned it on anyone."

"Is anybody working on Myda's case?"

"No, they have other cases to work on," he said sarcastically. "You think your wife will be next?"

"Yes."

"I hope she isn't, man."

"So do I."

"Thanks for your time, Javier." Oscar offered a hand. "We appreciate it."

Taking Oscar's hand, he said, "I'm sorry about getting in your face earlier."

Terry put out his hand. "I probably would have done the same. We weren't being very considerate. Please give our apologies to Mrs. Perez."

Javier vice-gripped Terry's hand. Terry felt his bones of his hand shift. "You and me, man, are brothers—family. We fight the same evil. You find this son of a bitch; you call me, okay?

We'll take care of this. There is plenty of desert out here. You call me."

Terry gave Javier a pen and a pad. He scribbled his telephone number down.

"You call me," Javier said again, seeing them to the Monte. It wasn't a question. It was a demand.

"Have no doubt," Terry said.

Oscar gunned the engine and pulled away.

"That was serious," he said. "Will you call him?"

"I will if I have to." Terry turned to Oscar. Fear and shock flashed in his friend's eyes.

• • •

Oscar had been quiet for ten minutes. Terry's promise to Javier was the cause, but he'd meant what he said. He couldn't help that. It was the way he felt. Terry broke the silence.

"What's our next step?"

"Myda's hospital is on the next street. Do you want to check it out?"

"We can, but I'm not sure it'll help much. Javier gave us all that we needed to know."

"Do you want to go home? We've got a good five-hour drive ahead."

Terry thought it over. "Let's see if we get lucky with the hospital. Then we'll go home."

Terry had been hoping to make it to Southern California to dig up what they could on Hope Maclean and Christy Richmond, but there was no way that happening this weekend. He was discovering yet again that America was a big place.

It didn't take long to reach the hospital. As they turned into the visitors' parking lot, Oscar said, "Another name change."

When Myda had exposed Dr. McKethen's malpractice, the hospital had been called Silver State General. Now the hospital was called the Nevada State University Children's Research Hospital. Whether Myda's action had caused the change, Terry wasn't sure.

Oscar switched off the Monte's engine and opened the door to get out. Terry didn't move.

"You coming?"

Terry had seen the hospital's name only few days ago on a piece of paperwork he'd signed. The children's hospital had been the sender of the urgent samples FedEx had delivered to Pamela Dawson.

"You okay? You look like you've just seen a ghost."

"Get back in the car, and let's get the hell out of here."

"What?"

"Just drive."

Oscar gunned the engine and roared out of the parking stall. Hightailing it out of the parking lot, they passed in front of the hospital. As the Monte sped past the outpatient exit, Terry kept his gaze fixed on the man leaving the hospital. He hadn't seen a ghost. It was much more disturbing than that. Frosty Frazer strode toward the parking lot with a refrigerated chest in his hand.

CHAPTER SIXTEEN

Six months earlier

Terry had left as late as he could. His London-bound flight would begin boarding soon. Sarah walked him to the security checkpoint.

"I suppose this is it," Terry said. "The honeymoon is over."

Sarah nodded.

"Don't look so glum. It shouldn't take long before immigration clears me to come back."

"You're not going to forget me, are you?" Sarah asked. She looked away and fiddled with the wedding ring, only days old, on her finger.

Her insecurity was ridiculous. Terry laughed and placed a hand under her chin to raise her face. "What makes you say that?"

"Well, our romance is hardly conventional."

"That's a good thing."

"Yes, because it's a novelty, but what happens when we have to settle for normality? Will the novelty wear off?"

He'd slipped an arm around her shoulder and squeezed her to him. "You have nothing to fear. There is no way I could get bored and forget you."

"Are you sure?" she asked.

• • •

"Of course I'm sure," Terry mumbled to himself in the confines of the bedroom. He couldn't stop replaying that day in the airport. He rolled over in bed and looked at the time glowing red in the darkness: 2:20. He couldn't believe he was still tossing and turning.

After he'd dropped Oscar off and driven home, he'd been ready for bed. It was after eleven by the time he closed the garage door and he was too dog-tired to do or think about anything. It took all his remaining strength to carry himself to bed. He thought sleep was seconds away, but the moment his head hit the pillow, insomnia struck.

Sarah was the source of his insomnia. He couldn't get her out of his head, for once. Finding her had become such a priority that he'd stopped thinking about her as a person. Sarah was no longer his wife. She was a goal, a prize to be attained when he'd solved the puzzle. Little day-to-day recollections that had seeped into his consciousness had dried up. How many times had *their song* played on the radio and not struck a chord with him? When had he last picked up a photograph to study her face? And what did her face look like anyway? He was having trouble recalling the nuances that made Sarah Sarah. He tried to summon an image of her in his mind, but managed only a hazy reception.

The road trip had been the wake-up call. All the women on Sarah's list they'd checked out so far were not only dead, but had been mutilated in the same way. He hated his pessimism, but he believed the chances of finding Sarah safe and sound were getting slimmer with every revelation. Death was courting her and it was only a matter of time before it snatched her. That realization sliced through all his thoughts. At last he was thinking about Sarah in the right context. She was his supreme concern. Life without her seemed inconceivable, but it was becoming a possibility.

He rolled out of bed and wandered into the kitchen, switching on the lights as he went. Reaching for a carton of orange juice, he spotted the bottle of French champagne with the red silk bow wrapped around its neck that Sarah must have bought for his arrival. He left the orange juice and pulled out the champagne.

He examined the label and had no idea whether it was a good vintage or not. He knew as much about champagne as he did about Sarah's whereabouts.

"Silly cow," he said with love in his voice and a sad smile. "You know I don't like this stuff."

Setting the bottle on the countertop, he picked at the foil covering the top until he exposed the wire and cork, then stopped. The champagne wasn't for drinking alone. It was for drinking with his wife. He returned the bottle to the refrigerator.

He reverted to the orange juice and wandered over to the wedding photo on the dining table. He picked it up and took it onto the patio. The patio lights sensed him and zapped him with a burst of blinding light. There was a chill in the air, a stark contrast from the heat of the day. The night was probably no warmer than a May night in England. The frigid concrete patio numbed his toes in seconds. He chugged the orange juice until the carton buckled.

He stared at their wedding picture again. It was a trivial image to represent their marriage. Taken outside the Luxor Las Vegas, the two of them were hugging while making rabbit ears behind each other's heads and flashing cheesy grins. He remembered the confused Japanese tourists who'd taken the picture. It seemed funny at the time, just another example of their disrespect for convention. They hadn't even gotten dressed up for the ceremony. They'd both worn jeans and T-shirts. They had made one concession to wedding convention. Sarah had worn a veil. Now he wished they'd done things right. Sensing no movement in a long while, the patio lights went off and plunged him into darkness.

He shifted position and the patio lights snapped back on. He moved to the warmer, sprinkler-moistened lawn to put some feeling back into his feet. He flopped into the garden hammock, safe from the glare of the patio lights. He hugged the wedding picture and orange juice carton to him and stared into the sky.

It was a cloudless night. The moon and constellations could be seen clearly. Lights as bright as stars blinked from a passing jet, its engines a distant roar. Jet trails scarred a perfect night sky.

He'd never felt so alone in his life.

• • •

Sitting at his lab bench the next morning, Terry felt left of center. He'd fallen asleep in the hammock and had been rudely awakened by the six o'clock sprinkler cycle. Regardless of the hot shower following his impromptu cold one, he still felt like an unmade bed. He sipped his coffee, hoping the caffeine would get his motor running.

He'd hoped to avoid Pamela and Frosty, but there proved to be no need. Pamela had signed herself out to some breakfast meeting and Frosty was nowhere to be seen. He found their absence disconcerting. He recalled his conversation with Oscar on the ride home from Nevada.

"So what does Genavax have to do with the women on this list?" Oscar had asked.

"I don't know. But something weird is going on there."

"Like what?"

"First, there was Sarah's argument with my boss. Then, a delivery I signed for at Genavax came from this hospital—Myda Perez's hospital. And now, Frosty Frazer is here leaving with a medical cooler."

"What's going on?"

The lab doors swung open and Frosty breezed in, making a beeline for his corner lab bench. He acknowledged various not-so-heartfelt greetings with dismissive grunts. Within a minute, his coat was off and he was already into the thick of his work.

Terry noticed Frosty wasn't carrying the refrigerated cooler he'd walked out of the hospital with yesterday. Terry guessed the cooler was already here, dropped off the same night. It was all too cloak-and-dagger for his liking. Pamela, Frosty, and Genavax were doing their damnedest to cover their tracks.

Frosty realized Terry was staring at him. He glared and Terry tried to determine whether it was just a dislike of being stared at or something more. He hadn't been sure whether Frosty had recognized him outside the children's hospital. But if he saw the Monte in the parking lot, it wouldn't take long for Frosty to put two and two together. Terry's phone rang.

"Terry Sheffield," Terry said.

"It's Oscar." Road noise interfered with the reception.

"Are you on the road?

"Yeah. I'm on I-5. I didn't get much sleep last night, thinking about what we'd talked about."

Terry knew the feeling.

"I can't wait until next week to check out Hope Maclean and Christy Richmond's stories. I should be in Delano by this afternoon."

"I wish you'd told me. I would have come too," Terry said.

"It's best you stay there. If you take too much time off, they might start to suspect you."

It was a fair point, but Terry didn't like it. "How long do you think you'll be?"

"A couple of days, maybe three. Today Delano. Tomorrow, Anaheim, then back."

"Just be careful, okay?"

"I will be, Mom."

"Shut up," Terry said, smiling.

Oscar laughed. "I'll give you a call when I've got something. And don't forget you've got a task of your own."

Terry hung up. Frosty was still staring at him. He left his bench and cut a path toward Terry.

"Yes?" Terry asked.

"Terry, you've got a visitor."

"Thanks."

"I think it's the sheriff."

• • •

Terry marched out of the lab. His blood was boiling. What new stunt was he trying to pull? He pushed open the door leading into the reception area.

"What the bloody hell do you want?" Terry demanded.

"In this country, we start a conversation with hello."

"And in this country, as in England, impersonating a law enforcement officer is a crime." Terry grabbed Jake Holman by the arm and shoved him through Genavax's main doors into the parking lot.

"Hey!" Jake stumbled but caught his balance before he went sprawling. "No need for the rough stuff."

"Isn't there?"

"Okay, I shouldn't have pretended to be my pop."

"Damn right, you shouldn't have."

"But would you have spoken to me if I'd said it was me?"

"No, and for good reason. Do you know what I've had to do to repair the damage your dad's done to my reputation? And your little stunt has ruined all that."

"Sorry."

Terry wasn't won over.

"I said sorry."

Terry glanced over his shoulder. They were drawing flies. Faces stared out from the reception area. He led Jake to the shade of a tree in the parking lot.

Terry crossed his arms and leaned against the tree. "What do you want?"

"To make up. Last time we ended things badly."

"You stormed off, as I remember it."

"Yeah, well, the prison crack wasn't funny."

"Because it was true?"

"Yeah," he sighed. "But that's not what I came to say. I wanted to say you did a number on my dad."

"And you're upset?"

"The opposite. Good job. It'll take a long time for him to get that egg off his face."

"And that's it? You've embarrassed me in front of my coworkers for that?"

"Hey, Terry, I'm doing my best here. I'm trying to make it up to you."

"You're a piece of work, Jake."

Jake frowned. "I'm not the smartest guy, but don't treat me the same way everybody else does."

Terry's alkaline compassion neutralized his acid anger. Maybe he was being a little harsh on the guy. "Jake, couldn't you have come to my house to tell me, or called?"

"I tried over the weekend, but I didn't get any answer. I thought you were avoiding me. I left a couple of messages."

"I was away all weekend."

"Oh. Have you heard from Sarah?"

"No."

"How long has it been…three, four weeks? That's a long time for someone not to come up for air."

Terry didn't need to be told this. "Look, Jake, I have to get back to work. Is there anything else?"

"Yeah. Be careful of my pop. You've bloodied his nose in public, and he won't forget it. He holds a grudge. He'll find a way to get back at you. He's not the upstanding keeper of the peace that people around here like to think he is."

It was obvious Jake was speaking from bitter experience. His father was a demon he'd never managed to exorcise. Terry had the feeling that his confrontation with Holman was satisfying Jake's desire to get back at his dad. He didn't like being the host for Jake's parasitic needs. It was a little too twisted. Frosty poked his head out from the doorway.

"I'll bear that in mind, Jake." Terry offered his hand. "I appreciate you coming."

"Are we cool?" Jake said, shaking Terry's hand.

"Yes." He smiled. "We're cool."

"Terry, I would like to be friends. Can we hang out?"

"Sure. Call me."

Terry pushed himself away from the tree. Frosty retreated back into the building.

"How about tonight?"

"I can't tonight. There's something I've got to do." Terry walked back to Genavax.

The rest of the day was a battle of wills. Terry wanted to be alone in the lab, but Pamela and Frosty wouldn't leave. Terry had the excuse of making up for Jake's stunt, but it was after seven and he hadn't been expecting to wait that long. The pressure intensified to see who would crack first.

Terry knew he had the edge. The other two were paper shuffling. It was obvious they wanted to do something, but they weren't going to do it in front of him.

"Terry, don't you want to call it a day?" Pamela asked.

"I want to finish running this gel before I go." He didn't really. He was robbing himself of tasks to do tomorrow. But setting up the agarose gel, loading it with samples, and running it to size the DNA fragments would keep him busy. He should outlast them, but he couldn't keep the facade up for long. If they didn't go soon, his gel would be finished and no excuse could warrant him staying any longer.

"We're going now." Pamela nodded to Frosty. He was slipping off his lab coat.

"See you in the morning, then," Terry said.

Pamela and Frosty exchanged a glance. They left together. *Maybe the rumors are true*, Terry thought. But he couldn't see them as secret lovers. Neither of them seemed to have the passion to be in heat with the other, unless it had something to do with Genavax. Maybe that was it. Genavax was their aphrodisiac. Terry hid a smirk.

"Good night," Frosty said. "Don't stay too late. It's only Monday."

From anybody else, it would have sounded lighthearted, but from Frosty, it sounded like a slur.

"I won't," Terry said with fake cheer.

Pamela switched off three out of four lights on her way out. Terry had the perfect mood lighting for what he had planned. Watching them leave, he bid them good riddance.

"Don't do anything the human race would do," he mumbled under his breath.

He carried on with his work. He couldn't risk Pamela and Frosty coming back if they thought he was up to no good. His prudence paid off. Fifteen minutes after their departure, Frank from security poked his head through the door.

"Terry, when are you going home?"

"Soon."

"Jeez, buddy, you Brits work too damn hard."

"It's what put the *great* in Great Britain."

"I suppose," he said, shaking his head. "Let me know when you go?"

"Will do," Terry said and saluted.

He still didn't make his move until his gel was done. He didn't have a choice. If he did, the data would be ruined. He was glad of the delay. It stopped him from being too impetuous. The clock nudged eight and his gel was done. He stained it, photographed it, and tossed it in the biohazard can. He didn't shut down his computer or put away his equipment. He needed props if he was disturbed again.

He opened the refrigerator where he'd put last week's FedEx delivery. It wasn't there and neither was Frosty's container from Nevada. He wasn't surprised. If the contents were anything remotely valuable, Frosty or Pamela would use them the moment they had the chance. Most likely, whatever was in the containers would have been tested and frozen or even incinerated in the autoclave by now. But the manifest should still be around.

Terry tried Pamela's office door first. It was locked. He didn't fancy forcing the lock, not just yet anyway. Frosty didn't have an office and offered less of a problem. Like Pamela's door, his lab bench drawers were locked, but the locks weren't bank-vault quality. Terry snatched a twelve-inch steel ruler off Frosty's bench. He jammed the ruler into the gap between the drawer and the bench top. Glancing furtively between the lab doors and the desk, he applied pressure on the lock, shredding the ruler's cork backing. The lock didn't budge.

"Sod it." He yanked out the ruler. It twanged as it exited the narrow gap.

Terry found a chunky paper clip, and he fashioned it into a crude skeleton key. He worked the tumblers with his paper-clip key. It stood up to the punishment, but it didn't trip the lock.

"Bloody thing," he growled, removing the now mangled key from the lock. He couldn't believe he'd wasted hours waiting for everyone to leave only to be thwarted by a crappy lock. Obviously, safecracker wasn't a skill he could add to his résumé. In disgust, he scooted Frosty's stool back. It collided with the coat rack that had Frosty's lab coat hanging on it. The coat jangled.

The jangle sounded familiar. Terry smiled. He delved in the pockets and tugged out a bunch of keys.

"You moron, Frosty. Why lock your desk if you're going to leave your keys in your coat?"

It was easy to tell which one he needed. He slotted the key in, turned it, and hey, presto, the drawer was open. He flicked through the various project files, careful not to disturb anything he couldn't return to its rightful place. The first drawer didn't churn up anything of interest, so he turned his attentions to the other locked drawers.

In a bottom drawer, he found a file. The file contained test procedures and results, the manifest for the FedEx delivery he'd taken in the week before, a newer manifest with Sunday's date, and a wad of others dating back several months. The deliveries had been regular and the contents the same. The file told him everything he'd suspected.

"Human tissue," he muttered under his breath. "Children's tissue."

Terry snatched up the file and ran the contents through the photocopier. While the copier duplicated the evidence of a federal crime, he powered down his computer and tidied his desk. When the copies were made, he locked the file in the drawer and put Frosty's keys back before pocketing his paper-clip key and tossing the cork fragments. He jammed the damning documentation into his backpack and got the hell out of Genavax.

Driving out of the parking lot, he spotted Pamela's car parked on the far side. Had she left her car there for the night or had she returned to the office? If she had returned, had she seen him?

CHAPTER SEVENTEEN

Terry's headlights lit up the sheriff's department cruiser parked across the street from his house. He groaned. *Not again*, he thought. Holman and Deputy Pittman weren't subtle. But it could have been worse. They could have been parked in his driveway. Terry hit the garage-door opener and guided the Monte into the garage.

He stood at the garage's entrance, waiting for them to approach. They didn't. They just watched him watching them.

"Have it your way," he muttered and closed the door.

It was a couple of minutes before they rang the doorbell, enough time for him to collect the mail, switch on the lights, and draw the curtains. He put down the mail and opened the door. The porch light illuminated two grim faces on the other side of the screen door.

"Sheriff Holman. Deputy."

"Mr. Sheffield," Holman said. "Could we come in?"

"No. For my own protection, it's best you stay out there on the doorstep. What's the problem now?" Holman sighed, but didn't argue.

"We've had a tip saying your wife has been seen entering the premises," Deputy Pittman said.

Terry aimed his remarks directly at Holman. "Not that one again. You've pulled that stunt before, and it didn't do either of our reputations any good."

Holman's tanned skin tightened, creating more lines on his face than normal. "Regardless of past history, I have a duty to investigate the allegation."

"Who made this claim? Another anonymous tip?"

"Not this time," Holman began before being cut off.

Osbourne appeared behind the police officers and barged past them in an attempt to open the screen door. "It was me who called."

Deputy Pittman did her best to hold back the neighborhood watch chairman, but his bulk and personality beat her. Holman was a different matter. He halted Osbourne's attempt with his arm. Terry did nothing to disguise his contempt.

"While you've been seeking public sympathy on TV, your so-called missing wife has been coming back and forth for days," Osbourne accused.

"You don't know what you're talking about," Terry said with a dismissive wave.

"Mr. Osbourne, this is a police matter, and it is being dealt with accordingly," Holman said in a commanding tone, putting a professional bearing on the brawl.

"I have a right to be here," Osbourne said.

"Do I have to listen to this crap?" Terry moaned.

"I'm an American citizen."

"Mr. Osbourne, please control yourself," Deputy Pittman demanded. She had both hands on the old man's chest, forcing him back. Holman rose above the fracas, letting his deputy deal with the interference.

"Ask him, Sheriff," Osbourne blurted. "Ask him to produce his wife."

"Sheriff, get that man off my property," Terry insisted. "This matter has nothing to do with him. I didn't invite him. He's trespassing."

"Mr. Osbourne." Holman's spoke with the commanding tone of God speaking from Heaven. Osbourne must have been a God-fearing man, because he finally did as he was told. "Mr. Osbourne, you've done your civic duty. It is time for law enforcement to take over."

"He lied to me."

"That may be so, but I would like to investigate without your obstruction."

"You want me to go?"

"Yes."

Osbourne hesitated. Deputy Pittman kept him restrained, just in case he launched a second attack.

"Will you update me, so I can report back to the neighborhood committee?"

"Yes," Holman replied. "Deputy, please escort Mr. Osbourne home."

She nodded.

"Sheffield, my offer to join our committee—consider it withdrawn," Osbourne said.

Deputy Pittman hooked one of Osbourne's arms in hers and led him across the street.

"We don't need criminal types contaminating our attempts to stop crime," he called.

"If we could only bottle that kind of energy," Terry said, "he'd keep us warm this winter."

Holman waited until his deputy returned. "Now that there are no distractions, can we come in?"

"Do you have a warrant?"

"No, I don't have a warrant," Holman admitted. "Would you like me to return with one?"

"What is it you want?"

"We just want to look around and ask a couple of questions. We'll be five minutes, maximum."

"You don't need a warrant. Come in."

Terry stood back and they let themselves in. Deputy Pittman overtook her boss and headed for the master bedroom. Holman checked the guest bathroom, then Sarah's office.

Terry let them do their thing and switched on the lights in the kitchen. He unhitched his backpack and put it on the countertop. Pouring himself a glass of orange juice, he noticed his hands were shaking.

"Home late tonight?" Holman called from Sarah's office.

"I had some work to finish." Terry steadied his trembling hand on the copied Genavax documents hidden inside his backpack. No one could know what he'd been up to tonight, but he wondered if he'd made a mistake and Holman knew. The thought did nothing for his nerves.

"You're a dedicated man," Holman said, returning to the living room.

So are you, Terry thought.

Deputy Pittman marched through the house and into the backyard.

"So is there anything to Mr. Osbourne's claim?"

Terry flung his arms wide. "Is she here?"

Holman nodded. "So what do you think Mr. Osbourne saw?"

"An alien invasion?"

Holman frowned.

"Okay, I don't know who the old bugger could have seen, but I know it wasn't Sarah."

"Not a girlfriend, then."

"I won't dignify that with an answer."

Holman shrugged.

Deputy Pittman slid the patio door back and let herself in the house. "All clear, Sheriff. She's not here."

"I told you that," Terry said.

"Thanks, Debbie."

Deputy Pittman stood at Holman's side.

"Can we look under the house?" Holman asked.

"Not without a warrant."

"Is there something you don't want us to see?" Deputy Pittman asked.

"No, but last time you were here, evidence magically appeared from thin air. I want my lawyer here when you do an in-depth search. And now that we're on the subject, that's something you haven't answered. How come there was evidence planted in my home for you to find?"

Deputy Pittman huffed and turned her back. Holman's jaw muscles flexed, but he kept his temper.

Terry didn't care that he was antagonizing them. He still needed their support to help find Sarah, but what had they done for him lately? He hadn't heard anything about the search for Sarah since they'd held him for questioning.

"So you have no idea who would have been poking around your house?" Holman said, keeping the questioning on track.

There were candidates. There was the person who'd broken in and stolen Sarah's confidential notes, the Honda driver who had a garage-door opener, the voice on the phone, and the person who planted Alicia Hyams's belongings in the house. But that could be four people or just one.

"There could be someone."

"Ah yes," Holman said, nodding. "If I remember correctly, you had an obscene caller."

"I never said it was an obscene caller."

"My mistake. You're correct. Let's call him your mystery caller, as he never told you his name."

Holman's tone was condescending. It wasn't surprising after the swipes Terry had made.

"And you think it was him, correct?"

"It's possible."

"Well, I'm willing to believe that Mr. Osbourne was overzealous and could've been mistaken, but I'm pretty sure he can tell the difference between a woman and a man, don't you think?"

Terry didn't reply.

"I think we're done," Holman said. "Deputy, please tell Mr. Osbourne the outcome of our investigation."

"Don't you want to tell him yourself?" Deputy Pittman asked.

"No, I've got something else to talk over with Mr. Sheffield."

She hesitated before leaving. Holman waited for Deputy Pittman to close the door after her. Terry flopped into an easy chair. If Holman was going to make some veiled threat, he might as well be sitting comfortably.

"I believe you've been getting friendly with my son."

"You could say that."

"I know it's none of my business with whom you choose to associate."

"It isn't," Terry said.

Holman frowned. "But take it from someone who knows Jake well, he's not the sort of guy you want to have as a friend."

"Are you telling me to stay away from him?"

"I'm not telling you to do anything. You're an adult and capable of making your own decisions. I'm just saying, watch your step. Jake isn't someone to be trusted."

Terry smiled.

"What's so funny?"

"That's exactly what he said about you."

Holman left. Terry eased the curtains to one side and watched the sheriff cross the street to Osbourne's house. The neighborhood watch chairman wasn't happy with the news Deputy Pittman was giving him. There was a lot of arm twirling and finger pointing, which was stemmed when Holman intervened.

"Sort it out, Holman," Terry said and let the curtain go. The last thing he wanted was Osbourne banging on the door all night demanding to conduct his own search.

It was getting late, and Terry was hungry, but he wasn't in the mood to start cooking from scratch. He found something packaged in the freezer and preheated the oven. While a limp version of the cannelloni pictured on the packaging bubbled in the oven, Terry dug through his notes from the weekend. He found the sheet with Javier's phone number on it and dialed. The phone rang. Terry knew if Oscar were here, he'd be trying to stop him. Oscar was a good friend, and Terry understood his reservations, but Oscar couldn't understand Terry's desperation. Javier Rivera could. Myda Perez's godson answered.

"Javier, it's Terry Sheffield."

"You find something out? You know who took our women?"

"No, but I might be on the right track."

"You're not holding out on me? We have an agreement. You promised me."

"I know, Javier, I know," Terry said. "When I know, you'll know."

"We are from different cultures, and you may not understand the value of a promise."

"Trust me, Javier, I do understand the value of a promise. We aren't as different as you might think."

"As long as we're clear. What have you found out?"

"A possible connection. Does the name Genavax mean anything to you? Did Myda ever mention them when she exposed Dr. McKethen?"

"No, I don't think so."

"Please think hard; it could be really important."

"The name means nothing, man."

"Okay."

"Let me ask around, though. Abuelita Perez might remember. Is there anything else?"

"Yes, see if anyone remembers anything about illegal testing, illegal organ donors, things like that."

"Okay, man. I'll do it. Give me your number, and I'll get back to you."

"Thanks." Terry reeled off his telephone number.

"No, thank you, man. For years I thought my godmother's death would go unavenged, but with you looking into it, I know someone will pay."

Terry hung up. He hoped Javier was right. The oven buzzer whined; his dinner was ready.

• • •

The next morning, it was business as usual at Genavax. Terry watched Frosty delve into the bottom drawer that held the file he'd copied. He showed no signs of suspecting anything untoward, and a weight lifted from Terry's shoulders. He seemed to have gotten away with his crime, and he eased into his workday, but he eyed his phone frequently. Oscar should have called by now. He tried his number a couple of times throughout the day and got his voice mail. Eventually, he gave up trying. He perked up every time the phone rang, only to be disappointed when it turned out to be someone else.

Oscar didn't call until that night, when Terry was in front of the TV. "Where have you've been? I've been trying your cell all day."

"I've been tied up. It hasn't been as easy I thought getting the dope on these women. I've burned through my free minutes for the next six months."

"Are you home?"

"No, I'm about twenty miles north of Delano, in a motel. I can't drive anymore. I'm totally knackered."

Terry smiled. It wasn't been the first time Oscar slipped in some English slang. Terry had first noticed it worming its way into Oscar's speech on their road trip. He wasn't sure if Oscar was aware of the Britishisms sneaking into his conversation. It warmed Terry to think he was corrupting American society.

"What did you find out?"

Oscar was silent for a moment before answering. "Hope Maclean exposed corruption in the City of Delano as the *Bugle* claimed. Five members of the city council were convicted of embezzlement, but the mayor wasn't."

"Was he innocent?"

"No, he was the ringleader. He skipped bail."

"How did Hope Maclean die?"

"Do you need to ask?"

"Yes."

"Okay. Two months after the convictions, she had her throat cut and her tongue removed. They had a suspect but never made an arrest."

"Who was it?"

"The mayor. The cops were closing in on him, and he'd made threats toward Hope at the time. They found him in his car in a Fresno vineyard with a gunshot wound to the head. In their opinion, they had their man and closed the case."

No, this couldn't be right. If the mayor had killed Hope Maclean, that torpedoed Terry's theory that the same person had killed all the women on Sarah's list. He didn't accept that. The Delano cops were wrong.

"Did they have a suicide note? Did he confess?"

"Hard to say. The note was vague, saying things like I am responsible. I am guilty of all crimes. Stuff like that. Nothing that actually said it was me, here are where the bodies are buried, yadda, yadda, yadda."

"He didn't do it."

"I know. It can't be a coincidence."

"How did you find all this out?"

"I got friendly with the city clerk. She gave me all I needed to know over a long lunch."

"How long a lunch?" Terry teased.

"Long enough."

"Okay, I won't pry. What about Christy Richmond?"

"That's what ate up all my time. I couldn't find any record of her. She wasn't in Anaheim. The cops weren't too cooperative for obvious reasons. They didn't want me poking into their dark past, seeing as she fingered four of their own."

"Did they want to know why you were asking?"

"Yeah, but I came up with some cover story and made like Carl Lewis. I did find out about her, but it wasn't easy. She led a life where you don't leave a forwarding address."

Oscar went into unpleasant details about how he'd descended into the seedy side of California life, chatting up hookers to see if anyone remembered Christy Richmond. But prostitutes were like milk—none of them had a long shelf life. There were no career hookers in Anaheim dating back longer than a tomato season.

While making a nuisance of himself, he'd run into a nasty pimp. The pimp knew Christy, and for another chunk of cash Oscar got a little piece of history.

"Jesus, I'm sorry to have gotten you mixed up in this stuff."

"Don't be stupid. It was my choice…and to be honest, it was exciting."

"That kind of excitement can get you killed."

"But it didn't."

"Okay, Dirty Harry, if she wasn't in Anaheim, where did she go?"

"Well, the cops didn't make it easy for Christy after the conviction, and she moved to LA, then Hollywood. She was murdered in April 2002—found in a Dumpster with her throat cut and her tongue missing. Because she had no identification and Hollywood vice had never busted her, she was reported as a Jane Doe."

"How do you know the Jane Doe is Christy?"

"From her physical description and her distinguishing death. The cops never had anyone else killed in the same manner."

"Did they pin it on anyone?"

"Nah. They didn't put too much effort into finding her killer. She was a hooker, and they guessed either her pimp or a john had killed her. If they found someone who did, then great, but if they didn't, it was no great loss to them."

"Is that the way of the world these days?" Terry lamented.

"Unfortunately."

Terry exhaled and sank into the couch. Everyone on Sarah's list had been killed in the same horrific way. Had she been investigating this series of missing and murdered women only to realize she'd put herself on the hit list? Is that why she'd gone missing? Had the killer worked out she was onto him and snatched her? He hoped not, because if the killer had her, there was nothing anyone could do to save her. He prayed she was in hiding. He felt old, tired and defeated.

"I need to go, bud," Oscar said. "I can't keep my eyes open. I need some serious sleep. Maybe if I sleep on it, I'll be able to make more of the connection."

"What connection?"

"The connection between the women and Sarah. Why has the killer targeted Sarah?"

"Because she was investigating their deaths."

"Maybe, but think about this. Besides all these women having been murdered the same way, they have one other commonality."

"They were all whistle-blowers," Terry said.

"Give that man a *see*-gar."

"But I don't see a connection to Sarah."

"Come on, Sherlock, take the next big step."

The fog that had clouded Terry's thoughts lifted and an explanation presented itself. "Sarah blew the whistle on someone."

"Bingo! Find out who and we find the killer."

• • •

Around four the next afternoon, the heavens opened and the storm was only warming up by the time Terry got home from work. As he pulled into the garage, the wipers made a final sweep across the Monte's windshield, and Terry could see again. Up until then, the world had been a smeared vision of reality.

Terry stood at the entrance of his garage and watched the rain bounce off the street. Water pitter-pattered off the Chevy onto the garage floor. He found the storm comforting. It wasn't as if he hadn't seen a storm before, but according to all the tourist propaganda he'd ever seen, California was meant to be sunny 24-7. The unexpected rain made California fallible, just like him. He'd seen enough, and he hit the button to close the garage door.

He switched on the television. It didn't matter which channel. He was tired of coming home to a silent house. He just wanted the noise. He stretched out on the couch and watched the news. The weatherman was apologizing for the rain. From the onslaught he was taking from the news anchors, Terry expected the weatherman would have to commit ritual suicide for bringing such shame on the station.

You think your problems are bad, Terry thought, a rainstorm is nothing. All day, he'd been preoccupied with Oscar's revelation that Sarah might have blown the whistle on someone. Could her words have angered someone enough to incite them to kill her? He wanted to say no, but he knew that if you backed a person into a tight enough corner, there was no telling what they would do. Whoever she'd potentially offended, it had to be recent. Sarah's run-in with Pamela came to mind, but none of the women on Sarah's list appeared to be connected to Genavax. But that wasn't true. He'd seen Frosty at Myda Perez's hospital. Was there a connection there? He shook his head. The connotations were driving him crazy. They left him with more questions than answers. All he knew was there was a vindictive killer out there. That thought put a bleak complexion on the situation. The phone rang and he grabbed the handset in the kitchen.

"Terry Sheffield."

"Terry, it's Marcus Beasley. I got your message. You think you know why Sarah's missing?"

Terry had called Sarah's editor the night before, but had gotten the answering machine. He might not have the answers, but Marcus might.

"I think she's in hiding. Well, I hope she is. Someone's trying to kill her."

"What makes you think that?"

"Amongst Sarah's notes, I found a list of women's names. All of them are dead, and they were all murdered in the same way. Alicia Hyams was the fifth victim." Beasley tried to break in with a question, but Terry didn't let him and plowed on, theorizing that the women had been killed for exposing a scandal and Sarah was next because she was guilty of doing the same.

"And you're wondering if it's connected to one of her stories?" Beasley asked.

"Yes."

"I can see why you'd think that. I don't know her past work that well—it's all I can do to remember my own."

"Do you know anyone who would?"

"Let me call around, shake a few trees, and see what falls out."

"I'd appreciate the help."

"Have you tried Tom Degrasse?"

"No."

"Well, he knows Sarah pretty well. They swam in the same ponds. He might be able to help."

"I've got his number," Terry said, remembering the card the news reporter had given him at the coffee shop.

"I'll call you back as soon as I have something."

Terry hung up, fished out Degrasse's card from his wallet, and dialed the cell number. He got voice mail.

"Doesn't anyone answer their phone?" The recorded message ended and a beep sounded. "Tom, it's Terry Sheffield, Sarah Morton's husband. I think I know why Sarah is missing, and I need to know if one of her stories ever exposed an embarrassing scandal. Get back to me, please. Thanks." He left his number and hung up.

Turning his attention back to the television, he knew the reason why Tom Degrasse hadn't answered his phone. He was on the TV screen, reporting on a controversial new road project, while the top of the screen blinked the word, "LIVE."

Ten minutes later the phone rang. "Tom, that was quick. I didn't expect an answer so fast. I was just watching you."

"It's not Tom."

Terry couldn't speak. His thick and inflexible tongue stuck to the roof of his mouth, and his heart raced. The sound of water gurgled in his ears, but it wasn't the sound of the rain cascading down the windows he heard. Tears welled up in his eyes.

"Terry? Are you there?"

"Yes," he croaked. "I'm here, Sarah."

CHAPTER EIGHTEEN

"Miss me?" Sarah asked jovially.

Terry choked on the question, not knowing whether to laugh or scream. How could she be so lighthearted about it? He'd been living on his nerves for weeks wondering if she were alive or dead, and she was asking whether he missed her. Anger boiled up inside him. He wanted to let her have it, both barrels, but he couldn't. Just the sound of her voice left him ecstatic.

He thanked God she was alive and well. Her image, hazy until now, snapped into sharp focus. He remembered her every facet, her light brown hair with the natural blonde strands forever rising to the surface whenever she touched it and her storm-gray eyes that consumed him. He smiled, thinking of her slightly rounded tummy, which she thought made her look fat, but he thought looked cute. He had a wife, and he could be a husband at last. Everything he'd come to America for could begin. The nightmare was over.

"Where are you?"

"Close."

Very close, he thought. The rain that rat-a-tat-tatted off his windows did likewise wherever she was.

"Why don't you come home?"

"I can't."

"Why?"

"It's not safe."

"Come home, I can protect you."

"Terry, you don't know what I'm up against."

"I don't care. Come home. If I can't help you, I'll get the police."

She dismissed his suggestion. "The cops are in no position to help."

"Come home, Sarah. Please."

"No. I can't. I just wanted to say hi and let you know that I'm okay. I'll call you again when things are safe."

"Oh, no you don't." Did she really think she could get away with a quick hello and good-bye? "I want an explanation."

"I can't."

"Jesus, Sarah, stop saying you can't. From the moment I landed in this bloody country, I've been wondering where the hell you are. You owe me an explanation."

"I know I do."

He didn't give her time to answer. He wanted to get it all off his chest. The cork was out and all the fear, and he had to release all his bottled-up anger. He didn't care about the mess.

"Have you been watching the news at all? Have you?"

She stammered, grappling for a response.

"I've been in jail because of your disappearing act. First for breaking and entering, then for murder. People think I offed you, just like Alicia Hyams. And it all could have gone away if you'd made an appearance."

"I know what I've put you through and I'm sorry, but I couldn't. It wasn't safe. My hiding, my silence, was protecting you."

"Not good enough. You have no idea to what lengths I've gone to find you."

"I'm sorry, Terry."

"Why are you calling now? Why break your silence?"

"Guilt, fear, you name it. I'm scared and alone out here and I hate what I've put you through. And I miss your voice. I was thinking about all the times we spent on the phone just talking about our lives together and now you're here, but we're still not together."

"It doesn't have to be that way. Come home now or tell me where to find you and we'll go into hiding together, but don't shut me out."

"No, no, no. it isn't safe. I do see this coming to an end. Really I do. I want to let you know I'm close to ending this. Just be patient and don't worry."

"How can I not worry, Sarah? I love you."

He went to say more, but found he was done. There was no more mud left to fling. His heart stopped pounding, and he felt his pulse slow to normal. His grasp on the phone relaxed.

Neither of them spoke for a minute. Terry listened to the stereophonic rain outside the window and on the phone.

"I guess we just had our first fight," Sarah said.

He smiled. "I suppose we did."

"I'm sorry, Terry. I've treated you badly. But it had nothing to do with you. It's the story I'm working on. It just landed in my lap, and when it did, I had to go for it. You were just caught in the middle. Bad timing, that's all."

"Sarah, is that how it's going to be every time? A story falls in your lap and you drop everything, including me?"

"You don't understand."

"I'll admit it, I don't."

"My work is important to me, Terry. Surely you see that."

"And I'm not important, is that it?"

"Now you're just twisting my words."

Maybe his friends back in England were right. He was too wrapped up in the romance of an international love affair to think straight. A whirlwind marriage with someone he hardly knew was a mistake. They would be hammering the point home if they knew what had been going on. Terry felt as dumb as they thought he was. He knew his relationship with Sarah might be rough and might not work, but he hated to think they were on the rocks already.

"If you love me, you'll come home," he said.

Her reply would either steer them aground or into safe waters.

"Because I love you, I won't."

"Sarah."

"Terry, this story could cost you your life. Five women are dead."

"I know."

"How?" She didn't hide her surprise.

"I found your notes."

"Then you know that I'm in danger. I'm not trying to be a heartless bitch, just a good wife. This story is big, but at the same time it's deadly, and I would never forgive myself if you got hurt."

"Sarah, I'm willing to take that chance. I want to be involved. Dammit, I am involved."

"No, you'll come to understand that I'm right."

"Tell me why these women were killed."

"It's complicated."

"Then tell me why the killer blames you."

"What?" Her voice trembled.

"You exposed someone. Who was it?"

"How do you know that?"

"Because those dead women exposed people, and you're a reporter—that's your job."

Sarah's phone picked up the noise of a car roaring past. "I've got to go."

"Give me your number?"

"I'll call you."

"Sarah, don't do this to me. Please give me your number."

"Speak to you soon." She was trying to sound as if nothing was wrong, but she failed. Her voice cracked. Tears weren't far away.

"Sarah, don't."

She wasn't listening. The investigative journalist in her took over. "I'll call soon."

"Sarah!" he shouted, but she'd hung up.

. . .

"Dude, you're wet," Oscar said, closing Terry's front door.

After Sarah's call, Terry had been angry with her for hanging up on him. He'd cooled off by standing in the rain, and he hadn't bothered to towel himself off.

"Sarah called," he said in a flat tone, all emotion drained from him.

"When?"

Noticing that he was dripping on the floor and a chill was seeping in, Terry tugged his shirt off and pulled out a towel from a closet. "About half an hour ago."

Oscar followed him to the closet. "Where is she?"

"She wouldn't say." Terry toweled off his hair and face.

"Why?"

"Too dangerous."

Oscar frowned.

"Yeah, well, that's how I feel about it too," Terry admitted.

"Did she leave a number?"

Terry shook his head and tossed the towel in the bathroom sink.

"What did she call for, then?" Oscar asked.

"Just to let me know she was okay." Terry went into the bedroom to put on a dry T-shirt.

"She should have thought of that a few weeks ago. What else did she say?"

"She said she was lying low because of the five murders."

"So we were right."

Terry nodded. "I asked her why the killer blamed her."

"What did she say to that?"

"Not much, but she didn't tell me I was talking crazy."

"What are you going to do now?"

Terry exhaled and shrugged. "Don't know."

"You should call Holman. He'll be able to find her."

"Will he want to?"

"At least it'll get him off your back. He'll stop thinking you have something to do with her disappearance."

"Yeah, but it's not like I can tell him anything."

"There are phone records he can check to prove someone called."

Terry shook his head. He couldn't call Holman. That made him a snitch. Sarah wanted her anonymity. And yet he knew Oscar was right. This was his first big test of their marriage, and he was about to fail it. If Holman took him seriously, maybe he could succeed where Terry had failed so far. What did it matter if she didn't get her story as long as she was safe and well? He found the cordless phone and dialed.

"Sheriff Holman, please."

CHAPTER NINETEEN

The following morning, Pamela Dawson took Terry by surprise when she touched him on the shoulder. He was totally engrossed in his work.

"Could I have a word?" she asked, smiling.

The saccharine tone again. That wasn't a good sign. "Sure," Terry said.

"Come with me."

She led him to a small conference room and held the door open for him. Frosty was there, sitting at one end of the conference table, a ring binder in front of him. He attempted a smile. It was a decent effort, but he didn't quite pull it off. Pamela closed and locked the door.

Terry stared at her hand on the lock, then at her.

"I don't want to be disturbed. Have a seat."

Terry sat down on the opposite side of the table from Frosty. Pamela bridged the gap by sitting at the head of the table. She smiled. She did better than Frosty, but only marginally. Terry didn't like where this meeting was going.

"Terry," Pamela began in a frank business tone. "I would like to talk about you, us"—she indicated to herself and Frosty—"and Genavax."

"My six-month review isn't for some time." It was an obtuse thing to say, but he wanted to play dumb.

"That's right," Pamela agreed. "But we want to skip past that, if you're agreeable?"

Terry shrugged.

"We see big things for you, Terry," Frosty said, giving him the chance to dispense with the smile.

"Good," Terry managed without the enthusiasm the compliment deserved.

"That's right, Terry," Pamela said. "We see you as an integral part of the Genavax operation." She interlaced her fingers, palms up.

The hand gesture reminded Terry of the "here's the church, here's the steeple" nursery rhyme he'd been taught during his first year of school. He'd always found the little party trick fun when he was a kid, but Pamela spoiled his childhood memories.

"Genavax likes to look after its more important employees," Frosty said.

"Is that right?" Terry asked.

"That's why we would like to promote you to senior scientist," Pamela announced proudly.

"Here are the terms and conditions." Frosty pushed the binder over to Terry.

Terry eyed his gift with suspicion. His name and proposed job title straddled a large Genavax logo on the cover. For a standard job contract the binder was overkill, but unlike a normal employer's contract, this one was over half an inch thick.

He flipped it open. After a pretty cover page was his new job title, enhanced salary, job description, and bonus scheme. His proposed job required him to do no more than he was doing now. In fact, it required less. It seemed most of his job would be done for him by other people. Ignoring the generous bonus, he was looking at an extra twenty thousand dollars a year. After a brief terms and conditions section came the meat of the contract— a privacy and confidentiality clause. It was twenty pages long. Even scanning the pages briefly, he could tell it wasn't actually a privacy and confidentiality clause. It was a secrecy clause, forbidding him from divulging any of Genavax's operations and promising the full force of the law if he did. They were buying his silence. He closed the binder.

"What is this all about?" he asked.

"It's a reward," Pamela said. "A show of appreciation for your hard work, if you will." She tapped the neatly packaged thirty pieces of silver. "It's a very good offer."

"I don't get it."

"What is there to get?" Frosty said. "Just take the offer."

"I've been here less than a month."

"So?" Pamela said.

"Don't you think the rest of the lab is going to think it's odd?"

"And that bothers you?" Frosty asked.

"It does a bit." Terry turned to Pamela. "A week ago, you threatened to sack me."

"And that would have been a mistake." She tried to smile the accusation away.

Terry had to be careful here. Pamela was pushing him into a corner. He knew Genavax was dirty and that Pamela and Frosty were just as tainted, but he didn't have all the answers he required to take action. He needed to buy himself time.

"Well, first off, thank you for this show of faith. I really appreciate it."

"You're welcome," Pamela said.

"Is it okay if I go through this and get back to you?"

"Why?" Frosty asked.

"Ideally, I'd discuss this with my wife first. As you both know, she's still missing; and I'll be honest, finding her is my first priority."

It was a nice bit of verbal gymnastics on Terry's part that silenced both Pamela and Frosty. It put them to a decision—push and risk forcing Terry's hand or back down. Terry didn't think they'd go for the former.

"You might as well sign now," Frosty said, "and get it out of the way so you can focus on your wife. Sarah, right?"

Terry was impressed with Frosty's subtle piece of arm twisting, but the suggestion drew a disparaging look from Pamela.

No overstepping your mark, Frosty, Terry thought. "I'd like to hold off, if I can."

"Of course you can," Pamela said. "Totally understandable."

Terry smiled, grabbed the offer, and stood. "Thanks. I really appreciate it."

"Just one thing," Pamela said. "There is a time limit on this offer. We need your signature soon. You understand, don't you?"

Terry did. He guessed he'd reached the point of no return.

• • •

Arriving home, Terry found the answering machine loaded with messages. He hit PLAY.

"Terry, Tom Degrasse." His tone was clipped and businesslike. "I don't know anything. Can't help. Sorry."

That was succinct to the point of nonexistence, Terry thought.

Beep!

"Mr. Sheffield, this is Sheriff Holman." His tone was as clipped as Degrasse's. "Just wanted to let you know I'm working with Pacific Bell to assist with tracing the call you received last night from Sarah. If you could let me know if she makes contact with you again, it would be greatly appreciated. Thank you."

Beep!

"Terry, it's Jake," the sheriff's son announced. "Just seeing when you're free, pal. Call me."

"You are far too needy, my friend," Terry said to Jake's overly chirpy voice.

Beep!

"This is Javier Rivera, Terry. Abuelita Perez doesn't remember Myda mentioning Genavax. Sorry."

It was all dead ends, but not a surprise. He was getting used to it. Not that their information mattered much. Sarah wasn't missing anymore. But was that true? She was alive and well, but she wasn't home. He replayed the messages, deleting them one by one.

Terry's finger hovered over the erase button when Tom Degrasse's message played again. He didn't erase the message and pressed the skip button instead. Beasley had suggested Degrasse and Sarah were close, so why was Degrasse's message such a big brush-off? The phone rang.

"Oh good, you're there. It's Marcus."

"Hi, Marcus."

"I thought I'd give you some news from the trenches. I've been putting some feelers out about Sarah's past triumphs. So far no one seems to remember anything of great importance. But that's not surprising. Laskey, the executive editor at the *Chronicle*, is a hack, and he wouldn't know a story if it shook hands with him. Did you know that when Watergate broke, he said it wasn't newsworthy? The *Examiner* people weren't much better, but I've pissed off a few of the editors in my time. Scooped their scoops and that sort of thing. I'm waiting for some of the TV people to get back. Tomorrow, I'll probably move the search out farther afield to Southern Cal and such. I know she knows some of the *LA Times* boys and girls. La-la land—why she went down there, I'll never know." Beasley paused. "I seem to be going on, don't I?"

"Just a bit, Marcus," Terry agreed.

"Rest assured, my friend, I will keep digging."

"There's not much need," Terry said, preempting a further wandering exchange.

"Why?"

"Sarah called."

"Is she there? Can I speak to her?"

"No, she's not here. She wants to remain in hiding."

"When's she calling back?"

"I wish I knew."

Beasley sighed, going silent for a moment. "Did she say what this is all about?"

"No, we didn't get that far."

"Damn."

"The other night you said Sarah and Tom Degrasse were close."

"That's right. Why?"

"He left a pissy message saying he didn't know anything. And when I met him he didn't have much in the way of compliments for Sarah." Terry went to the fridge and poured himself a glass of juice. "Does that sound odd to you?"

"I don't know what to tell you, Terry. I know they were colleagues once."

"He never mentioned that."

"Maybe there's a reason why."

Beasley's remark implied an office tiff, but Terry wondered if it was more—a grudge maybe.

"Marcus, do you know where I could find Tom at this time of night?"

"At his restaurant."

"His restaurant?"

"He bought into some fancy California cuisine place near Union Square. He always finishes his day there. He likes to use his fame to put butts on seats."

"Do you know what it's called?"

"I'm trying to remember. What did he call the damn place? It was something meaningless. Oh, I remember. It's called Rendezvous. It's on the corner of Bush and Powell."

"Sounds like a place a hungry man would go. Thanks, Marcus."

Terry hung up and grabbed his car keys. Reversing out of the garage, he thought better of his actions. He left the Monte running, half in the garage and half on the driveway, and raced back into the house. He stuffed all his notes on Sarah's women and the photocopied Genavax records into an envelope. His home had already been broken into, and evidence had been both stolen and planted. This time, he wasn't taking any chances. He needed a different hiding place.

When Terry pulled into the Gold Rush's parking lot, Oscar was closing for the night. A couple of the teenagers working for him were ushering kids out the door and shutting off the machines. Oscar was on the golf courses emptying the trashcans into a larger can on a cart. He saw Terry and smiled.

"Hey, buddy."

"Oscar, I need a favor." Terry held out the envelope. "Will you put this somewhere safe?"

"Of course." Oscar took the envelope and peered inside. "What is it?"

"It's everything we've dug up on the women on Sarah's list and the human testing stuff from Genavax."

"Why do you want me to hold on to it?"

"The stakes are being raised. Genavax knows I made copies. They tried to buy me off today."

"You shouldn't be giving me this. You should give it to Holman."

"I want to give it to Sarah."

"Has she called again?"

"No."

"I'm in no position to tell you about marital affairs, but…"

"Then don't."

Oscar frowned and shook his head. Terry knew what his friend was going to say. He was wasting his time on a woman who didn't have the courtesy to come out from the shadows when he was being accused of murder. He knew, because he'd thought the same thing. He might be a fool, but he still loved Sarah.

"Just let me do what I have to."

"Buddy, you're setting yourself up again."

"If you don't want to help, I understand."

"It's not that, pal. I'm just not sure how many more times I'll be able to help you."

"I can't do this any other way."

Oscar nodded. "I know. I'll look after this."

"Thanks." Terry smiled and backed away.

"I'll be finished up here soon," Oscar called after Terry. "Stay, we'll catch some dinner."

"I can't, I already have a dinner date."

• • •

Terry found Rendezvous more easily than he expected, but parking was another matter. He had to leave the Monte three blocks away.

From the outside, Rendezvous was understated. Its corner location was good for picking up passing trade. The blue neon sign was bright but tasteful, and the brick facade and wrought-iron finishing made the establishment stand out against the surrounding concrete and stucco. A doorman who looked more like a bouncer held the door open for Terry as he stepped inside.

The décor was style conscious. There was a preciseness to everything from the tables to the place settings. The place would have possessed a clinical feel, if it weren't for the warm color palate used to soften the edges. A tall and attractive hostess greeted him with a smile.

"Welcome to Rendezvous."

Terry smiled back. "Thanks. Is Tom Degrasse here?"

Her smile faltered. "No."

"I know he likes to keep a watchful eye over his pride and joy." Terry maintained his smile to make up for her shortfall. "When do you expect him?"

The hostess's gaze flitted from Terry to the doorman. "Is he expecting you?"

Terry understood her apprehension. He guessed it wasn't the first time she had a rabid fan clamoring for an audience with the great reporter. And he doubted any amount of explaining would help.

"He's a friend of the family. He and my wife work together."

She didn't look convinced.

"Do you have a reservation?"

"Afraid not."

She replied with a pained smile. "We're fully booked."

Terry cocked his head to one side to see a half-empty restaurant. "Too bad."

"We are very popular."

"Do you serve meals at the bar?"

"Yes."

"Good. I'll eat at the bar, then."

"Oh." She hesitated for the briefest moment before picking up a menu and escorting him to the bar. "He doesn't always come in," the hostess said, handing Terry a menu.

"I'll take my chances."

The hostess told him to enjoy his meal and returned to the reception area.

"What can I get you?" the barman asked.

"Just a lemonade."

"Designated driver?"

"Something like that."

"A lemonade for the designated driver coming right up," he said and tapped a hand on the polished bar.

Terry turned his gaze back to the hostess. She'd deserted her post and was talking to the doorman outside. The barman placed the lemonade in front of Terry. The hostess and the doorman glanced over at him. Terry raised his drink to them.

The barman said something.

"Huh?"

"Are you waiting for a table?"

"No, I'll be eating here at the bar."

"Then I'll be your waitress this evening," he said.

Terry scanned the menu for something appetizing. It boasted fancy fonts and even fancier descriptions, all of it enticing.

"I'd like a Caesar salad and the ahi, but can I substitute garlic mashed potatoes for the rice?"

"You got it," the barman said, taking the menu. He handed Terry's order to a passing waiter.

Terry's salad came and it was still a game of furtive glances between the hostess, the doorman, and him, but no one was making a play to remove him. Maybe they were waiting to see if he would get bored. He wouldn't.

"You waiting for someone?" the barman asked, making a cocktail.

"What makes you say that?"

"You've had your eyes glued to the front door since you sat down."

"I'm waiting for your celebrity owner."

"Tom Degrasse?" The barman placed the cocktail on the bar for the waitstaff to pick up, then he threw together another concoction. "He came in about fifteen minutes before you arrived."

"Is he still here?"

"Oh, yeah. He won't be gone until we close."

Terry smiled at the hostess's deception. She did her job well. No one could blame her for that.

"Could you get him for me?"

The barman shrugged. "I can try."

A breath of night air blew across Terry. The doorman headed toward him. The hostess looked worried for someone. Terry wondered for whom.

"Hold that thought, friend," Terry said. "I think Tom knows I'm here."

Terry smiled at the doorman. He leaned in close to Terry's ear, placing a thick hand on the bar.

"Excuse me, sir," he said calmly and quietly. "I believe you're waiting for Mr. Degrasse?"

"I am."

"It doesn't look like he's coming in tonight."

"I know for a fact that Tom is here as we speak."

The doorman aimed a disapproving glance at the barman. The barman stared right back, not exhibiting a hint of fear or embarrassment.

"Sir, we don't need any trouble."

"Neither do I."

"Good. Then why don't you settle your check and leave?"

"After I've spoken to Tom."

Unimpressed, the doorman sniffed. It was obvious he didn't like Terry using Degrasse's first name or his lack of compliance with his request. A vein in the doorman's temple pulsed.

"Sir, don't force me to make an embarrassing scene."

"Don't force me to shout at the top of my voice that there is a cockroach sharing my salad. And believe me, I brought one with me for such an occasion."

The doorman's face blackened. The vein spasmed.

"Now get Tom. Tell him it's Terry Sheffield. There's a good chap."

The doorman straightened and headed toward a door marked PRIVATE. The barman smirked.

"Do you really have a cockroach?"

"No."

He grinned. "That was slick."

A couple of minutes later, the doorman returned, but didn't stop to speak to Terry. He kept on going and returned to his post at the front door, ignoring the hostess's questions.

Terry's ahi arrived and a minute later so did Tom Degrasse.

"You wanted to talk, so let's talk. Follow me."

"What about my dinner?"

"I'll have it brought over."

The dining area was L-shaped. Terry followed Degrasse into a secluded corner of the restaurant. They wouldn't be overheard in the booth Degrasse chose. Other tables were close, but no one was seated within a three-table radius. A waitress brought Terry's meal after they were seated. Degrasse declined a drink.

"This is excellent," Terry said after his first bite.

Without much enthusiasm Degrasse said, "Our chef is one of the finest in California."

"No argument here."

When the waitress was out of earshot he said, "Okay, you've got my attention. What do you want?"

"I want to find Sarah."

"I told you I can't help you."

Terry put his fork down. "I find that hard to believe, seeing as you two were such close buddies."

Degrasse stiffened and leaned back. "Who told you that?"

"Does it matter?"

Degrasse said nothing.

"Sarah called yesterday," Terry said.

"Then what are you doing wasting my time?"

"Because she won't come out of hiding, and I want to know what you know about it."

"Nothing."

"Are you sure?"

"Yes."

Terry smiled. "You seemed to have all the answers in the coffee shop. Now, you know nothing. You barely left ten words on my answering machine. Are you two working on this story together?"

"No."

"I don't believe you. Convince me."

Degrasse huffed and gestured to a passing waiter. "I'll have a Jack Daniels on the rocks and whatever he wants."

Terry tapped his glass. "I'll have another lemonade, thanks."

The reporter didn't say anything until the waiter returned with the drinks. Terry didn't mind. It gave him time to savor his dinner. Degrasse didn't rely on his celebrity status to pull in the punters. He let the food do the talking for him.

Degrasse shot back his bourbon. "Many years ago, Sarah and I worked for the *Examiner*. We were both hungry and hoping for that one story that would get us a plum job with the *LA Times*, *Newsweek*, or whatever. We were both good, and it was a constant battle to outdo each other. We both wanted to be number one in the chief editor's eyes. After two years of sparring with each other, we ended up working different ends of a big story, so we combined forces. It was the first and last time we worked with each other."

He went quiet and stared at the ice melting in his Jack Daniels. Recollection knotted his face. Disgusted, he polished off what was left of his drink in one swallow.

"Why was it your last collaboration?"

"Sarah stiffed me."

Rendezvous's food was second to none, but Terry wanted to jam the plate in the TV reporter's face for trashing his wife's name. His good manners restrained him.

"How?"

"I told you Sarah liked to pull stunts, didn't I?"

Terry chose not to acknowledge the remark and swigged his lemonade instead.

"We had our story, and we were going to be there as part of a police sting operation. We had clearance, or so I thought. Sarah neglected to forward my name to the cops. When the moment came, Sarah went in, and I was detained until the story was in the bag. Sarah got the front page and an offer from the *Chronicle*. I got the shaft."

Terry indicated the restaurant with his fork. "You haven't done too badly with the setback."

Degrasse's smile was bitter and cruel. "Let's say Sarah was my inspiration not to let a setback be a disadvantage."

"What was the story?"

"Ten officers from the Oakland port authority were smuggling in illegal immigrants and drugs. The story changed port authority procedure."

Terry wasn't swallowing Degrasse's story. He didn't doubt the story's authenticity, but something didn't ring true. Degrasse exuded something more than bitterness.

"So what does that have to do with Sarah's disappearing act?"

Degrasse shrugged. "Not much. But it gives you insight into Sarah. I hope that helps."

It didn't. Degrasse's sob story was a fluff piece, nothing more.

"If you'll excuse me, I have some business to attend to. Don't worry about the check. It's on me." Degrasse rose to leave.

"What is it you're not telling me?"

Degrasse retook his seat. "You really want to know?"

"Yes."

"You won't let it go, will you?"

Terry shook his head.

"Are all English people as bullheaded as you?"

"You'll have to ask them."

Degrasse snorted. "Okay, don't say I didn't warn you."

"Just tell me."

"Sarah and I were lovers."

CHAPTER TWENTY

Terry drove with the Monte's window down. The chilled night air whipped his face as the Chevy raced across the Bay Bridge. He couldn't have been more wrong about Tom Degrasse if he'd tried. He felt such a fool for getting the wrong end of the stick.

Once Degrasse had admitted his affair with Sarah, he let his guard down and held nothing back. He and Sarah had been an item until she cut him out of the port authority piece. But their separation didn't last long. Neither of them could ignore their attraction for the other, and a series of casual flings had ensued. He admitted Sarah had finally broken things off for good.

Their final breakup had occurred the month before Terry met Sarah in Costa Rica. Degrasse had tried to revive their affair when she returned, but Sarah had rejected him for good once she had Terry in her life. It relieved Terry to hear that. At least she'd been faithful. The Bay Bridge came to an end and Terry pushed the gas pedal a little harder.

A disturbing thought scratched at the back of his mind. It hadn't bothered him at the time. The embarrassment he'd felt during Degrasse's revelation had blurred his concentration, but in the seclusion of his car with nothing but the Monte's engine whine and the wind flapping through the window, it occurred to him. Degrasse's preoccupation with Sarah bordered on the obsessive. He remembered the intensity in the reporter's eyes and the passion in his voice when he spoke of the moment he had realized he'd lost Sarah forever. Terry shivered and rolled up the window.

He replayed his conversation with Degrasse over and over in his mind. Each time, he tried to recall anything strange. The traffic thinned after the Carquinez Bridge and his foot squashed the accelerator into the carpet. He wanted to get home as quickly as he could—or did he just want to get away?

The phone was ringing when he arrived home. It was Sarah.

"Where have you been?" she demanded. "I've been calling all night."

He checked his watch. It was after ten. "I went out for dinner."

He decided not to tell her about meeting with Tom Degrasse, especially now that he knew about their past. It was something she should tell him about. Something to be shared during a carefree moment, not when she was hiding for her life.

"Are you coming home?" he asked.

"I can't. It's still too dangerous."

"Jesus, Sarah, I don't want to have this same telephone conversation every time you call."

"Terry, I've explained. I can't come home."

"Christ, you make it sound like a Tom Clancy novel."

She didn't dignify his snide remark with an answer. "I'm calling because I want you to know I'm okay, and when I have this story cracked, I'll come back home."

She made everything he'd endured sound like no big deal.

"And when do you think you'll have this story cracked?" he demanded.

"I don't know."

"Sarah, you can't keep expecting to me to live like this."

"Like what?"

"Honey, I'll be back soon. Our marriage is in the oven. Keep it warm until I get back."

"I thought you'd be supportive."

I would be, he thought, *if I knew what was going on.* He was tired of arguing.

"The cops know you're not missing."

"You told them?" An arctic breath followed her words.

"I had to."

"Terry, you don't know what you've done."

"You're right, I don't, because you won't tell me."

"Is this phone tapped?"

"Of course not."

"Are you sure?"

Terry couldn't imagine Holman having the resources to have organized and installed wiretaps in twenty-four hours. Besides, he would have needed a warrant and it seemed unlikely for a missing person's case, especially since Sarah wasn't a missing person anymore. He didn't know what to call her now.

"I know the phone isn't tapped."

"You're probably right, but I can't take any chances. I won't call back again until this is all over."

"You can't do this to me."

"You did it to yourself. You called the cops, not me."

"Meet me somewhere, Sarah."

She hesitated for a moment. "Give me your cell number. I'll call you tomorrow to arrange a time and place."

He gave her the number. "You will call, won't you?"

"Yes. But you've got to promise me you won't tell anyone."

"I promise. Scout's honor," he said, trying to lighten the mood.

Sarah hung up.

Terry exhaled. He was finally going to see his wife.

• • •

Sarah was true to her word and phoned him. He'd wondered if she'd really call. His ringing cell in the lab drew everyone's attention.

"Are you alone?" she asked.

A hello would nice, he thought. "No, but I can be."

He got up from his workbench and headed out of the lab. He spotted Pamela eyeing him with disapproval. He pretended not to see and kept on going. He left the building for the parking lot.

"I'm somewhere quiet," he said when he was outside.

"Do you know the Sunset Mall in Fairfield?"

It was a twenty-five minute drive from Genavax, but Terry would get there in ten if he had to. "Yes."

"Good. Meet me there at six tonight."

"Where?"

"Do you know the food court between the Barnes and Noble and the theater?"

"Yes."

"Wait for me outside the Mexican restaurant."

"I can't wait to see you."

"Me too." There was real affection in her words. Up until then, she'd been abrupt and businesslike. Now she was herself. The Sarah he knew. "I'll see you later."

Terry spent the rest of the day suppressing his excitement. He couldn't afford for Pamela or Frosty to guess that he was going to see her. He spent the day working on a speech that would force Sarah into coming home with him. Before he knew it five o'clock came and went. All he had to do was put his microtiter trays in the freezer and he was out of there. He checked his watch. It was 5:25 p.m. There was still plenty of time to get to the mall. He carried his rack over to the freezer and propped the door open with the wedge before walking inside. The arctic chill struck him, but not as much as the sound of the freezer door closing behind him.

"Hey, I'm still in here," Terry shouted and banged on the door.

He sounded good, not an ounce of panic in his voice. The door closing on him was an accident. Things like this happened from time to time. The sensible and rational Terry told himself these things, but too much had happened for him to be sensible. The new Terry didn't believe for one second that the wedge had popped out by accident or that someone hadn't realized he was inside and closed the door. He knew the moment the door slammed shut that someone had closed it on purpose.

Pamela or Frosty did this. They couldn't bribe Terry, so they were trying to kill him. He'd felt the vibe change after their botched payoff attempt. Pamela had asked him about signing the contract twice more after their meeting, but she'd let the matter drop. He'd searched for any other packages from the children's hospital and found nothing. They were covering their tracks and that included him.

Terry wasn't dead yet. If Pamela and Frosty wanted to kill him, they should have chosen a faster method. Freezing to death took time. Security was still on duty. A couple of guys in shipping and production worked late most nights. A few of the managers stayed through 6:00 p.m. All he needed was just one to come into the lab and hear him. Just one.

"Hey, I'm in here." His plea materialized as vapor. Like him, it went nowhere, blooming before him then dissipating into nothing.

His screams were pointless. The freezer was heavily insulated to keep the heat out, but worked just as well at keeping voices in. He was just wasting precious energy. In the short time the door had been closed the temperature had tumbled. The oppressive cold was already surrounding him, squeezing through his pores. His lab coat, a polo shirt, and chinos offered little protection. He probably had no more than thirty minutes before the arctic conditions got the better of him, but considering how he could already feel the freezer drawing the heat from his body, he thought the cold would kill him faster than that.

He'd never make it through to morning when his coworkers returned to the lab. He had to break his way out. There was no way he could beat on the door. The freezer walls were bare metal and he hadn't worn his protective gauntlets. If he touched the walls, the skin would be torn from his flesh. He kicked the door, placing a shoe heel where the door lock would be. He kicked again.

And again.

Every well-placed kick deformed the aluminum lining around the door. Each impact left a black rubber skid mark from his Doc Martens. Spurred on by his success, he kicked and kicked, lashing the door with ferocious energy.

But with every well-placed kick, Terry sucked in lungs full of arctic air. The freezing air clawed at his insides, burning like acid as it rushed down his throat. After two dozen well-delivered kicks, he stopped. The door's inner lining had buckled, but it hadn't broken.

He bent over, resting his hands on his knees and wheezing like an asthmatic. His chest bound up with each breath. The cold spread out from his lungs and wormed its way into his veins. His body seemed to be aging a decade with every minute.

Brute strength wasn't going to save him. Physics would. He needed a tool to bust the door open. But what was there in the freezer he could use? Like old Mother Hubbard's cupboard, the freezer was bare—except for the storage racks. The plastic trays were useless, but the steel racks had potential.

Like the freezer walls, Terry couldn't touch the metal racks. He tore off his lab coat, and with the help of his door key as a makeshift knife, he ripped off the sleeves and bound his hands.

Ignoring the value of the experiments frozen in suspension in the trays, Terry knocked over one of the racks. It clattered to the ground. Half the trays spilled out across the floor, frozen tissue samples and peptides exploding from the compartments.

Yanking out the remaining trays, he hoisted the rack free of the carnage. Raising it as high as he could, Terry smashed the rack onto the floor on its corner. The rack buckled, losing its box shape. He raised and smashed it on the ground again and again, ignoring the tingling shooting through his arms, until the rack splintered. The frame broke into three pieces, exposing the L-shaped runners the trays rested on. The runners weren't fully welded, only tacked at the corners. From the tangled wreckage, he twisted one off. He had to stand on the frame to break the final weld, but it came away easily.

Using the runner as a crowbar, he jammed it into the narrow gap between the freezer door and doorframe. It took three blows to wedge it into the gap. He worked the runner back and forth until it was good and tight before he heaved on his makeshift crowbar. It popped out of the gap without any effect on the door. He cursed.

Although his hands were bandaged in the sleeves from his lab coat, he held the runner so tightly the frozen metal scorched his palms. It didn't deter him. Without pause, he smashed the runner into the gap again. He leaned on it to spring the door. It popped out of the joint again. He tried again and again to force the door. Each time he failed, only succeeding in breaking the freezer's aluminum skin and exposing its insulation.

He changed his approach and used the runner as a spade. He dug away at the layers of insulation. He belched white vapor like a broken steam pipe, obscuring his view of what he was doing. The insulation came away easily, exposing the lock. He smashed at the mechanism in the hope of busting it and pushing the door open, but the lock was not as feeble as the aluminum sheathing. Terry's repeated blows failed to make an impact, and the frustration that had fueled him now drained him.

His blunted tool tumbled from his trembling hand. The cold had ahold of him, and he shook violently from head to toe. His fingers were claws, no longer able to grip anything his hands commanded. He glimpsed his reflected image in the polished surface of the freezer. It was distorted, not just by the warped imperfections of the aluminum sheeting, but by the cold. His sweat had frozen to his face, and frost dusted his hair and eyebrows. Tiny icicles hung from his bangs. He was a wretched figure.

It was a mercy when the light went out, plunging him into darkness. The freezer's florescent lighting was on a timer. Terry had used up the generous fifteen-minute time limit since opening the door. Fifteen minutes was a luxury for the simple task of putting away samples, but locked inside, the time allowance was a pittance. His only light source now was a dim glow coming off the luminescent numerals on his wristwatch. But he didn't need his watch to tell him the significance of the lights going out. He'd reached the halfway point of succumbing to the cold. In another fifteen minutes, his core body temperature would drop below the point of no return. At least it wouldn't hurt when the time came. Hyperthermia was kind in that respect. It was a quiet and painless death.

He scrabbled in the dark for his lost crowbar. He found the strewn trays, the racks, the floor, but not his makeshift tool. Not that he was sure he was touching what he thought he was. His hands were sensing muffled versions of the objects, as if they were wrapped in a blanket. The worst part was that he was no longer detecting the cold itself. His hands should have been screaming at him, but they weren't. Everything felt soda-can cold.

He gave up on finding his makeshift crowbar and searched instead for the broken rack and a new crowbar. He managed to tear off another runner. He tried again to bust open the lock, but in the dark, he had no idea what he was hitting. Arthritic with cold, he gave up.

Shaking so badly he couldn't control his limbs, he collapsed to his knees. He needed to keep warm. Palsied hands felt for his discarded lab coat and found it. It was frozen to the floor. He tore his coat from the floor and slipped the stiff material around his shoulders. Eventually, it softened to mold to his shape. He let his jaw go slack to prevent his teeth from bashing together.

He tried to keep warm by walking in place, but it wasn't working. His footfalls sent screaming jolts of agony through his bones into his groin, forcing him to stop. He wanted to sit, but he couldn't. The cold would get to him that little bit quicker. Eventually, he lacked the energy to remain upright and he sank slowly to his knees, hugging himself to keep what remaining body heat he had.

Time either sped past or crept by. It was impossible to tell. He felt he'd spent as much time in the dark as he had in the light, but he couldn't be sure. He tried checking his watch, but the humidity inside the casing had frozen and glazed over the face. Not that he could read his watch anyway; his ability to focus his gaze was intermittent.

At some point, he'd stopped shivering. He couldn't remember when. He felt neither cold nor warm, just uncomfortable in his own skin, and unbelievably tired. He wondered if the freezer was broken and was warming up, but he knew he was deluding himself. He knew shivering was the body's way of heating itself. When the body stopped shivering, it was time to worry. Hypothermia was setting in. Or was it exposure? He couldn't remember if they were the same thing or completely different. His brain was shutting down. He could feel his intelligence slipping away.

He had to keep his mind active. He couldn't let it hibernate, so he tried to remember his times tables. He managed his twos okay. His threes were a struggle. His fours were a disaster.

"Six fours are twenty...twenty...er. Dammit, six fours are twenty-six. No. Not twenty-six, twenty-four. Bollocks to the times tables."

He was wasting his time. He couldn't think straight. All he was doing was giving himself a headache. He had to think about something he cared about, like Sarah. He let his mind drift to Sarah and what he was going to say to her when he saw her again. He wanted to tell her how much he loved her and what she meant to him. He wanted to say, "I don't care how dangerous the story is, I just want to be by your side every step of the way." If she needed protecting, then he would be her protector. He'd promised to be that in his wedding vows, hadn't he? A hazy memory seeped in. They'd joked about it at the time, but it wasn't funny anymore. She needed a protector, and he wanted to live up to his vow.

"I'll be your knight in shining armor, Sarah," he said to four blank walls skulking in the darkness. "That's if I can get out of here." He laughed at his own ludicrous promise. "I'll protect you as soon as you break me out of here."

His laugh turned into a sob. He knew he wasn't getting out. He would die in the freezer never knowing why Sarah had gone into hiding, and knowing his killer would get away with murder. He detested the idea of losing. It wasn't fair. It wasn't right. A flush of anger rushed through him, but its heat was insufficient to the melt the cold that had eaten into him. He tried to shift his frozen joints, but he couldn't untangle himself from his crouched position.

He resigned himself to his demise. That last attempt to stand and save himself had drained him. Sleep was consuming him, but it was more than sleep—it was death. Death surprised him, though. He'd expected darkness without end or context. Instead, light flooded his vision. For a fraction of a second, he saw the freezer's interior and the damage he'd created trying to escape, but those sights evaporated as the harsh and intrusive light blanked out everything. He slammed his eyes shut, but the intense light was bright enough to burn through his eyelids until all he could see was pure white. He screamed for it to go away and slapped his hands over his face.

Hands grabbed him and yanked him over. They dragged him, but Terry tried to wrestle himself free. He didn't want to go. It wasn't his time.

"Jesus Christ, Terry! What the hell are you doing?"

"Leave me alone," he demanded and kicked out again.

"Terry, stop it. I've got to get you out of here."

The voice was lying. He knew it.

The hands had the better of him now. His attempts to save himself were pointless. He just didn't have the strength.

"Sarah!" he screamed. "Sarah, wait for me."

CHAPTER TWENTY-ONE

Terry awoke in a hospital swaddled in blankets and shivering. A headache threatened to split his head in two. He pressed the call button.

Light filtered through the window, so he guessed it was morning. He'd first awakened late the night before and was lucid enough to get the lowdown on his condition, then he descended back to the land of Nod. His extremities had suffered frostbite. Red-and-white blotches peppered his hands, feet, and face. His fingers were the worst affected. Frank from security had pulled him free of the freezer. Luckily, there was no serious damage done. He just needed time to thaw. The duty nurse, a slender African American woman in her forties, came into his room.

"Mr. Sheffield, you're awake." She smiled with motherly love.

"Yeah, I've decided the career move to replace Jack Frost wasn't for me."

She laughed. "I'm glad to hear it. How do you feel?"

"I've got a bugger of an ice-cream headache."

"I'll get you some Tylenol." She adjusted the blinds to let the day in. "You've got someone waiting. You up to a visitor?"

His thoughts rushed to Sarah. She would have panicked when he had missed their meeting last night. Maybe the silver lining in last night's freezer debacle was that it had brought her out of hiding.

Straightening, he said, "Yes. Please."

"Good. I'll be back in a second."

His heart sank when Frank appeared at the door a minute later. He wondered if Sarah even knew what had happened to him.

"Hey, Terry, good to see you up and around, man. You scared me last night."

"Frank, I hope you haven't been waiting all night."

"No. My shift finished an hour ago, and I thought I'd drop by to see how you're doing."

"That's really nice of you."

"Terry, I'm glad to see you're okay." He offered a hand and Terry took it. "You scared the crap out of me. I thought you were dead."

Terry smiled. "I would have been, if it hadn't been for you. I'm glad you were there. Sit down. Tell me what happened."

Frank dragged over a chair and sat at Terry's bedside. "I thought you could tell me."

"I was putting my plates in the freezer and the door closed behind me."

"You know they have that wedge there for a reason."

"I know. I used it."

"You didn't. It was in its usual position."

Terry squeezed out a grin. He didn't want to show his fear. He knew the wedge had been removed and he had a damned good idea who had done it.

"What made you open the freezer?" Terry asked.

"I was doing my rounds; when I got to the lab, all the lights were out, but I'd seen your car out in the lot. I switched the lab lights on, and I saw your computer was on and your backpack was there; I was just going to go back to reception to put a call out for you when I heard a thud from the freezer. I opened the door and there you were babbling away, kicking and screaming. For a second, I didn't think you wanted to leave."

Terry nodded, taking in Frank's account. "There was nothing blocking the door?"

"Nah," Frank said, shaking his head.

"Who was last out of the lab?"

"Frosty, I think." Frank grinned. "Hey, maybe that should be your nickname now."

The nurse returned with a clear plastic cup, four pills, and a smile. She poured a glass of water from a pitcher on the nightstand and handed the water and pills to Terry.

Frank stood and returned his chair to the corner. "I'd better go and let you get some rest."

"That's a good idea," the nurse said.

Terry gulped the Tylenol. "Thanks for dropping by, Frank."

"Anytime. I don't wanna lose the only Englishman I know."

Terry waited for Frank to leave. "Do you know when I can go?" he asked the nurse.

"When your body says it's time."

"When's that?"

She studied him with an examining eye. Terry smiled in the hope it would reduce his convalescence time. It didn't.

"When the doctor says," she said and walked out.

The second the nurse left, he phoned Oscar. He told him about being locked in the freezer and more awkwardly, about his promise to meet Sarah. He knew the reaction he'd get from his friend.

"Why didn't you tell me she'd called again?" Oscar asked in a soulful tone. "I could have met you there or even picked you up at Genavax, and this wouldn't have happened."

"I didn't call you because she asked me not to tell anyone."

Terry felt Oscar's frown from the other end of the line "Look, I need you to do something for me," Terry said.

"Sure, what is it?" Oscar said unenthusiastically.

"Go to my house. There's a spare key under the plant pot."
It was something he'd set up to prevent being locked out of his
house again. "Check my answering machine to see if she called."

"Sure," Oscar said and hung up.

Three hours later, Oscar strolled in with a paper sack full of
oranges. "Hey there, freezer burn."

"Ha, ha. I bet you worked on that the whole ride over."

He grinned. "I did."

"Well done, micro-amusing," Terry said.

Oscar perched himself on the edge of the bed and wiggled
one of Terry's feet, which were hidden under the bedclothes.

"They do have chairs," Terry suggested.

"Nah." Oscar bounced on the bed. "This is much more comfy."

Terry fingered the oranges in the sack.

"I thought about bringing flowers, but then…" Oscar screwed
up his face. "I didn't want people thinking we were…you know."

"Oh, yeah, I wouldn't want people thinking we were, you
know."

"So I thought: fruit."

"I thought that was what you didn't want people to think…
you know."

"You're a funny man. Anyway, I thought fruit, and you like
oranges, so I got you oranges."

Terry frowned. "I like orange juice."

"Then get someone to squeeze them for you."

"Did you check my messages?"

Oscar's grin slipped. "She hasn't called." Then he qualified
his statement to put a more positive spin on it. "Not saying she
hasn't, but she hasn't left a message. And if she's as spooked as
you say she is, I doubt she would risk a message."

Terry dropped his gaze to examine the weave on the blanket.

"You know you can't keep protecting her," Oscar said.

Terry nodded. "I know. I told her that Holman knows that
she's not missing anymore."

"What did she say?"

"Not a lot. It was all I could do to keep her on the line. She doesn't want to talk to me until everything is safe."

"She give you any clue as to what this is all about?"

Terry shook his head. "That's what she was going to tell me when we met."

"And you don't have her number, I suppose?"

Terry shook his head again.

"You're gonna have to wait until she calls again. There's nothing else you can do."

Terry knew Oscar was right. He hoped he hadn't blown his chance and she would call back.

"She'll call," Oscar said.

"What makes you say that?"

"She'll be scared. Worried that they've gotten to you."

"They nearly did."

"So she'll keep trying until she hears otherwise."

Oscar dug out an orange from the paper sack. He gnawed off a chunk of the peel, spat the rind into his hand, then dropped it on the bed before proceeding to gnaw off another piece.

"You're a class act, do you know that?" Terry said.

"What?"

"You've been divorced too long." Terry tossed him the saucer that his water jug sat on. "Put your mess on that."

"Thanks, Mom," Oscar said, doing as he was told. "So this freezer thing, you sure you didn't forget to use the wedge?"

"Someone tried to kill me. There's no way I would go into that freezer without propping that door open. It's a death trap. I have no idea how Genavax is allowed to get away with such a feeble safety device."

"They won't now. Cal/OSHA will be involved."

Oscar broke open his orange and tore off a segment. Juice sprayed everywhere, some of it landing on his pants, but most of it splashed the covers.

"It's going to smell like a fruit stand in here."

"Don't be such a girl. It's only a bit of juice." Oscar popped the orange segment into his mouth. He spoke while chewing. "You gonna tell Holman what happened?"

"No. I'm quite happy for everyone to think it was an accident." He tossed a box of Kleenex at Oscar to clean his face. "I can't take you anywhere."

"Thanks." Oscar wiped his chin. "Why do you want people thinking it was an accident?"

"Genavax did this to me. I want to see what its next move is."

Oscar pointed an orange segment at Terry. "Probably to do a better job of things next time."

Terry shrugged.

"Do you think Genavax killed those five women?"

It was a question Terry had been recycling for several days, but he hadn't been able to make any kind of connection other than Myda Perez. The other four women didn't seem to have any connection to Genavax. Terry had discarded the idea, but the attempt on his life changed things.

"I don't know," Terry said. "I can't make heads or tails of it."

Oscar chewed and swallowed. He hadn't given the slice of orange the requisite thirty-two chews before swallowing, judging by the strangled look on his face. "Okay, this is a wild one, but what if Genavax didn't try to off you in that freezer? You've got to admit it, it's pretty stupid to try to whack someone in your own backyard. Have you considered someone else?"

A name sprang to mind.

"Tom Degrasse."

"The TV guy?"

Terry nodded. He went on to explain the meal he'd had with the television reporter at Rendezvous and the queasy feeling he'd been left with.

"So he and Sarah had a thing, but it's over," Oscar said, unimpressed. "I don't think that makes him a killer."

"You're missing the point. His attitude was strange."

"It's never easy meeting the guy who's replaced you in the bedroom."

"It's not that. I don't think he's over it."

"Okay, he's still hung up on Sarah. So what? I've never gotten over the fact Farrah Fawcett married Lee Majors."

"Well, he was the Six Million Dollar Man."

"In body parts, not cash."

"This doesn't sound like a recent thing. How old were you when Farrah broke your heart?"

"That was in seventy-six—bicentennial year," he said, staring at the ceiling. "I was fourteen."

Terry grinned.

"Moving swiftly along, now you know which woman broke my heart. What makes you think Sarah dumping Tom Degrasse turned him into a serial murderer?"

"Maybe it had something to do with that story that busted them apart."

Oscar wiped his hands on another Kleenex. "The Oakland port authority bust?"

"Yeah. Think about it. Sarah was a whistle-blower, just like Alicia Hyams and the other women on her list. Tom Degrasse might be teaching her a lesson."

"Some lesson." Oscar dumped the remaining orange segments onto the saucer and wiped his mouth before pushing the saucer away. "Okay, let's say Genavax didn't try to kill you, but Tom Degrasse did. Could he have gotten into the building last night?"

"As much as anyone, I suppose. The place isn't exactly Fort Knox." Terry shrugged. "You don't look convinced."

"Well, it's not that I'm not convinced; it's that I don't have a clue what's happening." Oscar counted off on his fingers. "We've got five murdered women who have nothing in common other than the way they died and that they exposed some wrongdoing in their lives. We've got a biotech company conducting illegal experiments with children's tissue. We've got a lovesick TV newsman. And we've got your wife hiding in the wilds of the San Joaquin Valley." Oscar raised a finger. "But what we don't have is a clear-cut, honest-to-God motive that connects it all."

"You don't have to make it sound that bad."

"Unfortunately, that's the way it does sound."

Terry hated it when someone made perfect sense and he didn't.

"When do you get out of here, anyway?"

"When I've seen the doctor. Why?"

"Well, I hope he comes soon. We've got to find that connection." He smiled. "And I've got to get back to the Gold Rush. Call me when they discharge you."

Lunchtime came and went with no sign of the promised doctor. Just after two, Terry thought he was going to get his audience with the fabled doctor, but he was wrong. Pamela Dawson walked into his room instead, followed by Frosty and two guys in suits. None of them looked concerned for his health. Frosty closed the door.

Terry's visitors crowded his bed on both sides.

"You try anything, I'll raise hell." Terry picked up his call button. The remark was more in jest than seriousness, but nevertheless, the button could still be used to alert help if necessary.

Pamela ignored his threat. "These two men are Genavax attorneys." She indicated to the men in suits. "They are here to sort out matters between the company and you."

One of the suits used the end of Terry's bed to rest his attaché case on while he opened it. He removed the binder Pamela and Frosty had used to bribe Terry and tossed it to him. "I think you've seen this."

"Wow, you let him speak, Pamela."

The crack impressed no one.

Terry picked up the binder and glanced at the contents. It was the job offer, but it had been revised. The salary had been scribbled out and a new one had been written in and initialed. The new salary had been hiked another ten thousand dollars.

"It's Genavax's last offer," the other suit said. "It also includes a generous settlement for the pain and suffering you incurred last night."

"So you'd better take it," Frosty said.

"What if I don't?" Terry tossed the binder back at the suit.

"You'd be making a big mistake," Pamela warned.

"Am I? I don't think so. I think it's you who's making the mistake."

Frosty leaned on the bed and stuck his face in Terry's. "We can make life very difficult for you."

The cheap gestapo act wasn't intimidating him, and Terry waved a dismissive hand in Frosty's face. "You and whose army?"

"We don't need an army." The first suit returned the binder to his attaché case. "We have the law."

Terry snorted and crossed his arms. "What law?"

The second suit intervened. "You've stolen intellectual property from Genavax."

"That's just for starters," Pamela said. "There's the ICE to contend with. We can fire you, and you can kiss your visa good-bye."

"Fire me. Go to the ICE. I dare you. My visa isn't dependent on my job status. I'm married to a US national."

"Not if she never turns up," Frosty said.

The remark ignited Terry's anger. "What the hell is that supposed to mean?"

Frosty shrugged. "No one's seen her in quite a while, and maybe no one will."

Terry tasted metal in his mouth. He wanted to wipe that smug leer off Frosty's face. "Get out of my room."

No one moved.

"Didn't any of you scumbags hear me?"

Pamela nodded to her troops to leave. The suits didn't hesitate and filed out. Frosty remained until Pamela indicated to him to leave as well. He left reluctantly.

"There's a good doggy," Terry said to Frosty's back. He waited until his colleague closed the door. "You need to put a muzzle on him."

Pamela sat on the bed next to Terry, her feet dangling over the edge. Her arm slipped around his shoulders and she leaned in close, like a lover.

She whispered in his ear. "What is it you think you can do to us?"

Terry turned to look her in the eye. "Plenty. I can do more damage to you than you can to me."

She laughed. "You think so, do you?"

"Pam, let's cut the foreplay. What is it you want?"

"I want all the copies you made of our files, and I want you to leave Genavax. Don't worry, we'll keep you on the books. You'll get a regular paycheck, and you'll keep your benefits until you find another position."

"And if I don't, you'll get Frazer the lapdog to shut me in the freezer again?"

"I'd watch what you say, Terry. That's slander."

"We both know it isn't. Either you or Luke locked me in that freezer."

Pamela smiled. "Which is it—Luke or me? You need proof, and you don't have it. Any accusation you make, I'll shoot it down."

Pamela was right, and Terry hated her for it. "Get the hell away from me."

Terry shoved his boss off the bed. Grabbing the bedclothes, Pamela caught her fall. She snapped to her feet.

"If there's dirty work to be done, I do it myself."

"And does that dirty work include stealing tissue from children?" Terry demanded. "Do you wait for them to die or do you help them along?"

Pamela shook her head. She had the expression of someone trying to explain quantum mechanics to a three-year-old. "How long have you been working in the biotech industry?"

Terry didn't answer.

"Have you learned nothing? Nine out of ten biotech firms fold before ever coming up with a viable drug. Genavax will only survive by being better than the rest and more important, faster than the rest. Animal testing only goes so far—human testing is the final answer. Many times the results from animal tests are misleading. Human testing is what will get Genavax to the finish line first."

"Have you been practicing that speech long?"

None of what Pamela said was new to Terry. He knew the facts of biotech life, but he knew the rules too, and Genavax had broken them. Human testing without FDA approval was illegal, and if the FDA knew, it would hang Genavax from the nearest tree.

Genavax's human testing wasn't there to advance its research, but to keep it on track. It was a parity check, a cheat sheet with all the right answers. If animal testing led them off the straight and narrow, Pamela and Frosty made sure a miraculous breakthrough put them back there. Even in his short time at Genavax, he'd seen Frosty come up with foresight in research that sent them in a different direction.

"So what's it to be?" Pamela asked. "Are you going to return the copies?"

The doctor let himself in without knocking. He looked sheepish when he realized he was disturbing something serious. He apologized for his intrusion.

"That's okay, Doctor," Pamela said. "I was just leaving. Terry, you've got until five thirty tomorrow evening."

The uncomfortable moment passed when Pamela left. The doctor made his examination and duly discharged Terry with express instructions to take it easy and to check in with his primary-care physician. Terry agreed, but had the feeling he wouldn't be taking it easy for some time.

Two hours later, Oscar was whisking Terry home. Oscar went to make a turn off Solano Dam Road toward Terry's house, but Terry stopped him.

"Let's carry on to the Gold Rush. I need something."

"What is it you want?"

"I want those documents that you hid for me."

At the Gold Rush Oscar carried a maintenance sign to the fourteenth hole—the windmill hole. He told the disappointed preteens who were about to play the hole to move on to the next one and promised them free sodas when they finished. From the looks they gave him, the compensation didn't go far enough. Terry put out the CLOSED FOR MAINTENANCE sign and Oscar cut the power to the novelty.

Terry looked on incredulously. "You put it in there?"

"Yeah. Why not?" Oscar said. "Who would think to look there?"

Terry couldn't deny Oscar's logic and smiled.

Oscar rooted around inside the replica windmill, then handed Terry the envelope. Terry removed the Genavax documents and handed the rest back to Oscar for safekeeping.

Oscar restarted the windmill and asked, "What now?"

"Take me home. There's something I have to do. Pamela's waiting for an answer."

CHAPTER TWENTY-TWO

The following day, Terry pulled into Genavax's parking lot for what he guessed would be his last time. He walked into the reception area.

It was five and his coworkers were leaving. A couple of familiar faces said hi and asked how he was doing after his freezer ordeal. Terry made small talk, but not wanting to make a meal of it, he cut his conversations short. He smiled when Frank appeared from the direction of the restrooms.

"Hey. The new Frosty," he said.

"The one and only," Terry replied.

"What you doing here? Surely you're not starting work?"

Terry grinned, shaking his head. "No. I came to drop something off."

"Go straight through." Frank indicated to the corridor leading to the research lab.

Terry frowned. "I prefer not to. Can you do me a favor and give this to Pamela?"

"The Ice Maiden? Sure thing." Frank took the envelope Terry had prepared the night before. The security guard gave the package a cursory exam. "Do you want me to give it to her now?"

"Give me time to get out of range."

"No problem." Frank leaned back in his chair. "Don't want to get dragged into talking shop for the next couple of hours, eh?"

Terry smiled. "You know it."

"I'm glad to see you're finally learning the American work ethic."

"You taught me well, Master."

Frank held up his wrist to read his watch. "Okay, the clock is ticking. Now, take a hike."

Returning to the Monte, Terry grinned. He wished he could be there when Pamela opened the envelope. Instead of finding the copied human-testing data she expected, she would find three Polaroids. The photos were a series, each one numbered on the bottom right-hand corner. The first was a close-up of his letter to the FDA, the second was of the photocopied data going into the envelope, and the last was of him dropping the envelope into a mailbox. He didn't leave a note. Pamela was a smart woman. She didn't need it spoon-fed to her.

Slipping behind the Chevy's wheel, Terry's euphoria leaked away through a hole in his conscience. For his colleagues leaving for home, it was just another day, just one in a long series of uneventful workdays—but not for long. Once his letter hit the FDA, every day after would be a train wreck. The FDA would serve Genavax with a consent decree, allowing it to chain up the facility and throw away the key. The FDA wouldn't care that its fines would drive Genavax to financial collapse. Genavax wasn't strong enough to weather the tornado coming its way. By the time the FDA was finished, Genavax would be dust and all of its employees would be jobless—and all because of him. It was going to be bloody, but he didn't have a choice. He gunned the engine.

He hoped his coworkers would understand that he was doing the right thing, but he doubted it. Principles were a precious commodity that most people were forced to give up for a cheap price—but he couldn't follow suit. He put the Monte in drive and shook off the guilt. He didn't have time for it. He had Sarah to meet.

She'd called late the night before when he was tired and chock-full of the hospital's drugs. She was still paranoid, and kept the phone call brief. He barely managed to get a word in before she hung up, but he did manage to say he'd been attacked. He thought he heard a hint of shock and fear in her voice, but she did her best not to show it in her reply. Her response was simple: "Same place, same time, tomorrow."

Terry crossed the Sunset Mall's north parking lot on unsteady legs. He felt like a teenager again, suffering the symptoms of first-date nerves. Adrenaline was pumping and control over his own motor functions was minimal. He was a passenger in his own body. A mom held the door for him after a gaggle of her progeny of varying heights poured out.

The air-conditioned air—a stark contrast to the heat outside—wafted over him and made his frostbite tingle. He stopped and scanned the foyer for Sarah. He half expected a spotlight to shine down on her. But there was no spotlight and no sign of Sarah.

Someone brushed past him, grumbling. Terry followed the grumbling man into the mall. He checked his watch. He was on time. The Mexican restaurant was in the far right corner of the small mall, to the left of the UA Cinema. He did as arranged. Ignoring the other stores, he took a seat at a table outside the restaurant.

He had the SFO jitters again. It was all too reminiscent of the airport incident. He was there and she wasn't. He kept scanning the mall, from the Barnes & Noble opposite to the Panda Express Chinese restaurant at the entrance, to see if she was hiding. He didn't notice the waitress until she spoke.

"Welcome to El Tiburon. My name is Kirsten, and I'll be your server this evening." She handed Terry a menu he didn't look at. "Can I start you with a drink—a margarita, maybe?"

"No, I'll just have a lemonade, if you've got it."

"Of course." She beamed. "I'll get it for you right away."

Kirsten returned in less than a minute, far too efficiently for Terry's liking. She put the drink before him with a basket of chips and small dish of salsa.

"Have you decided?"

"Er...Um." He flashed through the short menu without reading. "What are your specials?"

Kirsten ran through them.

Terry didn't know why he was asking. He didn't care. All he wanted was Sarah.

"Decided?" she asked.

"Actually, I'm waiting for someone."

"No problem. An appetizer, then?"

He hesitated for a moment. "What would you suggest?" he asked to get rid of her.

"We have a very nice chicken quesadilla." Kirsten went on to describe an overelaborate Californian interpretation of the Mexican dish.

"That sounds great."

She left him alone at last, allowing him to keep lookout. He checked his watch. The numbers meant nothing. All they told him was Sarah was late.

Terry didn't spot her until she put a hand on his shoulder. He didn't have to turn around; he knew it was her just by her touch. She smiled. He jumped up and embraced her in a crushing hug.

"Oh, Sarah." He couldn't say any more.

"I know," Sarah said. Her eyes reflected everything he couldn't say.

She returned his embrace, and he reveled in the contact. After what seemed an eternity, they let go of each other and sat. They held hands across the table. Terry lazily rubbed a thumb across the back of her hand.

He was glad to see she hadn't come to any harm. She looked the way she had the last time he'd seen her, albeit a little tired. There were rings under her steel-gray eyes, but the keenness wasn't tarnished. Her hair needed some TLC, but she was still Sarah. He couldn't stop smiling.

Kirsten returned with the quesadilla. "Ah, your party has arrived. Would you like to order your main meal?"

"No," Sarah said. "We've got some catching up to do. This will be all for now."

"Would you like a drink? A margarita, maybe?"

Sarah glanced at Terry's drink. "Lemonade, please."

Sarah amazed Terry. She was so collected. He was a wreck.

Kirsten returned in double-quick time with the lemonade. "I'll leave you guys to get reacquainted."

"Thanks," Terry said.

Sarah touched the frostbite on his forehead. She smiled painfully. "Is that from the freezer?"

He nodded and held up his wounded pinky finger. "So's that."

"I'm sorry."

"It doesn't matter. You're here now. God, I've missed you."

"Me too."

"Does this mean you're coming home?"

"No, I'm not coming home." Her face was apologetic, but her tone was brusque.

"Then I'm coming with you."

"No. It isn't safe."

"I don't care."

"What about your job?"

"It doesn't matter."

"It does."

"As of an hour ago, I probably don't have a job. And in a couple of months, neither will anyone else at Genavax."

"Why?"

Terry explained in detail what he had done, including his letter to the FDA. "The FDA won't mess about," Terry said. "It'll lock the doors and fine Genavax into extinction."

"No wonder Genavax was willing to kill you."

He was still uncomfortable with the idea that Genavax was willing to kill him to ensure word didn't get out. He didn't want to believe they could stoop that low, but people had killed for less. He glanced down at the table. Neither of them had touched the quesadilla or lemonades.

"Do you know who closed the door?"

"I think I do. It was either my boss, Pamela Dawson, or a guy called Luke Frazer."

"I met Pamela."

"You argued with her. Was it over Genavax's illegal drug testing?"

"In a way. When you asked me to check out the company to see if it was in good financial shape, I looked beyond its balance sheet. I came across a biotech industry rumor mill on the web. It's mainly a bitch session for ex-employees to trash their former employers, but some people did post some valuable industry data, like who was in rough financial shape and whose drug wasn't living up to the hype. Well, there was some dirt on Genavax."

"Like what?"

She picked up her lemonade and sucked on the straw. "A number of people—ex-Genavax employees—felt that Genavax was falsifying its data. Its fast-track progress rang alarm bells."

"Being able to do human tissue testing from the beginning would allow that."

"Well, a couple of ex-Genavax workers I got in touch with through the website confirmed the suspicions, but didn't know how the company was doing it. They gave me what they could, and I was getting even more when I got into that fight with your boss. I shouldn't have let her catch me asking about illegal practices."

"You never mentioned any of this before I accepted the job. Why didn't you tell me?"

"I wanted a reason to check out the company, and with you on the inside, I had a direct line to the heart of the beast." Sarah looked impressed with herself.

"Sarah, I'm your husband, not your mole. They tried to kill me."

"And I'm a reporter. I had to know."

"You put me at risk."

They were silent; neither wanted to let the rift escalate into an argument that would spoil their reunion. Terry got proceedings moving again.

"Is Genavax why you were hiding?"

She shook her head.

"Is it the women on the list?"

"Yes."

"Are they tied to Genavax in some way?"

"I don't want to say."

"C'mon, Sarah. You have to. You've been skulking in the shadows for nearly a month, and people have been killed. I was nearly killed."

Sarah moved in close and checked over her shoulder to make sure they weren't being listened in on. Terry noticed they were under Kirsten's watchful eye, but she wasn't within hearing distance—the ambient mall noise was too great. Sarah went to speak, but instead, her grip tightened on Terry's hand.

"What is it?" he asked.

Sarah's gaze was fixed on something. Terry craned his neck to see. Holman and Deputy Pittman were cutting a swath through the mall worshippers from the main entrance. They separated to go around the concession stand in the center of the mall. Terry cursed.

Sarah whipped her head around to face Terry, her expression murderous. "You told them," she hissed. "I can't believe you told them."

She shook off his hand and stood.

"I didn't." He reached for her, but she recoiled. "Believe me."

Holman and Deputy Pittman had been striding, but they stepped up their pace to a jog when Sarah stood.

"I thought I could trust you."

"You can."

Holman and Deputy Pittman broke into a run, and Sarah bolted. Terry raced after her, but kept a watchful eye on Holman and Pittman. Kirsten flew out of El Tiburon, screaming for Terry and Sarah to stop. Shoppers stopped and stared in prairie-dog fashion.

Sarah clipped shoppers and chairs, knocking them aside to escape. Terry couldn't believe what was happening. He was concussed by the enormity of it all. Life didn't happen this way for people like him. Holding a marriage together shouldn't be this dramatic. What the hell was he doing?

Unfortunately for Holman, he'd taken the long way around to intercept Sarah, and he wasn't going to make it. He crashed into a mother and child, getting tangled up in the stroller. All three went down heavily—Holman the heaviest.

Deputy Pittman wasn't as impeded as her boss. Although weighed down by the array of cop toys hanging from her belt, she cut Sarah's lead. Sarah wasn't far from the four pairs of glass doors at the south exit, but the deputy would get to her before she reached the doors.

Terry couldn't let Deputy Pittman take Sarah down. He didn't want Sarah thinking he'd betrayed her, not when he was this close to holding on to her. He had to stop the deputy.

Deputy Pittman closed in, preparing to tackle Sarah from the side. Sarah glanced back and from the look on her face, she knew she was screwed. Her look of desperation nearly split Terry in two, but it spurred him on not to let her down. He kicked a chair out of the way, giving him a clear run at the deputy.

Deputy Pittman was within arm's reach of Sarah. Terry made his move. He dropped into a soccer-style sliding tackle.

He struck the mock-marble floor and accelerated on the highly polished surface. He stuck his feet out, chopping Deputy Pittman at the ankles. She crumpled, collapsing on top of him. Sarah smashed through the doors, flinging them wide.

Deputy Pittman flailed on top of Terry, fighting to get to her feet. Terry rolled the deputy off him then rolled on top of her and used her as a springboard to get up. He spotted Holman steaming toward him like a force-ten gale. Deputy Pittman got to her knees, and Terry booted her in the backside, pitching her forward.

He blew through the same doors Sarah had and raced after her. She'd just crossed the crosswalk and was disappearing into the field of cars in the south parking lot.

"Sarah!" he bellowed. "Wait up!"

She threw a glance in his direction, but kept on running.

"Sarah!"

"Sheffield, stop!" Holman ordered, blasting through the doors with Deputy Pittman at his side.

Terry charged across the crosswalk and into the parking lot. He called Sarah's name again. She didn't look back this time.

He heard Holman shouting his and Sarah's names. The sheriff and his deputy had their weapons drawn but not aimed. They were way behind. There was no way they would catch up and he couldn't imagine them opening fire in such a public place.

Sarah threaded her way through the parking lot, but an endless family pouring out of a minivan halted her. The human obstacle allowed Terry to catch up. When she took off running again, he was on her heels.

"Sarah," he panted. "You've got to take me with you."

"I can't."

"You've got no choice."

"Damn you, Terry."

Terry was at full pelt, and his lungs burned. He hadn't realized how out of shape he was until he had become a fugitive. Only adrenaline and fear gave him the fitness of an athlete.

"Sarah, what is this about?"

"You want to know now?"

"I want to know what I'm running from."

They raced between a long row of vehicles before darting down a pedestrian path that separated the cars from the people. With Sarah ahead by a few feet, they charged across yet another crosswalk. She made it across fine. Terry didn't.

He didn't see the Toyota, just as the Toyota didn't see him until it struck him. The sedan wasn't going fast, but the impact sent searing pain up his thighbone and into his pelvis. His legs shut down and he went sprawling.

Sarah stopped at Terry's scream. Her face was a mixture of frustration, shock, fear, and concern as her eyes flitted between him, Holman and Deputy Pittman, and her escape. Terry saw the emotions ripple across her face as she struggled with a decision. He made it for her.

"Go."

She hesitated.

"Go," he repeated.

She glanced at the sheriff and deputy. "In my home office. If you want to know what this is all about, it's in my room."

Sarah didn't need telling a third time and she darted off, never looking back. As the thudding footsteps of Holman and Deputy Pittman slapped the asphalt around him, he heard a car scream to life and saw it peel off out of the parking lot. He knew it was Sarah. He'd lost her again.

CHAPTER TWENTY-THREE

Terry just lay there where he had fallen. Deputy Pittman aimed her gun at the back of his head. It was getting to be a habit for her.

The Toyota driver was upset. She was pissed as hell at the damage Terry's body had done to her car. She wanted justice. She wanted to sue. She jabbed a finger at Terry. "I want to press charges. I want this son of a bitch in jail. Look what this idiot has done to my car. Look!"

Terry looked and so did Holman and Deputy Pittman, who let the woman rant. Terry found it hard to see the damage he'd done to the Toyota. The car was at least a decade old. The sedan was blue—once. Now it was a sliding scale of shades and the original color was hard to determine. And if Terry had put a dent in the front of the car, it was lost among the others the car sported.

The woman threw her hands up and stared into the clear sky. "Why, God? Why do this to me? Am I not a good servant?"

God didn't answer her, but Holman did. "A good servant of God wouldn't have hit someone crossing a crosswalk."

"But he was running," the woman said, recovering from being knocked from her high horse.

"Running, walking, crawling—doesn't matter. In a crosswalk the pedestrian has the right of way. The driver doesn't."

"But—"

Holman silenced her with a raised hand. "And a good servant of God wouldn't have expired tags."

The woman glanced at her license plate. Her mouth flapped in reply, but the words didn't come, only a blubbering noise.

"Now, I think you should get into your car, consider what you've done, and see how you can fix things so this doesn't happen again." Holman spoke in a condescending fashion that adults usually reserved for disobedient children. "Deputy Pittman, please escort this lady to her car and make sure to get some details in case we need to talk to her at a later date."

Deputy Pittman guided the woman to her driver's side door while the woman delved for her license. Holman stood frowning over Terry. He put his hands on his hips and shook his head.

"Are you hurt?"

Terry throbbed from his feet to halfway up his side. He had the urge to use the bathroom, but to do what, he wasn't sure. His bladder and bowels kept changing their minds. He took comfort in the fact that nothing appeared to be broken.

"I'll live."

"Can you stand?"

"With help."

Holman stuck out a hand and Terry took it. The sheriff hoisted him to his feet. Terry put weight on his bad leg and it went numb instantly. He struggled to maintain his balance and tottered. Holman caught and steadied him. Pins and needles raced up and down Terry's leg and side. Nausea turned his stomach inside out.

"I don't think you're going far," Holman said.

Shocked and white-faced, the Toyota driver dove into her car and hightailed it out of there with a screech of tires. Deputy Pittman closed her notebook and came back to Terry and Holman.

"Deputy Pittman, he can't walk. Bring my car around."

"Do you want me to call an ambulance?"

Holman wrinkled his face and shook his head. "I don't think so. Not just yet, anyway. Mr. Sheffield has a few questions to answer."

Deputy Pittman jogged off in the direction of the north parking lot, and Terry became aware of the crowd of onlookers that had built up since the incident. They were treating the lull in proceedings as an intermission between acts. Holman brought the show to an end.

"C'mon people, move it along. The carnival is over. Move about your business, please."

At the fringes, people broke off and dispersed, but a core still expressed their constitutional right to free assembly. Holman grimaced, and that did the trick. His displeasure cleared the hardcore fans. Terry wondered where he could get a stare like that.

A few minutes later, Deputy Pittman returned with Holman's cruiser. Both officers eased Terry into the back of the car. He was glad to be off his feet and stretched out across the seat. All compassion ended the moment he was in the cruiser and the doors were shut.

"What the hell were you playing at back there?" Holman shouted, pointing in the direction of the mall.

Deputy Pittman drove the car toward an exit.

Terry fought fire with fire. "What the hell was I playing at? I was having a meal with my wife. What the hell were you playing at? My God, I can't believe you tapped my phone."

"We didn't tap your phone."

"Didn't you? So you're expecting me to believe you just happened to come across us?"

"We didn't tap your phone, because we didn't have to. Since you told us that your wife had contacted you, Deputy Pittman has been following you."

Deputy Pittman smiled into the rearview mirror and waved at Terry. She made a left onto a side street, parked on the side of the road, and switched off the engine.

"Why were you following me?"

"To find your wife," Holman said.

"Well, you did a bang-up job, didn't you? Because she's right by my side now, thanks to you two clowns."

"Mr. Sheffield, you came to us," Deputy Pittman said.

"I know, and I also told you when she was back in contact."

"Do you have any idea the world of crap you're in?" Holman demanded. "We've got obstruction of justice, assaulting an officer, wasting police time—and that's just for starters. There's a lot more I could throw at you if I decide to."

Terry stared at the world outside the car. "Sarah isn't missing anymore. I don't know what your interest is in her now."

Losing his patience, Holman said, "Mr. Sheffield, your wife names five murdered women in her notes."

"So does the telephone book," Terry snapped, "but I don't see you hounding AT&T."

Holman ignored the wisecrack, but Terry couldn't ignore Holman's remark. The sheriff knew about the murders, which made Terry wonder what else he knew. Terry's surprise must have shown.

"Did you think I wouldn't check out the names?" Holman asked. "We're a small unit, but we're not dumb, Mr. Sheffield. And by the look on your face, you know the women on your wife's list were murdered. Why don't you tell us what you know?"

Holman had really sucker-punched Terry. He hadn't expected Holman to do his job and follow up on the list. He didn't really see any way to bluff his way out. He knew he was already blushing. There was nothing for it; he would have to come clean—to a certain extent. He had to be careful. He didn't want Holman knowing that Oscar was part of his private investigation. His friend shouldn't have to face Holman's wrath—or else who would be around to call Schreiber?

"You know as much as I do," he said.

"I doubt that," Deputy Pittman said, pursing her lips.

Terry ignored her. "The women on Sarah's list were all killed by the same method."

"And don't pretend that this doesn't have anything to do with your wife," Holman said. "She's at the heart of this mess."

"Why has your wife been tracking the murder victims?" Deputy Pittman asked.

"I don't know. Honestly, I don't."

Holman frowned. "At best, your wife is a material witness. At worst, she's an accessory. We want to speak to her."

"Mr. Sheffield," Deputy Pittman said, "tell us where she is. If we can speak to her, we can find out what's going on, and she might even help us find a murderer."

"I can't."

"Why?" Holman demanded.

"She didn't tell me where she was going."

"I thought your wife had come back," Deputy Pittman remarked.

"She isn't missing," Terry said disdainfully, then continued more humbly. "It's just that I don't know where she's staying."

Holman sighed. Everyone was silent for a few minutes while they all tried to think of something to say. It allowed time for tempers to cool. Holman spoke first.

"Do you have any idea where Sarah might be?"

Terry wished he did even more than they did. He shook his head.

"What did you two talk about?" Deputy Pittman asked.

Her tone was supportive; her face, caring. It was the first time she hadn't been confrontational with Terry. It felt like she was a friend.

"We asked each other how we had been." Terry half smiled. "Original, eh?"

Deputy Pittman smiled too. "You must have asked where she's been this whole time, right?"

"I did. She wouldn't tell me."

"Why?" Holman asked.

"Because she thought it was too dangerous."

"Damn, I wish you would let us in," Holman said.

Terry shrugged.

"What's too dangerous?" Deputy Pittman asked.

"The story she's working on."

"Is it linked to Alicia Hyams and the other women?" Holman asked.

Terry could feel them clawing the information from him, but he didn't mind. The more time they wasted on him, the farther away Sarah was getting.

"I believe so," he said.

"Christ," Holman muttered.

"And she told you this?" Deputy Pittman asked.

"Sort of. Some I've worked out for myself. Some she told me."

"Does she know who's doing this?" Holman asked.

"I think so."

"Did she tell you?"

"No."

"Because it's too dangerous?" Holman suggested.

Terry nodded.

"Do you have any idea who it is?" Deputy Pittman pressed.

Terry did have a good idea who it was—the man who'd laughed at him on the phone without saying a word, the "friend" who wanted to get in touch with Sarah and knew that she was in hiding. But that man was just a voice on a phone. He had no face or name.

"I don't know who it is, but I do think I know why Sarah went into hiding. I think the killer blames Sarah for something she did."

"Something she did to the killer?" Deputy Pittman asked.

"I think so. I think the other murders were showpieces to draw Sarah out."

"And she took the bait," Holman said.

"Yes. And I also believe the killer's been in contact with her—feeding her bits of information. But once he showed that he could get to her, I think she panicked and fled."

"Do you have anything to back this up?" Holman asked.

"Gut feeling. Coincidence. All the women died the same way Alicia Hyams did."

Holman nodded, mulling over Terry's reasoning. Deputy Pittman looked soulful, disturbed by the revelations.

"Do you want to press charges, Deputy?" Holman asked.

Deputy Pittman shook her head. "I don't think it would help matters, and there was no real harm done."

"Thank you," Terry said.

"Can you walk?" Holman asked.

Terry's leg throbbed, and he imagined a nasty bruise was hiding under his jeans, but the pins and needles were gone and the feeling had returned to his side. He wouldn't break the hundred-meter world record anytime soon, but he was okay.

"Yes, I can walk."

"Drop him back at his car."

Deputy Pittman fired up the cruiser and drove back to the mall.

Holman and Deputy Pittman didn't speak to each other or to Terry. It was obvious they wanted to plan their next step without having him around. Deputy Pittman stopped behind the Monte, boxing the Chevy into its parking spot. The rear passenger doors couldn't be opened from the inside, so Deputy Pittman got out of the Crown Victoria to let Terry out.

"You speak to Sarah again," Deputy Pittman said, "get her to speak to us."

"I wouldn't get your hopes up." Terry smiled thinly. "She thinks I sold her out to you two. But if she does, I'll try."

Terry got his keys out and hobbled over to the Monte Carlo. He had unlocked the door and was starting to get in when

Holman stopped him by rolling down his window. "You've neglected to mention something," Holman said.

Quite probably, Terry thought. "Have I?"

"Your wife went into hiding before Alicia Hyams was abducted, but her name was on Sarah's list."

"So?"

"If she knew anything that could have prevented Alicia Hyams's death..." he trailed off, doing little to hide the anger blazing in his eyes. "Then goddamn your wife, Mr. Sheffield."

• • •

Terry went into Sarah's home office. He felt bad for not telling Holman and Deputy Pittman what Sarah had said before she'd run off, but he still wasn't sure whether he could trust them.

He studied the room. The closet was stacked with papers and the computer was packed with articles and stories. The bookshelves bulged with past work. The answer was hidden somewhere within the room. Sarah had said as much. He'd missed it before. He would find it this time.

He flicked on the PC and immediately shunned it for the closet. Retracing old ground, he pulled out files of notes and old news copy and examined them. He searched for stories related to the five women on Sarah's list, hoping to find a reference showing that Sarah had foreknowledge of their actions. If he came across a name of a contact that occurred in more than one piece he kept it to one side, making a pile. He topped the piles with hastily scribbled notes explaining the connection. Anything that seemed to have no bearing on the situation he tossed out of the room and into the hallway to reduce the confusion. The hours passed, and the evening gave way to the night with the closet yielding little that made much sense.

He turned his attention to the bookshelves. He sifted through their apparently unconnected facts applying the same meticulous attention he'd paid to the data in the closet. His reward was frustration. He found even less of value than he had in the closet.

He went to the computer and scanned directories filled with story drafts and rewrites. He printed anything that reminded him of any of Sarah's whistle-blower cases. When he was finished, he was left with two small and untidy stacks of paper, sore eyes, and a raging headache. He pushed his seat back from the PC and rubbed his eyes with his palms.

Terry stood and backed away from the computer until he was leaning against the wall. He fixated on the piles of papers he'd extracted. It was pitiful compared to the amount of work Sarah had amassed over the last decade, and he still had nothing to show for it. He didn't have to examine what he'd collected to know that. All he'd unearthed was a couple of stories that had taken place in Sacramento and Anaheim, where Alicia Hyams and Christy Richmond were from, and the Oakland port authority story Sarah and Tom Degrasse had worked on. Other than that, there was nothing. He kicked the files across the floor.

Sarah had said the answer was in her office, and Terry didn't have a reason to doubt her, but he just wasn't seeing it. Frustrated, he banged his head against the wall.

He nudged a framed picture hanging on the wall, and it fell. He stopped it from hitting the ground by trapping it between the wall and his back. He grabbed the picture frame from behind him and examined it. The picture, like many in the room, was a framed newspaper story Sarah had written. The one he held was a fly-on-the-wall piece about death-row prisoners. He stared at the other framed stories when a realization struck him: What if he'd been staring at the answer all along?

Dropping the framed death-row piece, he went from picture frame to picture frame, scanning the stories. A chill washed over him as he stopped in front of the Oakland port authority exposé.

The *Examiner* led with a banner headline and Sarah's byline. Below was a picture of the police bust as it was happening. Port authority workers were being led away to unseen police vehicles. Some held up hands to hide their faces from the photographer's aim. One man closest to the camera, held a hand out to block the camera lens, but the photographer was just out of reach. In the corner of the photo, small but visible, was Tom Degrasse with his hands in his pockets and looking distinctly pissed off.

"You son of a bitch," Terry said to Degrasse's captured image.

Degrasse fit the bill perfectly. He'd lost Sarah and he couldn't let it go. His delusion had pushed him to murder. He'd started a killing spree, murdering women who'd wronged others, and then he'd sent Sarah the clues. The thread that ran through all the murders was whistle-blowing, Sarah's career trademark. Something shifted inside the frame.

Terry didn't have to be told; he knew the answer to Tom Degrasse's guilt was sandwiched inside the picture frame. He flipped the frame over. Screws and clips kept the cardboard back in place.

He didn't have the patience to disassemble the frame—he swung it against the corner of Sarah's computer desk. The glass in the frame exploded, spraying shards over the desk and carpet. Knocking the remaining glass free, he ripped the cardboard border off and the Oakland port authority story tumbled out, along with another newspaper clipping.

Shaking off the glass fragments, Terry picked up the hidden clip. It was an old edition of the *Santa Rita County Courier*, dating back to the late nineties. The front page explained everything. He didn't have to turn a page for confirmation. But it wasn't the answer he was expecting. Tom Degrasse wasn't the feature story. Sheriff Ray Holman and his son Jake were.

"Oh, God," he muttered.

Filling the front page was a picture. Holman looked distraught in the face of duty as he led his handcuffed son to a waiting squad car. The banner headline read "Sheriff Arrests Son." This was what she wanted him to find. He went to read the story, but the ringing phone interrupted him. He answered it.

"Terry," Sarah said.

"Sarah, thank God. I found it. I found the newspaper."

"Terry, listen."

"I found it, but I don't know what I've found. What are you saying?"

"Terry, please listen."

Her voice was on the verge of breaking. She was close to tears. He hadn't noticed at first. He'd been too pumped up from finding the newspaper.

"What is it?" he said softly. "Are you okay?"

She broke. The sound of her crying poured down the phone line. She tried to speak, but couldn't stop sobbing. She gulped in uneven breaths, which rushed out just as untidily. It was impossible to understand what she was saying. She blurted out multiple words as one and chopped others in half.

"Sarah, hush now." He tried to sound soothing—given the chance to be the good husband at last. "It's okay. Whatever it is, tell me, and we'll sort it out."

"Terry," she managed to say through the tears. "I'm so sorry."

"You've got nothing to be sorry about."

"I do. Oh, God, I do. It's all my fault. We...should...have never...gotten...ma...ma...married." She broke down again and her words dissolved into an incomprehensible babble.

"Sarah, what are you talking about? You're not to blame for anything. Tell me where you are and I'll come get you.

"She's with me," a male voice answered.

Terry turned to stone. He choked on his next breath. The newspaper slipped from his feeble grip. The pages caught on a draft from the air conditioner and separated as they tumbled to the ground.

"Jake," Terry said slowly.

CHAPTER TWENTY-FOUR

"Terry," Jake said, mocking him. "You're finally taking my calls."

It sounded like Jake Holman and it didn't. He'd dropped his downtrodden persona and revealed his true self.

"What's going on, Jake?"

He inhaled. "Let me see…payback, revenge, murder."

"Please don't hurt her."

"Don't hurt her?" Jake snapped.

His rage turned Terry's stomach to slush.

"Why the hell not? Huh? She deserves it. She deserves a few hours of misery before she dies to make up for all the years of misery she's given me."

"I don't know what this is all about."

"Terry, Terry, Terry. Still in the dark after all this time," Jake said, calm again. He sighed. "I thought you were on to me a few times, but I can see I was wrong. Even with the evidence before you, you still don't get it."

"Just tell me, Jake."

"Maybe you should come join us and we can have big long chin-wag. That's an English word isn't it? *Chin-wag.*"

Terry was silent.

"Terry, I'm talking to you."

"Sorry. Yes, *chin-wag* is an English word."

"That's better. Yes, I think we should have a chin-wag."

"I would like that." Terry's throat was dry and his voice cracked, the words snagging on his parched tongue.

"Then it's a date. See you later."

"Wait! Where? You haven't said where."

"You're right. Silly me." Jake took in a deep breath before proceeding. "Where would be a good place for old friends to get reacquainted? Any ideas?"

"Anywhere that's good for you."

"That's the marvelous thing about you English people—you're so accommodating. I think that's something we Americans have lost. There are a lot of things we could learn from you people. But let's get back to the matter at hand. Where should we meet? Hmm." Jake drifted for a minute, humming some meaningless tune. "Where's a good place where people can socialize, have fun, and forget all about their daily troubles?"

"I don't know."

"Oh, c'mon, Terry, you're not even trying. Have a go."

Terry's brain seized up. He couldn't think of a single place. His mind couldn't comprehend entertainment when his wife was being held hostage.

"Jake, I really don't know a good place."

"Terry, do you want me to cut her throat right now? Is that what you want, huh?"

"No. No, it's not, Jake." Terry spoke quickly, hoping not to give Jake time to think about killing Sarah. He heard her whimper in the background. "But Jake, I'm new to town; I don't know any good places."

"Okay, Terry. I was forgetting myself. You're right. I shouldn't have put you on the spot. Accept my apologies."

"It's okay, Jake." Sweat trickled down Terry's neck. "Don't worry about it."

"All right, then. Let's see…where can we *amuse* ourselves?" Jake emphasized the word amuse, saying it long and slow.

Terry's sweat turned icy cold. He had an idea about what Jake was insinuating.

"Where we can have some *fun times*? But we don't want big fun. We want little fun or even *mini* fun. We want somewhere we can have some *gold-en* times. Any thoughts now, Terry?"

Terry's heart raced, crashing against his rib cage. Fear seeped in as it dawned on him: he knew where they were meant to meet. The words nearly stuck in his throat as he said them.

"The Gold Rush."

"Good idea."

"When?" he asked, hoping to give Oscar time to get away.

"How about now? We're here already. Aren't we, Sarah?"

Sarah moaned somewhere not too far from the phone.

"Don't be long. I'm not sure how long I have." Jake paused. "Correction, I'm not sure how long Sarah has."

"Please don't hurt her. I beg you. Please."

"Don't beg." Jake was cold and unforgiving. "It's not becoming."

"I'm on my way."

"Terry?"

"Yes."

"No cops. They'll only screw things up, okay?"

Cops were the last thing on Terry's mind. Jake was a hair trigger. He needed only the slimmest of reasons to kill Sarah. Terry was not about to take any chances.

"And one last thing: bring all the evidence your bitch wife compiled on me."

• • •

Terry made it to the Gold Rush in ten minutes, but the journey seemed to have taken a lifetime. He skidded into a parking stall and the Monte slammed into the curb. When he switched off the engine, he noticed his hands were shaking. He got out, leaving the keys in the ignition.

He hadn't bothered bringing a weapon to defend himself. He'd gone as far as grabbing a butcher knife, but there'd be no point in bringing it. Terry possessed no fighting skills with a knife or anything else, and Jake had proved he could kill a person quite easily. Besides, Jake had Sarah, and Terry couldn't take any chances with her life by doing anything stupid. All he could hope for was that if he went in unarmed, he could prevent the situation from escalating.

Terry limped over to the Gold Rush's main doors, which had been kicked in. He slipped between the drunken-looking doors, his feet crunching on broken glass. Inside, the lights were off but the arcade machines were on. They ran through their demo programs, casting flickery shadows. Mechanical voices enticed players who weren't there. Revving engines, explosions, and snapping bones simulated the end of the world. Terry had no stomach for simulations. He'd seen too much of the real thing lately. The minigolf course's floodlights glared, pushing back the dark on the far side of the arcade. He guessed Jake's party was out there.

Terry crossed the arcade to the golf course entrance and kicked something on the ground. Before he looked he knew he'd found Oscar. His friend was an untidy heap of clothes and flesh. He was unconscious and cuffed to a steel column. Terry knelt by Oscar's side and felt for a pulse. In his fear, he couldn't find it, but he heard shallow breathing. In the gloom, Terry made out Oscar's face. He'd been beaten, and his face was blood-streaked from a head wound above his hairline. Strange markings blighted his face. It took a moment for Terry to realize they were shoeprints. Terry didn't have the words. His overloaded emotions had shut down. He left his friend where he lay.

Terry pushed open the doors to the golf course and walked into the blinding brightness cast by the floodlights. The minigolf course's sound effects played. All the course's feature holes were operating. Their electric motors whined eerily loud without any players having fun to mask the sound. On the other side of the course, Sarah sat slumped on a chair in front of the windmill hole. The scene had been set, but one thing was missing—Jake.

Terry knew he was walking into a trap, but it didn't matter. He'd tripped it the moment he'd stepped off the plane. The snare was around his throat. It was all a matter of whether he could slip out of it before it became too tight.

"Sarah," he called across the course.

She didn't respond.

"Jake." Terry waited for a reply. "I'm here."

Jake didn't answer.

Terry wasn't going to give Jake time for a second invitation. He charged across the carpeted course toward Sarah, leaping over the multitude of obstacles. Jake was out there ready to pounce, but if Terry was lucky, he would reach Sarah before Jake cut him down.

But nothing happened. Jake didn't pounce. A thought crept into Terry's head. Realizing he couldn't keep a lid on the situation any longer, Jake had simply delivered Sarah to him and fled to start anew elsewhere. Terry wished he could believe this. But Jake wasn't going anywhere. He wouldn't miss this nightmare for the world.

Terry closed in on Sarah and his world ended. From the arcade, he'd thought Sarah had been wearing a red-and-white T-shirt, but with every stride, he realized his eyes had deceived him. She was wearing a white T-shirt drenched in blood. He willed his legs to stop pumping to prevent him from seeing any more, but they betrayed him and carried him all the way to her.

Terry collapsed to his knees before Sarah and stared up at her. Her head rested on her chest, her hair hanging down, hiding her face. Her blue jeans were stained black with blood and a puddle soaked the nylon carpeting at her feet. His eyes burned before the tears came. He gulped in breath after breath without exhaling, but no air made it to his lungs. A force he couldn't control shook his body from head to toe. She was dead.

He cupped Sarah's chin in one hand. Blood spread across his palm. He lifted her head. Hair matted to the blood on her chest broke its bonds. More blood spilled from the gaping wound in her throat. Sarah stared back at him with vacant eyes. She was forever trapped in a single snapshot of time, her expression capturing the moment of her death.

He'd never seen death before he had seen Alicia Hyams. He'd never known its impact or understood its devastating power. But he was seeing death now roaming in Sarah's eyes. The spark that was Sarah had gone. The intensity of her smile was absent. Her excitement when life consumed her didn't burn anymore. Whatever a soul or spirit or life force looked like, it had left Sarah. Releasing her head, Terry crumpled, collapsing at her feet.

He couldn't hold it in anymore and his misery exploded from his chest in one convulsive breath. Sobs rocked his body. "No. Not her. Not now. Please God, no! Why?"

"Because she deserved it," Jake answered.

Terry rose to his knees. Jake emerged from behind the model windmill, one hand holding a bloodstained hunting knife, the other casually hidden in his pocket. He stood behind Sarah and stroked her hair from her face.

"You bastard," Terry spat.

Jake sighed. "Stick and stones, Terry. Really."

Terry cuffed his running nose. "You didn't have to kill her."

"Are you crazy?" Jake stared at Terry like he was insane. "She's the cause of this." He pointed at Sarah with the knife. "She destroyed my life."

Terry shook his head. He reached behind him and tugged from his back pocket the newspaper he'd discovered hidden inside the picture frame. He tossed it on the ground at Jake's feet. It fell open to the front page with Jake's shame splashed across it.

"She just reported the news. You were a rapist. She didn't make you into anything that you weren't already."

"It was statutory rape." Jake jabbed the knife in Terry's direction. "The girl was a high-school senior. She lied about her age. Nothing was forced."

"That's not what it says in there." Sarah's report alleged that the girl had pleaded for Jake to stop, and he'd ignored her.

"That's because that bitch wife of yours made me out to be a pedophile." Jake kicked the newspaper back at Terry. "Christ, you've got no idea the humiliation of being busted by your own dad." He stared at the ancient newspaper, reliving old nightmares. "And do you know what it's like to be a sheriff's son and a rapist in the joint? Do you?"

Terry didn't answer. He didn't care.

"You're the lowest of the low. No one gives a damn whether you live or die, and don't think the correction officers step in to help."

"My heart bleeds for you."

"It should, Terry. Because, guess what? During every beating, one thing kept me alive. Through the pain, I saw a face. Just one." His stare bore into Terry. "Your wife's."

"So why the other women, Jake? What made these other women so special to you? They didn't have a part in your conviction."

"But they would have, given the chance." Jake sneered. "When I got out of jail, it was no better. No fresh starts for Jakey-boy. Someone always found out about my past. In every city I moved to, Megan's Law ratted me out." He laughed bitterly. "Christ, by making sex offenders' information public, Megan's Law was meant to save lives. What a joke. It forced me to take them."

God, it was pathetic. Jake's excuse for all the misery and pain he'd inflicted was feeble. It was no better reasoned than one from a child striking out at an unwanted punishment. Did he honestly expect Terry to feel sorry for him when he'd just murdered his wife? It was beyond ridiculous.

Terry watched Jake work himself into a frenzy, losing control of himself and the situation. Jake realized it too. He snapped out of it, sniffed, and smiled.

"Do you want to know why I killed those women? Huh?"

Terry didn't answer.

"Because they were just like Sarah. They all liked to point the finger. They made the headlines by destroying other people's lives. They poked their noses into things that had nothing to do with them."

"Those women pointed the finger at people who broke the law."

"Don't make me laugh." Jake shook his head. "Are you saying a whore who blew the whistle on cops was right?"

"They were dirty cops."

"A know-nothing nurse exposed a doctor who saved lives every day for a mistake he made."

"A person died because of that doctor."

"You're a piece of work, Terry. Do you know that? You've got an answer for everything."

Terry glanced at Sarah. He didn't have an answer for tonight. He didn't have an answer for anything anymore and he shook his head.

"A couple of times, I really thought I'd be able to settle down, you know?" Jake said. "I thought, this time I'm going to get on all right. But just as I would get settled, someone would yank the rug from under me. They'd find out about the conviction, and they'd want me to go. Jesus, I'd paid my debt to society. I should have been left alone." Jake palmed away a tear. "Soon I found I wasn't the only one being given the shaft. I'd notice the likes of Alicia Hyams and Judith Stein sticking it to others like me. I've moved every year after getting out of prison. But it wasn't until I saw Hope Maclean that I decided to even things up."

Jake smiled and nodded to himself, reveling in his past achievements. He exhibited the smug warmth of a job well done. Terry couldn't help but wonder at the depth of Jake's sick delusions.

"Did you really think no one was going to catch on to you?"

Jake snorted. "It wasn't meant to be a secret."

Terry was incredulous. Every time he thought Jake couldn't shock him any more, he said something to drag the nightmare another level lower.

"At first, it didn't matter. It wasn't until I killed Judith Stein that I realized these bitches' deaths needed to be recognized. People have to understand there are consequences for their actions. So I gave myself a crusade."

"And you contacted Sarah."

Jake snorted. "You know what? Of all the women I wanted to teach lesson, the one woman I really needed to teach was your wife, and it never crossed my mind until I spotted her back in town. I've been sending her notes for months."

Terry's insides turned to stone. Sarah had known about the murders all along and kept them to herself. She'd played a stupid, stupid game with a killer and paid the price. He hated to admit it, but she deserved Sheriff Holman's damnation. If she'd gone to the police earlier, Alicia Hyams might not be dead.

"At first, I was pretty cryptic, but she wasn't connecting the dots, so I had to spell it out for her. She wasn't as smart as she liked to think she was." Jake pointed at Sarah. His finger touched her head, which lolled to one side.

Revulsion clawed up Terry's throat. He wanted to puke at the sight of that monster touching his wife. How dare he? How fucking dare he?

"Don't touch her."

"Excuse me?"

"Don't touch her," Terry repeated.

"Terry, listen to yourself." Jake pointed the knife at him. "You are in no position to make any demands here. You are here as a courtesy. Remember that."

Terry didn't reply. There was no arguing with Jake. Not that Terry was trying to reason with him. They were all beyond that stage.

Jake frowned and lowered the knife. "I wanted her to work it all out and know that she was responsible. I wanted her to suffer the way she'd made me suffer. Suffer like all the people she'd wronged."

Terry could only imagine what it must have been like for Sarah. The shock and exhilaration of communicating with a killer must have seemed like a journalistic gift from heaven. But that excitement must have turned into a fear-driven sweat when she realized Jake had orchestrated the murders for her benefit—and her demise. No wonder Sarah ran.

"Jake, why have you brought me here? If you're going to kill me, just do it."

Jake frowned. "I could have killed you a thousand times, but I wanted you to see what kind of woman you married and what she did to me." He ran a hand through his hair. "We could have been friends."

Terry felt nothing but hatred toward Jake Holman. "I knew what kind of woman Sarah was. I didn't need you to show me."

"You really piss me off, Terry. Do you know that? You kept giving me the brush-off and that's why I didn't just kill you. I wanted you to experience this pain, this suffering"—Jake pointed at Sarah with the knife—"so you might just find some compassion for me in that pea brain of yours."

"Are you finished?"

Jake sneered. "No. This is only the beginning of your agony. I killed Sarah just so I wouldn't have to listen to her bleat." He came behind Sarah and lifted her head. "But I wanted you to be here when I hacked her blabbing tongue out."

"No!"

Terry wasn't going to let it happen. He'd failed to save Sarah, but he'd be damned if he would let Jake desecrate her any further. Adrenaline ignited in his veins, and he propelled himself at the killer. Jake's eyes widened, but for only for a second. He wasn't expecting the attack, but when he realized it was happening, he grinned, relishing the challenge.

"C'mon," Jake beckoned and dived out from behind Sarah.

Terry body-slammed Jake, sending him sprawling into the windmill. The structure tottered on its foundations, and a rotating windmill sail thudded into Jake's side, stopping the sails from turning. He didn't show any sign that the sail had made an impact on him.

Terry snatched both of Jake's wrists. Jake shoved Terry backward. They danced a surreal death waltz with Jake leading. Terry's grip was tight on Jake's wrists, but his effect was negligible. Jake's strength was overwhelming, and Terry had no option but to follow his partner's lead.

Terry backed up another step and his heel clipped the shallow step at the edge of the carpeted fairway. He lost his balance, but he didn't let go of Jake. He went down hard into the landscaping, taking the killer with him. The sandwiching impact of Jake and the ground blasted the air from his lungs. His ribs flexed under Jake's weight and at least one rib broke, draining Terry's strength.

Jake shook off Terry's feeble grasp and straddled him. He had the advantage, and they both knew it. That knowledge was aflame in Jake's eyes. Terry fought to regain his grasp on Jake's wrists. Jake head-butted Terry, and pinpricks of light twinkled in his vision. Jake head-butted Terry again and again, until Terry's hands slipped away. He grabbed Terry's throat, choking him. Terry tore at the restraining hand. Jake raised the knife high, his mouth open with anticipation. Terry gurgled.

"This is it," he said. "End of the line, old chap. Are you ready?"

"No," Sheriff Holman bellowed.

The sheriff stood a few yards away with his gun aimed at his son's chest. Relief washed over Terry, although he didn't relax his grip on Jake. He was far from being out of the woods. A gun was hardly the thing to strike fear into Jake.

Jake laughed. "Come to do the right thing again, Dad?"

Terry squirmed under Jake's choking grasp. The sheriff's son tightened his grip, keeping him pinned. Starlight burned in Terry's vision.

"It doesn't have to be this way, son."

"Doesn't it? Do you think you're going to make things better by taking me in?"

Holman cocked the long-barreled revolver.

"You'd better do it. I'm not doing a second stretch, not for you, not for anybody. It's your call. What you gonna do, Dad?"

Holman was frozen, petrified in a moment of decision that would determine all of their fates.

"This is a tense moment. There should be music." Jake delighted in his father's pain even more than he delighted in Terry's. "C'mon, Dad. Ticktock."

"Put the knife down." A faint tremor contaminated Holman's speech. "Don't kill him."

"You disappoint me, Dad." Jake shook his head. He flung his arm back again to plunge the blade into Terry's chest.

"Don't, Jake," Holman said with overpowering compassion. He wasn't a law officer. He was a father reaching out to his son in a moment of supreme need.

Jake hesitated. "Why?"

"If you don't kill him, I'll stand by you."

"You'll hold my hand in the gas chamber?"

"No, I'll help you."

"Help me, how? You can't prevent me from going to prison."

"Yes, I can."

"How?"

"I'll pin it all on him." Holman nodded at Terry.

CHAPTER TWENTY-FIVE

Jake stood, dragging Terry to his knees. He came behind Terry and rested the knife against his throat. Holman trained his gun at Terry.

"You'll make him the killer?" Jake asked.

Holman nodded. "He's been under suspicion before. This time, he was apprehended red-handed and killed during his arrest."

Terry couldn't believe they were planning his demise in front of him. They spoke of him as if he weren't there—an imbecile too stupid to understand. But it was hard to be much of a force with a knife pressed to his neck and a gun pointed at his head.

"Holman, you son of a bitch. You're an officer of the law, for God's sake."

Holman ignored Terry. Jake pressed the knife a little harder against Terry's throat.

"Jake, I didn't do enough for you last time. I can make it up to you this time."

Jake smiled. "You're really going to come through for me?"

Holman didn't return the smile. He was grim faced. "Yes. This time, yes."

"Thanks, Dad."

"Jesus, Holman. Your son has killed six people. You can't condone this. You can't let him get away with this."

Jake snatched a fistful of hair and yanked Terry's head back. "Shut up."

"We need to make this look like he killed his wife. Did his friend see you?" Holman jerked his head in the direction of the arcade and Oscar.

"He saw me."

Holman inhaled, mulling over Oscar's significance as a witness. "I'll take care of him."

"You'll kill him?" Jake asked.

"There's no other way."

"No, you leave him alone," Terry yelled. He pinwheeled an arm back to slip Jake's grasp, but Jake brought him back into line by slamming a fist into his left kidney. The blow sent a burst of pain up through his spine and into his brain. "You bastard!"

"Behave yourself, Terry. I won't ask again," Jake said. "How do we do this thing?"

"You give me the knife."

Terry felt Jake tense. He knew what Jake was thinking, because he was thinking it too. Was Holman playing his son? Was he lulling him into giving up his weapon so he could take him down? Terry hoped the sheriff was a good man after all.

"Why?" Jake asked. Caution hung thick in his question.

"Because I need it to be in his hand." With his gun Holman pointed to Terry. "And not in yours."

"Where's your deputy?" Jake checked behind him.

"Off duty. At home. I don't know. Now give me the knife."

The knife fell away from Terry's throat. He swallowed, clearing his airway, and sucked in untidy breaths. He fell forward, his hands resting on his knees.

"Okay," Jake said.

He stepped back from Terry. He and Holman circled Terry in a counterclockwise arc until they swapped places. Holman eased in behind Terry and gripped his shoulder with the strength of a pipe wrench. The shadow of the sheriff's gun darkened the corner of Terry's vision.

"Now the knife," Holman instructed.

Jake hesitated. "I'll give it to you when he's dead."

"Give to me now, Jake. I don't want you here when I kill him."

"What?"

Jake's actions said everything. He took a step backward. His doubts were now suspicions. Holman was losing his grip on his son, and Terry didn't like being in the crossfire.

"Jake, I don't want you here. If there are any questions, I want you to be elsewhere with an alibi. I don't want anything to go wrong, son."

The razor edge of panic nicked Holman's composure. Terry could hear it. Holman knew he didn't have a leash on his son, and any control he thought he did have was slipping away. The sheriff was playing catch with a lighted stick of dynamite. There was no telling when Jake would go off.

"How do I know I can trust you?"

"Jake, please. Look, I'm here, aren't I? Would I be doing any of this if it weren't to help you? I'm putting everything on the line for you."

To Terry's amazement, Jake wavered. He glanced down at the knife, weighing the situation. He bounced the blade on his open palm.

"C'mon, Jake. We don't have all night. Give me the knife. You know I'm right."

Jake smiled and nodded.

Then it went all wrong. Terry saw how it was going to happen before it did. And there was nothing he could do to stop it.

• • •

Oscar sprang up from behind Jake, jack-in-the-box style, with a golf club in his hands, the handcuffs flailing from one wrist. Jake was totally unaware of Oscar's presence. Oscar swung the club back to bring it down on Jake's skull.

Holman had a clear view of Oscar and reacted like a machine. His actions were simultaneous and fluid. He jumped back from Terry, raised his gun, and drew a bead on Oscar. Terry lunged for the sheriff, but snatched air. "Jake!" Holman screamed.

Jake misread everything. Betrayal and anger blackened his features. He guessed his dad had sold him out and had strung him along for a spectacular arrest. Jake drew back his knife hand and threw.

The knife wasn't meant for Terry, but he saw the flying blade coming straight for him and threw himself to the ground. He heard, then saw, the blade bury itself up to the hilt in Sheriff Holman's stomach. Blood blossomed across his groin, the bloom doubling in size by the second.

Oscar was primal and his yell voiced his baser instincts. The golf club's head connected with the side of Jake's skull. The sound was hollow and overshadowed by the crack of his skull giving way.

Jake's face was thick with pain and shock. A realization overwhelmed his features. He realized that he'd been wrong and he'd made a mistake. He'd turned on his father when his father was trying to save him. There was nothing he could do for his dad, but everything he could do to his attacker. He turned to see who had dared to harm him.

Fear swept across Oscar's face when he saw Jake wasn't going to be stopped with a single blow. He swung for a second shot, but Jake grabbed the end of the club—the end greasy with his own blood and hair.

Holman groaned and collapsed, his gun clattering to the ground before him. He tugged the blade out of his stomach, opening the floodgates.

Jake had Oscar's club and was about to return the favor Oscar had dealt him. Oscar cowered, covering his head with his hands.

Terry snatched Holman's gun, just as the sheriff's blood threatened to soak it. His grasp was clumsy. He'd never handled or fired a weapon before, but his instincts took over. Terry aimed and squeezed the trigger.

The bullet halted Jake, freezing him in the moment. His arms were outstretched with the club over his shoulder, but he wasn't moving. He didn't deliver Oscar the fatal blow and he never would. For a long moment, he managed one thing and only one thing. He bled.

Terry kept Holman's gun aimed.

Slowly, Jake turned. He tottered toward Terry, threatening him with the club.

Terry fired again. And again.

Jake absorbed each bullet, but three was his limit. He crumpled and struck the ground only inches from his slain father. He stared at his father and mumbled something. He clawed at the ground, sucking in an untidy lungful of air, but for all his tremendous efforts, he covered precious little ground. Jake came to a halt at his father's feet, their spilled blood colliding.

Terry wasn't satisfied and never would be while Jake Holman still had the strength to breathe. He stood over the dying man. Jake looked up and managed a smile. Terry fired the gun and kept on firing until it dry-retched with every squeeze of the trigger. He wanted to make sure all six rounds stopped Jake, one round for each of his victims. And even then, he didn't stop firing until Oscar grabbed the revolver.

In a quiet voice he said, "It's over."

Terry stared at Oscar. Oscar's complexion was ghost white. Terry nodded and let his friend take the gun.

Oscar took the revolver from Terry and dropped it, wincing. His dislocated thumb hung slack against his hand. Terry saw how his friend had escaped the handcuffs. With a sharp tug, Oscar snapped his thumb back into position.

"Sometimes a disability isn't always a disability," he said, shaking the cuffs dangling from his other wrist.

"She's dead, Oscar."

"I know. I'm sorry, buddy."

Terry glanced over at Sarah. "I hope she isn't disappointed in me."

Oscar rested a comforting hand on his shoulder. "How could she be? She loves you."

In the distance, sirens wailed, and Oscar held Terry as he cried for his dead wife.

CHAPTER TWENTY-SIX

The blue golf ball rolled in a shallow arc, catching the downward slope just right. The ball completed its thirty-foot journey, missing the bumpers guarding the hole, and dropped into the tin cup.

"You jammy git," Oscar announced.

In the three weeks since Sarah's murder, Oscar had rarely been out of Terry's company. He had made sure Terry hadn't been allowed to dwell on Sarah's death too much. He'd also helped out with the police and the funeral arrangements. But in that time, he'd picked up a lot of English slang. The words sounded fine coming out of an English mouth, but when an American said the same words, they sounded comical, even juvenile. Terry wondered if he sounded as ridiculous.

"Only you can turn a crappy first shot into gold."

Terry shrugged. He wasn't enjoying the game. It was just something to do—something to take his mind off Sarah. Every moment he had alone, he replayed the events leading up to her death and how he could have prevented what happened. He still hadn't accepted Sarah's death. He knew that. And he wasn't sure he ever would.

Oscar took his shot and missed. He took a third and sunk his putt. He noted their scores on the scorecard, and they moved on to the next hole.

Oscar lined up his ball to tee off. "Has Javier gone?"

"Yes."

Terry had called Javier Rivera as promised to let him know he'd found Myda's killer and that he was dead. Javier asked to pay his respects and arrived the day after the funeral. He'd said a prayer over Sarah's grave and laid a wreath. Afterward, Terry took him to Jake's grave and they spat on it.

At the grave Javier said, "You're my brother. If you need anything, it's yours."

Then they'd drunk themselves into a stupor. They told each other stories about Sarah and Myda. They laughed, cried, and sat in silence, just remembering. They didn't stop drinking until they'd drunk themselves sober. A tequila hangover felled Terry two days after their binge. The effects had only worn off today.

"He went this morning. He asked if he could bring Myda's mother to see Sarah. I said it was okay."

They played the next two holes without speaking. That suited Terry fine, but he could see Oscar still had questions.

"What is it?" Terry asked.

"Holman. I know blood's thicker than water, but I still can't believe Holman would kill, lie, and plant evidence for his son."

"I don't know that he did."

"What do you mean?"

"For sure, Holman wasn't playing it by the numbers that night, but I wonder if it was all for Jake's benefit."

"To get Jake to drop his guard, you mean?"

"Maybe. We'll never know for sure. I don't even know how he ended up here that night. He either followed me or he was following his son. But I know Holman didn't plant the evidence in my house."

"How?" Oscar asked, retrieving his ball from the hole.

"It was Sarah. She'd been coming back and forth for days. I think she was taking and hiding evidence in the crawl space as and when she needed it."

"How do you know?"

"More than once I came home to find something in the house moved. Osbourne claimed he'd seen Sarah entering the house. And do you remember the old Honda that opened the garage?"

"Yeah."

"When Sarah and I were outrunning Holman at the mall, the car she drove off in was the same old Honda."

Terry holed his putt and they moved on. They skipped the next hole. It was the windmill hole. They always skipped the windmill hole. He was sure a psychologist would tell him that when his emotional scars were healed he would play the windmill hole again, but Terry didn't think so. As long as he lived, he knew he would never play it.

"Do you regret coming to America?" Oscar asked. "It's hardly been a fairy-tale welcome."

No, it hasn't, Terry thought. The company he'd worked for had broken the law and he'd brought them down. People had been murdered and he'd avenged them, but not in time to save Sarah. He never could have conceived this nightmare. But was that America's fault? Hardly.

"No, not at all."

"That's good."

Oscar paused for a long moment before asking, "Do you regret marrying Sarah?"

That was a question that required no deliberation. Sarah had taken his breath away when they'd met and had never given it back to him. She made him more than he was without her. Even now, with her gone, he was still a better man for knowing her. He touched their wedding rings on the chain around his neck and smiled. It was the first to cross his face in weeks.

"I don't regret marrying Sarah, regardless of how short a time we had together. One day, one minute—it's not important how long we were married. I'm proud to have been her husband. She may have done some questionable things, but I fell in love with the Sarah I met in Costa Rica, and she fell in love with me—that can never be changed."

"I'm glad for you, buddy." Oscar smiled. "Let's blow this game and do something else. Whaddya say?"

"Okay."

"Good man," Oscar said and headed for the arcade.

In the arcade, Oscar handed Terry a drink, and they sat at the same table where they'd first met. Oscar pushed his drink to one side.

"What are you going to do now?"

"I don't know at the moment. There's still some insurance stuff and other of Sarah's affairs I need to sort out. My family and friends have asked me to come back to England. I suppose I should."

"You're not going to stay and find another biotech job?"

Terry shook his head. Genavax was finished. The FDA was all over the company. Evidence was being gathered and charges and arrests would be announced soon. There were rumors that one of the international drug conglomerates was waiting in the wings to buy Genavax for pennies on the dollar and absorb it into its operations. He hoped the rumor was true. He didn't want to see his innocent coworkers lose their jobs. Out of respect, he'd resigned.

"I'm finished in the biotech industry in this country. I'm a corporate leper. No one will want to employ a whistle-blower."

"I suppose you're right. But dammit, buddy, I don't want to see you go. I'm just getting used to having you around."

"I don't really have a choice. What else could I do?"

"I guess…" Oscar stopped himself midsentence to flash a naughty-boy grin. "I know what we need and I know what you could do."

Terry was puzzled. "What?"

"We need a new sheriff." Oscar could barely contain his excitement. "Are you up for it?"

The End

AUTHOR'S NOTE

The city of Edenville and the county of Santa Rita are wholly fictional. Those familiar with the I-80 corridor between the Bay Area and Sacramento might recognize some of the locations stolen for this book.

ABOUT THE AUTHOR

A former racecar driver, licensed pilot, animal rescuer, endurance cyclist, and occasional private eye, Simon Wood is also an accomplished author with more than 150 published stories and articles under his belt. His mystery fiction, which has appeared in numerous magazines and anthologies, has earned him both the prestigious Anthony Award and a CWA Dagger Award nomination. In addition to *No Show*, his books include *Accidents Waiting to Happen*, *Working Stiffs*, *Asking for Trouble*, *Paying the Piper*, *We All Fall Down*, and *Terminated*. Originally from England, he lives in California with his wife, Julie.